A Star of Ash: A Child of Magic

Parker James

ISBN: 979-8-218-24600-6

DEDICATION

To my wife Lisa, with you I am whole, with you, I am better, with you I am in love.

To my Parents, without whom I would never have been able to achieve my dream.

To my brother and sister for helping to shape me into the person I am today.

To my friends on Discord, thank you for answering all of my hyper-specific questions and refining my work.

To my Orthodontists at Dr. Abbot's office in Rochester Hills. I keep my promises and thank you again for fixing my teeth.

CONTENTS

Prologue — 1

1 The First Day of A Long Year — 3

2 Day of Rain — 17

3 Day of Choices — 32

4 First Sàbaid, Day of Gillian — 48

5 Second Sàbaid, Day of Umba — 62

6 Day of Changes — 71

7 Night of Terrors — 85

8 Souls of Saints Day — 96

9 Day of Regrets — 119

10 Night of Hunting — 134

11 Night of Gathering — 140

12 Day of Journeys — 149

(Sneak Preview) — 155

Follow the Author — 159

THEN

"Morning time is gold in the mouth," Kalby's big sister said as she woke him up. Kalby could never tell when it was morning. He wasn't even sure what morning was. His big sister had told him about it once.

"A time outside where a big ball of light brightened the world and made it warmer."

He tried to imagine it but couldn't. Too big. Big things like those didn't seem real to him. He liked to think smaller. Like imagining the light looked like his sister. Her skin had a faint yellowish glow and was warm when he touched her. Perhaps it was like that? It was the only light in their black cell. It helped if he imagined they were living in a larger cell room. It might have been closer to what she meant.

Kalby's skin was pale, but it didn't glow like hers. His hair was never allowed to grow long, but his sister told him it was blonde like hers used to be. He'd never seen his face but could feel his slightly pointed nose, and his sister told him he had brown eyes. His ears were rounded, unlike her sharp ones. He couldn't picture the rest. His sister had golden eyes and a soft round face, which was gaunt like the rest of her body after being here for almost two decades. She was taller than Kalby, but he was slowly catching up. She liked to tease him and called him "My little Kalby." Kalby believed he could be taller than her if they provided him more to eat. And she never changed as he did. They weren't related by blood, as she explained to him. She just decided to take care of him since no one else here would. She also gave him his name so she wouldn't have to call him by the numbers they assigned him.

If it was morning, then they would be getting food soon. The slide on the cell door opened, and Kalby and his sister were told to stand back. A tray of food paste was shoved in, and the slide closed again. Kalby tried to scramble for the food, but his sister held him back. Considering how little food they normally gave them, it could only mean one thing. It was Kalby's turn again.

Whatever he ate now would just be wasted. His stomach started to clench up, but she was right. Kalby wouldn't have much time anyway. In a few moments, someone would come for him. His big sister hugged him while they waited. When the masked ones came, they stuck something sharp in his neck before he could fight back, and his mind was addled with a concoction of unknown chemicals. Not to stop the pain, but it would stop him from resisting.

CHAPTER 1
THE FIRST DAY OF A LONG YEAR

NOW

It was early in the morning. The sun had yet to rise past the cloud-breaking Tower of Babel on the horizon, and the air was cold from the autumn night. Nearly every day, Freya and her father woke up at this time and ventured deep into the woods, away from their town. When they walked through the woods, her father would carry her on his bony back, and she would wrap her arms around his neck.

Although this was a daily routine for Freya, she was always still sleepy. When the birds sang, Freya had little chance to stay awake. At this hour, their songs would sound like lullabies. Coupled with the soothing sounds of the stream, she was practically napping.

The woods always looked peaceful, even through the darkness of the early morning. Almost as if it were still asleep, and the rustling of the leaves was its way of snoring. Freya wished her father would feel the same way, though she understood why he didn't. He taught her well to be afraid of the Sanctus Venatores. When they ventured farther, her father would stop every few minutes to look around, especially if something was scurrying behind them. Sometimes Freya had needed to remind him where they were, but he was fairly present today.

After what Freya had guessed was an hour, she and her father finally made it to their clearing. In this empty space, there were stones and old, torn-up scarecrows. Freya and her father would use them as practice dummies, placed in arrangements of groups and individuals.

Her father made sure Freya was awake before setting her down. She was not up to his waist yet, though few adults were up to his head. This was further exacerbated by her father always wearing his big, black, pointed hat.

He once told Freya they were called scholar hats, but Freya was sure he only wore the oversized thing because it kept people away. Her father moved toward the stones and practice dummies and made some quick changes and fixes to ensure they were in the right place for today. Freya rubbed her eyes and looked for her favourite tree stump to sit on while she waited for her father to prepare everything for practice. Freya tucked her whole body into her large, dark purple robe, like her own little tent, keeping herself warm.

The sun had started to peek out over the Tower when her father had finished setting everything up. The woods were showered in bright golden sunlight. Her father called for her, so she popped out of her robe tent and ran to him as fast as she could. Nearly tripping over herself in excitement, she was finally getting more awake now.

Freya faced the four scattered stones as she stood next to her father. Her father knelt down so he could talk to Freya, eye to eye. He spoke to her, his voice hoarse but gentle and quiet with an accent like no one else in town, "All right, vennen min, let us work more on finer control today." He pointed to the stones and continued, "I rounded out the stones yesterday. They will not have any flat sides. Try to stack as many as you can. Keep the spell simple and take as much time as you need." He paused briefly. "Remember you do not need to use your hands. That is just in your head."

Freya nodded energetically. She prepared herself by keeping balance, her body relaxed. Freya focused on the rock closest to her. In half a second, Freya had mentally measured everything she needed to know about the stone: the size, density, mass, and current force of gravity, all down to the exact decimal, as assigned to it by the Rules of Reality. She configured the rules for how gravity would work on the stone, adjusting the pull in different directions. Allowing the rock to vibrate and then slightly hover above the ground as the pull of gravity on it was just as strong as the natural gravity holding it down.

Magic of this school caused an effect of a pale blue ring that illuminated and encircled Freya's feet, rotating and pulsating. Within the radiant ring, symbols, and equations appeared, matching the ones in her head. Reverberating with the same rhythm as the ring itself.

Freya thought of another configuration, and another symbol formed on the ring. The rock she focused on was pulled toward another stone. It appeared there was an error in Freya's configuration as the pull was too strong, causing it to move too fast and overshoot its target. Freya nearly dropped it in her pa nic to overcorrect. When Freya tried to fix the rock's course, she forgot to keep the configuration and lost the upward pull, causing it to fall back down too low, and knocking over the rest of the pile.

Freya let out a huff of frustration and just barely avoided stomping like she used to do when she was younger.

"Nope, this is too hard. I'm not ready to use Gravomancy without my hands." Freya thought as she reached out her arm and used her hand to guide the second rock. This time, she was able to pull the rock with far greater control and successfully stacked it on top of the first stone. The third and fourth stones took more time to stack, even with her hands as a focus.

By the time Freya had finished, the sun was barely out. When Freya released her control over the final stone, the ring around her faded, and she took a deep breath of chilled air before turning to her father. Her father gave Freya a mirthful smile through the shadow cast on his face by his big pointed hat.

"I'm sorry, Pappa," Freya said, pacing back and forth, trying not to let her frustration show.

Her father gently patted her head, "It is all right, vennen min; we are in no hurry. Magic is altering the Rules of Reality. It is not a physical task, but a mental one."

"But how am I supposed to control it if I can't use my hands?"

"Vennen min, you are not actually holding the rocks with your hands." "I know, but it feels like I am."

For Freya, it was easy to comprehend the changes needed to do a lifting spell in Gravomancy. Even spells lifting heavy objects her own weight made sense to her even if it was harder. Trying to do something so precise, such as rotating them, did not. There were numerous changes to keep track of and focus on. Especially when she can't use her hands to remind her what she is doing. "Why can't I figure this out? Pappa is able to do it all the time so I know it's possible. Am I not smart enough? What is wrong with me?"

"I am sure you will understand with enough practice. We are not in a rush," her father said as he scanned the area once more. Freya looked up at him with big brown eyes that mirrored her father's.

"Pappa, since I finished early, could I please do quick throws before we leave?" she asked, hoping they could have more fun before going to school. He looked back down at her and nodded.

Freya joyfully ran back to the stones and faced the scarecrows. This exercise was easy for her. All she had to do was levitate each rock and configure the rules to launch them at the scarecrow as fast as she could and in quick succession. Using a similar spell from earlier, Freya pointed her hand at a stone, and it hovered in the air. She whipped it at the scarecrow, hitting one of its arms and causing it to spin rapidly. She pulled another stone from the stack and flung it again, this time grazing the head of the scarecrow.

For the last two stones, Freya decided to pick up both at once and threw them one after the other. The first stone missed and slammed into a nearby tree, causing splinters to scatter while finches soared off from their perch. The final rock hit the centre of its straw chest and knocked it flat on the ground.

When Freya had finished, she looked back at her father. He pulled something from one of the bags tied to his belt. It was a small vial of azure

liquid her father had made. She hadn't realised her mind had clouded until she recognized the potion as Xatralt.

He took a sip of it himself. Waited, testing it before letting Freya have some. She began to drink it as soon as he handed it to her. Xatralt doesn't have a taste, much like water. Yet it had a thickness that made Freya gag each time she drank it. Knowing this, her father had mixed in various fruits to try and give it a better taste hoping it would be easier for her to drink and it worked for the most part.

As she drank, the usual coolness of the liquid Xatralt splashed the back of her throat, and it tasted like peaches today. Freya chugged down faster, trying to taste more of her favourite flavour. As the cloudiness in her mind receded, Freya realised if she hadn't taken the potion today, she would have been lucky if she could recall how to spell her own name. She must have been overcomplicating her spell if it had gotten this bad.

"Could you do the exercise, Pappa? I want to see how you would do it," Freya asked.

If it just so happened to stall time from getting to school, then it would be merely a happy coincidence, according to Freya.

Her father looked past her and at the stones for a brief moment. He pointed toward where the rocks had been, and Freya turned to see all four stones restacked and balanced in what appeared to be impossible angles.

Freya's eyes widened. Freya had watched her father the whole time. Not even for a moment did it look like he was doing anything. Freya didn't hear a single stone move, nor had she noticed the glowing ring that should have surrounded him whenever they used Magic. Freya turned back to her father and looked at him dumbfoundedly. He smiled again and headed back toward town. She gazed at the stones one last time before running after him.

When she caught up, Freya and her father walked side by side along the dirt path as she drank her potion. Freya's eyes wandered around the now brightly lit woods. It appeared to be glowing with amber-orange and golden yellow, the effects of which made her teal, waist-length hair pop out in contrast. All the animals were now wide awake. Squirrels scurried across the oak tree branches, deer trotted around them, and a brown-furred mamma bear took her cubs out to gather berries.

After a couple of minutes, Freya finished her drink and handed the empty vial back to her father. Freya grabbed her father's gloved hand and swung his long arms back and forth as they walked along the dirt trail.

On the way, they passed a group of tiny pointy-chinned and pointy-eared Clurichauns, the nocturnal cousins of the Leprechauns. They were singing an unintelligible song and drinking what her father called "potions only for grown-ups." They were returning to their homes deep in the woods after a long night of working at the Starboard Tavern.

Up ahead, they walked under one of the signs outside of town that arched only two feet above them. "Welcome to Valour" was written on it. Not too far from where they stood, yet away from the rest of the town, laid their little, wooden hilltop house.

The two walked through the marketplace, where most traders and craftsmen lived and conducted their business. The marketplace was a four-way intersection of dirt roads with buildings lining each side. Toward the west end of town were the docks. It was known as the Port District. Ships for trading and fishing would come from the sea or through the large Thirds Rivers.

To the north, toward the Bow District, is where the schoolhouse was. Freya's and her father's house was outside of town but nearest to the Starboard District. The street was empty except for a few dozen shopkeepers setting up their stores and wares displays and some sailors preparing to travel. It was still early enough in the day that everyone already awake was still eating their morning meals.

Freya and her father eventually passed the house of her best friend Brigid and her father, Mister Conall. Mister Conall was the town blacksmith. He made and repaired tools for people and built weapons and armour for some of the older boys and girls who would leave town. Or to adventurers who passed by now and then. The stone house was two stories, with the upper being where they lived connected to a chimney that puffed out black smoke during working hours. The bottom floor had a fenced-up opening facing the road instead of a wall, showing the forge and workshop with all the tools he used as displays on the back wall.

Freya and her father stopped at the bottom of the steps outside the schoolhouse. Freya turned as her father knelt down to give her a big hug and handed her a bag he had previously tied around his waist. Freya watched as her father left before entering the red wooden schoolhouse. Freya's teacher, Missus Aibrean, was sitting behind her desk at the front of the room. She wore a puffy white blouse and shuffled through papers while twirling her greyish-red curly hair between her fingers. Missus Aibrean did not seem to notice Freya as she left her boots by the door and made her manners to Missus Aibrean by doing the curtsy all the girls in her class were taught. She went to her assigned desk by the window, a few rows behind the six - to eight-year-olds row. Freya placed the bag her father gave her inside the desk and pulled out her chalk and slate. It would be at least twenty minutes before anyone else came to school, so she would either read or doodle heroes from her stories to pass the time.

***

As her schoolmates started arriving, the room became gradually louder with the sounds of talking and roughhousing. Then Brigid came in. She wore a   beautiful sunflower-coloured gown. Her copper-coloured hair was up in a fancy knot that twisted and twirl like a tiara, all of which complemented her juniper green eyes. Brigid waved excitedly, and Freya waved in kind. Brigid had made her way to her assigned desk in the row with the older kids immediately behind Freya. Brigid started to braid one of the sides of Freya's hair as Freya began yawning.

"You wouldn't be so tired if you slept more instead of getting to school so early," Brigid suggested. Freya did not know how to respond. "What are you doing up so early anyway? I'm sure Missus Aibrean would be fine if you showed up at the same time as everyone else."

"Pappa says morning time is gold in the mouth," Freya answered using her father's odd phrases. She hoped it was weird enough for Brigid to avoid asking further questions.

Freya hated it when she had to lie, especially to Brigid. As much as she loved her best friend, Freya couldn't risk even half a percent chance of word reaching the Venatores. If they found out what Freya or her father could do, there was a good chance she would never see her home, her friends, and her father ever again.

"If you say so. Is your Da teaching you his job or something?" Brigid asked as she finished one side of Freya's hair and moved on to the next.

Freya hadn't considered much about what she wanted to do as a grown-

up.

"Not yet, but I suppose it wouldn't be so bad," Freya answered.

"I can't imagine you sitting still for that long. You would go mad with boredom within the week. You need something with adventure! Like a Venatores in shining armour! Or a rough and tough mercenary."

"No, no, no! T-there's no w-way. I'm not b-brave enough for that." Freya bashfully stuttered.

"Quit selling yourself short, shorty."

"Do you still want to work with your Da?" Freya asked, hoping to change the subject.

"I'm not gonna just work with him, I'm gonna be the best smith there is! Them kings and noble folk from all over the Known World will come to me for forging things before anyone else! There's gonna be legends of the weapons I craft that will last forever!" Brigid exclaimed.

Hearing the passion in Brigid's words, Freya couldn't stop herself from giggling. "Oooh? And what's so funny?" Brigid teased while playfully tugging Freya's hair.

"Nothing," Freya chuckled, trying to stop herself from laughing.

Freya had no doubt her friend would be a great blacksmith. Brigid had an eye for detail, knew a great deal about the histories of weapons and armour, and was one of the strongest kids in school, surpassing a bunch of older boys. Freya found it funny. Despite these qualities, Brigid made sure to look as if she were attending a fancy party. She took every opportunity to be clean and dressed in the most colourful clothes she owned. And never left home

without her hair having minimal proper care for an hour. Yet, Brigid wanted to work with coal and steel in a hot mucky workshop.

"You're damn right, nothing," Brigid replied with a goofy grin. After Brigid finished braiding her hair, Freya sat up straight and let the two twisted hair ties fall down in front of her shoulders.

***

"Aidan Corith?" Missus Aibrean called.

He stood and answered, "Here!" then sat back down, and Missus Aibrean continued down her list of names.

"Oh, Freya, I just remembered something," Brigid

whispered. "What is it?"

"Da says he would take us to the sweets store after school if you wanted to come."

"Freya Pantar?"

"Ooh yes! Oh, but I need to ask my Da first."

"No problem, we can stop by your place first," Brigid said.

Then Freya noticed something. Missus Aibrean was staring at her for a few seconds, but it felt like hours to Freya. Missus Aibrean adjusted her small glasses and asked in a jokingly dramatic tone, "I could've sworn I saw Freya here earlier. Did she leave without saying anything? I suppose we will have to go on without her."

Everyone stared at Freya, and some chuckled. Freya timidly looked at the ground as she realised she wasn't paying attention, and she meekly mumbled, "I'm here… S-sorry Missus Aibrean."

"It's all right, Freya, I was only teasing," Missus Aibrean said with a light-hearted smile.

She continued calling the rest of the students as Freya slowly sat back down. Brigid asked if she was all right. Freya nodded while burying her face in her arms.

Class officially started with the first lesson being math—the subject that got under Freya's skin. It wasn't difficult for her, but rather the opposite. In fact, she could even solve the most "advanced" equations faster than she could blink. The problem was her father had told Freya she would need to purposefully make mistakes, or else it might draw suspicion. Yet every time she gave a wrong answer, it was like being bitten by bed bugs, and today was no exception.

The class had done several warm -up problems, and then they were given a surprise test. As Freya filled out the answers, she would look at each question and think to herself, "This is so simple. It's just a tiny problem I could easily solve." Then she would remind herself of what her father told her and would reluctantly write an incorrect answer. After ten minutes of boiling frustration, she finished the test and waited for someone else to turn theirs in so she wouldn't be the first. Her father had told her this urge would go away as she got older, and she certainly hoped so.

It wasn't too long before her schoolmates finally finished their tests, thus allowing Freya to turn hers in without appearing to answer too quickly. The other lessons like Adamic Language, her second despised subject for the exact opposite reason of being too confusing. Like learning the three consonant roots. After they finished the lesson, it was time for lunch recess. When they were dismissed, Freya and the other kids grabbed their lunch sacks from their desks and put on their boots by the door as they ran outside.

Once out there, Brigid kept busy playing ball and listening intently to all the daily gossip, while Freya spent her time devouring the food her father packed her.

***

Once lunch recess was over, everyone came back inside the schoolroom and sat back at their desks. The class continued on with their last two lessons. Reading being first, everyone took turns reading the assigned book out loud. This particular book was one Freya enjoyed, and she was having a fun time. There was a humorous part in the story where a light-haired boy named Fionn ate some fish grease and gained all knowledge of everything everywhere. But then Ronan Gallagher had to ruin it, as he always does, by mocking one of the little boys up front who couldn't read well yet. She had half a mind to walk over to the boys' side of the room and smack Ronan across his thick head. Thankfully it didn't have to come to that as Missus Aibrean kicked him out of the room for the rest of the lesson.

Afterward, they went on to history, which started as it always did with everyone standing up and reciting the opening passages from the holy scriptures Libri ex Dii. "At the beginning of our world's time, the Goddess of creation, Gillian, and her husband, the God of order, Umba, felt alone in their heavens. And so, Gillian gave birth to life itself while Umba gave each life purpose. Gillian started with plants, and Umba gave them cycles of growth and decay. But they were not enough, for they were indifferent to all things, including love. Then Gillian created the animals. Umba categorised them as herbivores to eat the plants when they threaten to overgrow. And carnivores to stop the herbivores from starving. But the animals were controlled by primal instincts. Love always came second to survival. And although Gillian loved them all, they could not love in the way she desired ..." - Partus Vitae 1:1-10

Freya's mind numbed each time they had to read this passage.

When they finished the passages, Missus Aibrean would begin her lecture, but today's lesson was different. They would normally learn about the formations of nations around the Known World and even their home country of Bastiel, or they would learn about the heroic quests of the Sanctus Venatores.

***

Today, the lesson was about the Second Grand Crusade. Freya knew plenty about the First Crusade with the Angelic rebellion against the Gods led by The Star of Ash because it was written in the Libri ex Dii they recited. The only information Freya knew about the Second Crusade was what she overheard adults gossiping about, and some of the stories Ronan's father liked to tell everyone. Freya remembered hearing of the wild tales and bizarre legends, though nothing specific.

Missus Aibrean started the lesson with the events of sixty years ago. Corruption was rampant. Monsters of all kinds were overpopulated and unleashed. Barbarians and criminals from around the Known World became organised on national scales. Magic users, or Draoi as they are called in Bastiel, went mad and wreaked havoc with their vile dark spells and experiments. Prefectures, city-states, kingdoms, and empires all over began to fall one after the other.

Even the former monarchy of Bastiel fell after the old Queen was revealed to be a traitor and a monster herself. There was chaos. After forty-seven years of suffering, just about everyone had enough of it. From simple farmers, Demi-Humans, mercenary companies, and even the entire Order of Sanctus Venatores gathered together. They created the Divine Militia to fight back. After four years of brutal warfare, they were victorious and put the world back to how it should be.

It didn't take Freya long to realise she was born barely a year before the Second Crusade ended. This made her curious about a few things, but she knew asking such questions here could draw suspicion. In a war that affected everyone, how come Missus Aibrean didn't mention any Draoi helping? Her father told her not to believe everything Missus Aibrean taught when it came to history, but this seemed ridiculous. The other kids asked their questions and the lesson continued as usual.

***

As the final lesson ended, everyone grabbed their belongings from their desks and rushed out the door, more than ready to leave. Once outside, the other kids would head home to their families. Freya normally walked with Brigid until they got to her house. From there, Freya would walk the rest of the way home, following the path her father showed her through the marketplace. Today, however, Brigid's father was waiting for the two of them, and it didn't take long to find the jubilant portly man in the crowd of her charging schoolmates.

As the three walked across town, Freya peered at the shops that surrounded the roads as Mister Conall, in his usual deep gravelly voice, asked: "So lasses, how was school today?"

Brigid cringed and groaned, "Bah, she made us take a pox-bottling maths test without letting us know at least a day before!"

"I'm guessin' it didn't go well then?"

Brigid crossed her arms and grumbled.

"You need to take this more seriously. When I was your age, only the nobles could afford an education back when we still had nobles."

"I know. I know. You also couldn't learn how to read at night because fire wasn't discovered yet."

"Good Gods, the head on you! I ain't that old. Perhaps you can learn to count my age better if you asked Freya to help you."

"But Freya's worse at maths than me!"

Mister Conall scratched his thick curly copper coloured beard and continued. "Really? Freya, I could have sworn you had a knack for it. Just the other day you …"

"No, I- I uh … M-maybe you're thinking of someone else?" Freya interrupted, trying her best to sound calm.

Mister Conall looked confused but quickly went back to his usual jolly self. "Perhaps I am. Heh, maybe all the heat and smoke from the furnaces is messing with my head, aye?"

"I wouldn't mind asking Aidan to help me," Brigid whispered to Freya.

"I guess he's smart enough," Freya thought, just glad they weren't asking about her anymore.

After a little bit of walking, they were at the shoulder of the hill. Freya and Brigid reached the peak while Mister Conall struggled behind them to keep up. At the top, Freya could see her house and her father. His face was still obscured by the shade cast from his big hat. Her father was seated behind the small wooden stand he used as his shop. Freya ran over to him as he stood up and walked around his potion stand to catch her in a hug.

Once Mister Conall finally caught up and regained his breath, he asked, "How's the craic, Kal?"

Her father shrugged and Freya broke the awkward silence by asking, "Mister Conall said he can take me and Brigid to the sweets shop. Can I go, please?"

He looked back at Freya and told her, "Ja, hold on." Her father let her go, stood back up, and grabbed a small sack from the stand. He then unwound the tie and pulled out one silver coin. It had an imprint of Bastiel's symbol: an armoured horse head with a sword and a woodcutter's axe crossed together behind it. Before he handed the coin to her, he said, "Be sure to be back here before dark, vennen min."

"I will. Tusen Takks, Pappa." He nodded, and Freya gave her father one more hug before she headed off.

***

"I can't believe out of every sweet in the store, you used all that money to buy only one peach candy," Brigid said as they were walking back from the sweets store.

Freya was in too much bliss from chewing on the peach gummy to

answer.

"Leave her be. If she wants to buy peaches, that's her business." Mister Conall retorted.

"Thanks a million for letting me join you!" Freya said between chewing. "Don't mention it, lass."

"So Da, there's been an interesting rumour floating around school," Brigid said with a mischievous grin.

"What have I told you about listening to rumours, Brigid?"

"But I heard we're having a new student and not only that, but they're also a Demi-Human."

Freya nearly choked on the gummy from the surprising news. Luckily she was able to swallow it before asking, "Akh …Why didn't you tell me?"

"Because I wanted to get it straight from the horse's mouth before you started freakin' out."

Mister Conall shushed the two girls before Freya had a chance to respond. He whispered, "Yes, lasses, it's true. You'll be havin' another schoolmate and yes, she is a Demi-Human."

"She?" Freya asked as her curiosity grew.

Mister Conall mumbled a curse to himself and continued, "She's an Elf, specifically an Aos Sí from the Fay Forest way down south in the bogger."

"I thought so," Brigid said with obvious satisfaction.

Freya, on the other hand, was excited. She had known plenty of Demi-Humans like the Clurichauns from the woods. Mister Brian, a Leprechaun and a local cobbler, whom Freya and her father go to when they need new shoes. And Mister Cadhla, a local bard for hire, whom Mister Conall called a Gancanagh, though he didn't look different from a human. This would be the first time Freya got to meet an Elf. As well as being her first Demi-Human schoolmate.

"Why's she here? Don't they have their own schools in their mounds or whatever it is they live in?" Brigid asked, matching Mister Conall's volume.

Mister Conall looked around again then back to them before saying, "Look, you have to promise me you won't bring this up again to anyone, all right?"

They both nodded in agreement. Brigid had done so indifferently, and Freya couldn't stop grinning.

Mister Conall crouched down to meet their eyes and continued, "From what I know, her parents were killed by brigands who were trespassing the forest. Thankfully, she managed to run away and find the nearby village. And they took her to our church where Saint Orlaith and her priestesses are watching over her."

"That's horrible!" Freya said, and quickly glanced back at Brigid and realised she was feeling the same. The two had lost one parent, but to lose both of them was something unimaginable. Mister Conall looked at them and continued, "She is going to be scared, alone, and confused, so I'm hoping I can count on you two to try and be her friends since not many of our kind will. Gods know she needs some."

"Absolutely! And bollocks to any thick head who tries to give her trouble!" Brigid said.

Mister Conall gave a proud smile and rubbed his hands on both their heads. "Glad to hear it." He looked at the setting sun and said, "Welp, it's about time we take Freya back."

***

By the time Mister Conall took Freya back home, her father had dinner ready for her inside. It was soup with assorted vegetables and herbs that he most likely found when collecting ingredients for potions in the woods.

The inside of the house itself was made with dark brown wood on the ceiling, walls, and floor. It only had two rooms. One was Freya's bedroom. The other was the main room, which served as everything from the kitchen, to her father's apothecary, and his bedroom. A long table, made of a brighter wood, took up most of the room's space and was where they would eat most of their meals, and on the wall, right above the table, hung a map of the town.

In the back of the room, furthest from the door was a stone stove. Her father used it to cook either food or ingredients and sometimes keep the house warm during winter. Slightly above the stove was a window that would bring light inside during the day.

As she went inside, her father was eating from his bowl at the table. Her bowl was waiting for her on the opposite side. He had left his large hat on the hook by the door, revealing his ghostly pale, unlined, thin face and short, unkempt sandy-coloured hair, so unlike her own. He had flat eyebrows that Freya remembered playing with when she was much younger. A slightly pointed crooked nose she liked to poke. And a squarish jaw he had recently shaved, though he could barely grow facial hair. Freya thought of her father's looks as plain, but not without some handsome qualities.

Freya sat down at the table on the opposite end and ate for a bit. Freya wanted to ask him about the history lesson on the Crusade, but she hesitated.

Her father turned up from his soup bowl, looked at her with his familiar gentle smile, and asked, "What's in the way, vennen min?"

Freya was worried her father would get scared again, so she decided to beat around the bush a bit and see when to stop. "We've learned about the Second Grand Crusade today." Freya waited for her father's reaction. He stared blankly for a while; Freya wasn't sure at what.

"Pappa? Pappa, are you still here?"

"Huh … Sorry. I did not … I did not think you would learn of that so soon." Her father finally spoke, his voice sounding more hoarse than usual.

Freya wondered, briefly, if nine years could be considered soon. "You know about the Crusade?"

Her father looked back at her. Freya assumed he was going to change the subject as usual, instead, he told her something she would have never expected, "Ja, I was with the Militia."

Then he went back to eating as if she asked how his day was.

"What! Why? Were you forced to?" Freya covered her mouth. What he said was jarring for her, but she was afraid it was a question too far.

Her father stopped eating and looked back at her, "Nei, as far as I know, they did not force me or anyone. I joined willingly, though I'm not sure why. I was … lost perhaps? Maybe I believed that if I helped them, they could keep me safe from … something."

Freya allowed herself to breathe again, and a surge of questions barged its way into her mind. However, she noticed her father was starting to look uneasy. Freya calmed herself before she would accidentally ask something she shouldn't. Freya decided to start with the questions she had at school.

"So were Draoi helping others too?"

Her father cocked his head slightly. "What did Missus Aibrean say?"

"Only that Draoi were going mad and hurting people with Dark Magic,
but that can't be true because you were there!"

Her father had taken on a more solemn look, which made Freya nervous. He said, "You are right, vennen min. There was Draoi that helped; however, Missus Aibrean was not wholly wrong either. There were Draoi that hurt other people, yet most were not crazy, and many were not really evil, or so I think."

Freya relaxed a bit as her father appeared comfortable with this question. "How could they not be evil? They were hurting people!"

Her father rested his elbows on the table and his chin in his palms. "I was told it was a scary time before the Crusade, and I was definitely scared during it." Her father leaned back in his chair and looked up at the ceiling. His relaxed posture reassured Freya. "From what I have seen, when people are afraid, it does not matter who or what they are, we all can react in ways that get others hurt, which scares even more people."

Freya tried to understand what her father was saying, but it seemed backward to her. Freya had been scared plenty of times but never thought about hurting someone. Then again, she has killed plenty of scary gross bugs that tried to get in her room.

"Maybe that's what Pappa meant?" Freya thought.

When they finished dinner, her father took off his worn-out gloves, his gnarled wrists no longer hidden, and placed the bowls, along with his beakers and vials, in the wash basin to be cleaned later. Unfortunately, whenever her father stood inside their house, he had to crane his neck because of how low the ceiling was for him. He then cleaned out the soot on the stove while Freya helped by sweeping the floor.

As she was sweeping, another thought came to mind. It was something that popped in her head once in a while, but it wasn't until she was told about what happened to the Aos Sí girl she began to wonder, "Did you meet Mamma there? The Crusade I mean."

He stopped what he was doing. He took a deep breath and nodded. "It was right after I joined the Crusade. A few of the soldiers felt the need to express their … dislike of Draoi to me after one of them saw me use Magic. Your mother is not a Draoi like you or me, she was just an ordinary soldier, like them, and yet when she saw that they were about to get violent, she stepped in and saved me. From then on, we became friends and, over time, something more. I think."

Freya couldn't help but grin. "What was she like?"

Her father didn't look back at Freya and instead continued to clean, though Freya noticed the smile he had before returned, yet it somehow seemed sad at the same time. "She was remarkably outgoing, wanting to be friends with everyone she met." Her father whispered to himself, "Even someone like me." He spoke up again to say, "She was very pious and wanted me to feel the love of Gods as she did. She was brave no matter how dangerous things got. And above all, she was the kindest person I have ever met."

Hearing all this made Freya imagine her mother as one of the brave knights from the storybooks she loved to read. When Freya was little, she had asked why her mother wasn't around like Brigid's was before she got sick. Her father had told Freya her mother had to leave for something important, but he never found out what.

CHAPTER 2
DAY OF RAIN

Freya opened her eyes, slowly sat up, began to yawn, and stretched out her arms. She wondered why her father didn't wake her, then noticed the rain pattering against the roof, and the answer became clear. Freya wanted to practice her control again, but it looked like it would have to wait till tomorrow. She climbed out of bed and pulled open the clothes drawer underneath. Freya grabbed a pair of clean trousers, an undershirt, and her favourite fluffy, dark purple robe her father had given her. Whose sleeves, no matter how often Freya rolled them up, dangled several inches past her fingertips, and the hem reached down past her knees. The robe was always soft and warm, and it was like a blanket she could wear. Freya got dressed, and once she had finished, she went back to the main room, where her father was doing his apothecary work by the stove. A hot bowl of porridge was sitting on the table for her.

As she ate the mushy morsels, her father took a sip from one of his potions. He waited a minute, then walked over to Freya and kissed the top of her head before routinely asking, "What do you do if you think you're in danger and I'm not around?"

Freya restrained herself from shovelling another spoonful before answering. "I try to find you."

"And if you cannot?"

"Run or hide. Try to find help, and only use Magic as a last resort."

"Utmerket! And what do you do if a Sanctus Venatore manages to capture
you?"

"Make sure to not use Magic around them and refuse to say or do anything until they let me see you."

"Perfect."

Her answers had come almost instinctively and automatically over the years, just as her father seemed to have hoped. Her father wanted Freya to come to these answers as easily as breathing, so he quizzed her on them every morning, usually before Magic practice.

***

Her father had put on a wool cloak and his big hat while Freya had finished her morning meal and left the empty bowl in the washbasin. He grabbed his umbrella, and the two headed out the door. When they went outside, the rain crashed down as if the whole town was under a large waterfall. They rushed across town, taking shortcuts through the less muddy alleyways to the schoolhouse. The umbrella sounded like war drums as the rain pounded on top of it, and they still managed to get drenched from head to toe. She would have had so much fun in this rain if it weren't so cold. Freya started to climb up the schoolhouse steps when she noticed her father resisting her pull to follow. She looked back at his dusty brown eyes that wandered around anywhere else.

"It's all right, Pappa. Missus Aibrean should be the only one there right now, and you need to get dry and warm."

He wordlessly followed her inside, and they both took off their soaked boots by the door and carried them to the stove in the centre of the room. Luckily for them, Missus Aibrean had the fire burning already.

"Oh!" Missus Aibrean flipped through her notes, "Mister Kalby Pantar?" she asked while Freya and her father were huddled by the stove trying to get dry. He turned sharply, which seemed to startle her.

"How are you two doing?" Missus Aibrean asked, trying to fill the silence.

He looked at Freya, then back to Missus Aibrean, and shrugged in response.

It looked like she was about to ask something else, but instead, she said. "Well, since you're here, could you please help me carry some firewood out of the supply closet?" Her father was still and silent for a moment, so she continued. "It's over there in the back corner to yer right." Missus Aibrean pointed toward the closet door, and he turned to face it. Freya's father cautiously walked toward the door, avoiding each desk as if it would break if he bumped into it. When her father reached the supply closet, he looked back at Missus Aibrean. "Yes, that's the one."

As he went inside, Missus Aibrean tried to make small talk asking, "I don't think I've ever heard about where you …"

"Please don't ask him stuff like that! It makes him scared." Freya interrupted with a harsh whisper.

"Scared? Freya, what do you mean?"

When her father came back out, he had an absurdly large bundle of firewood in his arms he brought back hurriedly. He seemed to be able to carry them with little difficulty despite his wiry frame.

"I know he isn't that strong. But if he is using Magic, why can't I see it?" Freya thought and it wasn't the first time. She just needed to think of the

correct way to ask him.

"Thank you, Mister Pantar," Missus Aibrean said, keeping an eye on him as he plopped the piles next to the stove. After they spent a while longer drying off, her father handed Freya her lunch sack for the day and hugged her before he grabbed his boots and headed out the door. Freya looked out the window by the door, and her father got soaked again the second he stepped outside.

"Is everything all right with you and your big brother?" Missus Aibrean asked as she grabbed bowls from the supply closet.

"Yeah, we're all right, but he is my Pappa. I don't have a brother," Freya replied as she curtsied to Missus Aibrean and headed back toward the stove.

"Ah, that's right. Forgive me, I think this was the second or third time we've met, and he looks ... Well anyway, I'm going to be making breakfast for everyone who tried to outrun the rain. Feel free to have some yourself if you didn't eat."

"I'm good, thank you. But what do you mean? Did he look hurt or sick?"

"Oh goodness, no! He's just younger than the other parents. Or at least looks like he is."

"Younger?"

"You don't need to worry about it. It's not unheard of after the Crusade. Not many expected to return home, so often they wanted to leave something behind if they couldn't make it back. Go ahead and take your seat."

When her schoolmates came in, they grabbed a bowl and ate at their desks. Freya tried to focus on each one to see if the Aos Sí girl was among them. She stared at each girl she didn't immediately recognize to see if maybe they had longer ears or were wearing some forest-looking clothing.

Freya was electrified to meet her. "What would she look like? Are Aos Sí as pretty as other Elves I read about? Is her voice different? Does she have any special abilities like Magic?" She had no idea what to expect and wanted to learn everything about her. Freya was so focused on finding her she hadn't notice Brigid had sat at the older kid's desk just behind her.

"Freya, what have I told you about acting quare?" Brigid asked as she was fixing Freya's hair.

"I'm only trying to see the Ao ..."

"By looking at everyone like a blood-starved Vampire?"

"No, no, no! Please don't talk about monsters! You know they give me nightmares."

"You're going to give her nightmares if she sees you staring at her like that. Just relax Freya, I doubt she would miss her first day at school."

"If you say so," Freya conceded. Brigid was rough with Freya's hair because of how damp it had gotten. After she managed to get it untangled, Brigid gave up and decided to let it hang down. It wasn't long after everyone finished their breakfast when Missus Aibrean began the roll call. Freya paid

close attention to hear what the new girl's name was. As well as to avoid a repeat of yesterday. Missus Aibrean called out their names. With each one, Freya's anxiety grew. She kept looking around for the new girl and her imagination began to wander. "She is new here, what if she doesn't know where the school was and got lost? She might not have a map like I have at home; could she have wandered into one of those bad spots Pappa warned me about?" Freya frantically thought.

Thankfully, Missus Aibrean began to speak before Freya's anxiousness got the better of her. "Class, I have a special announcement to make. We are having a new student join us."

Missus Aibrean walked over to a map of Bastiel hanging on the wall. Bastiel was a united country divided into four land masses by the great Three Thirds Rivers. Valour, Freya's hometown, is on the western coast of the northern land. Right above the First Third River.

"Your new classmate comes from the far south of our country, just below the Final Third River. In the Fay Forests with our good neighbours, the fair folk."

Freya nearly tipped over her entire desk from leaning too far forward in an attempt to see the new girl. Luckily Brigid managed to grab Freya's chair before she fell over. Missus Aibrean opened the door and greeted two priestesses as she taught her class. The priestesses wore their usual white robes with red-and-green hooded cloaks. They spoke quietly to each other and bowed before they left. Missus Aibrean closed the door and then headed back toward the chalkboard. Freya could almost see there was someone smaller next to her. Missus Aibrean came to a stop, moved to the side, and revealed the new student.

The class faded to silence. The only noise was the rain hammering on the roof. The girl was definitely not how Freya would have imagined her. Her hair was a deep dark blue, which almost looked black in certain lighting. It appeared someone had tried to put it in a fancy knot. Instead, they were met with strong resistance, making it look scraggly and mangy. It also seemed like they were trying to use her hair to hide her ears, which were at least four inches longer than Freya's. Her face was thin with prominen t cheekbones. Her skin was pale. Her legs were short, and her arms were uncommonly muscular. Freya thought this made her look top-heavy. She wore a white puffy dress, similar to what Brigid would wear. Due to her non-human proportions, it fitted poorly on her. It was clear the Aos Sí girl was uncomfortable in the outfit. This was likely why the dress had tears in the sleeves and two buttons missing. Even though Freya couldn't see Brigid's face, she knew Brigid would be wincing at the mangled dress.

Missus Aibrean asked the Aos Sí girl to introduce herself. When she spoke, she mumbled and pronounced every word, replacing her S and C sounds with an SH sound. Freya could barely understand half of what she was saying. Then Missus Aibrean grabbed the Aos Sí girl's wrist and swiftly smacked it with a hickory stick by her desk. It made a loud snapping noise and startled the whole class.

"Class, she needs to learn to speak properly so she can fit in better with us. If you notice her speaking like this again, please let me know."

The Aos Sí girl rubbed her red wrist, showing she had thick sharp claws instead of nails on her fingers. She scowled at everyone as she struggled to slowly say, "They call me Jash … Jacinta Kelly." There was an uncomfortable moment of silence in the room before Missus Aibrean showed Jacinta to her desk.

At first, Freya noted how peculiar it was that Jacinta was sitting up front with the little kids. She wasn't sure if Jacinta was her age or slightly older like Brigid. Then again, in all likelihood she hadn't been to any school before, so she wouldn't be at the same level as Freya or Brigid. The class began, and math was first this time. It wasn't as terrible for Freya today, mostly because she was too busy thinking about how to approach Jacinta when she had the chance. Jacinta seemed rather upset, and Freya feared she might worsen things.

"Perhaps she gets shy sometimes like I do?" Freya thought to herself.

***

In Adamic class, they studied spelling by copying down passages from Libri ex Dii. "At last, she created us. The humans. We were perfect in Gillian's eyes. We had true free will. We had the capability of the great love she had so long sought. But we were ignorant. We were unaware of the common virtues of morality, such as empathy, sympathy, generosity, and peace. We created chaos. We took more than what we needed, and when we couldn't get something ourselves, we took it from others. We began killing for hate, greed, lust, and jealousy. Gillian was patient and hoped that over time, we could become what she wanted, but as the decades turned to ages, she began to despair. Umba could no longer bear witness to his beloved's suffering any longer. So, he devised a monumental plan. Umba had convinced her to help him create beings with the Gods' laws imprinted on them. They would bring order to the humans. Their final creation. The Angels. When they arrived, they ended the wars among us humans, with blazing swords and holy light, and gave us peace. They showed us how to be loving to one another through example and taught us how to bring about justice instead of revenge. But after centuries of prosperity, Fraxineus, the highest Seraphim, conductor of the Angelic choir, and the eldest Angel, The Star of Ash, started to feel discontent. Fraxineus believed the Angels should rule over us humans, and that humanity should serve them, and he was not alone in that corrupted thinking. When Umba refused their demands for power, Fraxineus and his fallen followers revolted and started enslaving and killing us humans. The loyal true Angels gathered warriors of faith and dubbed them the Sanctus Venatores and led them to battle against Fraxineus in the Grand Crusade ...” - Partus Vitae 1:11-33

“Wait! If Angels were the last things the Gods created, where do Demi-Humans come from?”

“Excellent question, Aidan!” Missus Aibrean said. “Since it is not written in the Libri ex Dii, many scholarly priests believe the Demi-Humans were created by the planet itself. Hence why they fit so well in the land of their origin. Like how the Leprechauns and Clurichauns are just the right sizes to make homes in our trees.”

“What makes them different from Demons or Undead?” Ronan asked, more than likely to try and scare everyone.

“Well prior to the Second Crusade, we didn’t have a clear set way of telling. This led to a lot of distrust since many are very unhuman-like. However, at the end of the Crusade, our own Saint Orlaith helped to make a legal definition in the Doctrine of Amnesty. Simply put, any non-human creature was considered a Demi-Human if th ey don’t eat humans or other Demi-Humans, are able to understand human speech, are able to follow our laws, and overall be a productive citizen. If such a creature is unable to fulfil any of those qualifications, they would be labelled as something else more fitting like an Undead, Demon, Beast, etc.”

***

It was still pouring out, and it didn’t look like it would calm down anytime soon, so lunch recess was inside today. The stove continued to burn, making the room uncomfortably humid and stuffy. Ronan and his friends were talking amongst themselves. They took glances at Jacinta, who was eating alone at her desk. Freya knew it was only a matter of time before he caused some trouble. Brigid headed toward her, and Freya followed. They were about to sit by her and introduce themselves when Jacinta got up and walked away from them in a strange, hunched way as if she was about to hit her head on the ceiling. “Did we do something wrong?” Freya asked.

Brigid, just as confused, said, “I dunno. Maybe a quare Fay thing to leave if someone else is about to sit down? Let’s try to introduce ourselves first.” They walked over to Jacinta to try again.

“What’s the story? The name’s ...”

“I don’t care,” Jacinta interrupted as she started to move again.

Freya tried to stop her, but when she was up close to her, she noticed Jacinta’s eyes were an odd amber colour and were slit like a cat’s, which made

Freya immediately nervous.

“I ... uh, I’m sorry, are we doing something wrong, J-Jacinta?” Freya managed to ask.

Jacinta glowered at Freya. Her teeth bared and revealed a sharp point on her cuspid teeth, making her look more like an animal about to attack. Jacinta took a deep breath and slowly spoke through her fanged teeth, which

reminded Freya of her fear of Vampires. "That ish not my name. Do not call me that."

"S-sorry, I …"

"I don't care if yer shorry. Pleash shtop bothering me and go away."

Brigid stepped in front of her and asked, "What is yer problem? We only
wanted to be friends."

"I don't want to be friendsh! Now go away!"

"Jaci … I uh m -mean," Freya stuttered. Soon after, Jacinta sprung over to Freya. Although Jacinta was a little shorter than her, Freya suddenly felt small. Jacinta began ranting, and as she went on, it became harder and harder to understand her as if the words started to meld together.

Everyone was staring at them while Missus Aibrean moved out of her desk. She was about to head toward the three of them when Brigid pulled Jacinta away by her shoulder and stared down at her until Jacinta stepped back.

"Jusht … Leave me alone," Jacinta struggled to say before angrily walking away. After a moment of uncomfortable silence, everyone returned to what they were doing, and Jacinta sat alone to finish her lunch. When Freya and Brigid went back to their desks to eat, Ronan had his smirk that she knew meant he had a terrible idea forming, which she was sure would somehow make things worse.

***

The rain had started to calm down ever so slightly when the class had finished. Even so, everyone's parents came by to pick them up with an umbrella in hand. Freya's father had also waited outside and listened to Mister Conall as he tried to chat with him.

Freya headed down the steps of the schoolhouse. When she looked at her father, she was reminded of his peculiar appearance. Her father always preferred avoiding crowds, so it was rare to see him around this large a group of people. But when he was, Freya couldn't help but notice how her father tended to stand out despite his best efforts. Compared to someone like Mister Conall, who despite being unusually brawny with a beer belly to match, was still average in height. His balding head wasn't unusual for the other fathers in town, and he didn't seem to mind it.

Freya's father was at least a head taller than the other parents. Freya often wondered if the reason her father rarely made eye contact with people was that his neck would hurt to constantly look down. When he was out in the town, he tended to walk with long strides and kept his feet anxiously moving when he stood still. Her father had a bad habit of shaking his leg whenever they sat on a public bench. His arms also seemed disproportionately long and scrawny, making him look lanky. And he never seemed to know what to do with them when he was around the other townspeople.

The rain trickled down on Freya and Brigid, so they hurried toward them

to get under their umbrellas.

"Hvordan har du det, vennen min?" Freya's father quietly asked.

"I'm doing fine. Takks, Pappa," Freya replied.

"So, what're you two chatting about?" Brigid asked her own father.

"I was telling Mister Pantar here about your new schoolmate."

"Bah! Don't get me started on her," Brigid groaned, not hiding her exasperation.

Mister Conall sighed as he asked what happened.

"I have no bloody idea!" Brigid said. "We tried to be polite and stuff, despite her awful puss. Then she loses the rag and starts yelling crap at Freya. I thought she was going to pounce on her, so I got in her way before she could try anything," Brigid answered.

Freya recollected the terrifying moment, of Jacinta's frightening fangs, of the glowering slitted eyes, and the look of utter contempt she had toward everyone. Freya couldn't stop herself from shivering.

"You ought to be more careful with Elves, lasses," came a voice from behind them.

Freya jumped and turned around with Brigid to see it was Mister Gallagher, Ronan's father. Ronan and Mister Gallagher both had shoulder-length brown hair and bright blue eyes, but that was where the similarities end. Mister Gallagher's face was a bit craggy with scars scattered across it. His nose was snubbed and slightly bent off-centre. He also had a bruised lower lip. Freya looked around to see if Ronan was with him. Instead, he was talking to his friends elsewhere, which was more than fine with her. Freya definitely did not want to deal with him after the day she had.

"Very unpredictable. I've encountered all sorts around the world during the Crusade. Ljósálfars in the giant tree land of Yggdrasil, Weiße Wesens of Graburg, Patupaiarehe while sailing the seas, but nothing worse than our homebred Aos Sí. When you get too close to them, they hide underground and use their fangs to bite at your ankles."

"Stop trying to scare them, Fao," Mister Conall said.

"Best they learn now before they learn the hard way as I did." Mister Gallagher lowered his head and then looked to the left so that Freya and Brigid could see his torn ear.

"See this, lasses? I got this nasty bite back when I was in the old mercenary company. It was thirteen years ago, I think, during the Crusade, and we were hunting down a gang of Demi-Human marauders."

"They don't need to hear any damn war stories, Faolán!" Mister Conall said sternly before Mister Gallagher could continue.

"It's all right, Tom. I'll leave out the messy
bits." "Every bit of the Crusade was messy."

Mister Gallagher ignored him and continued, "Anyway, we managed to ambush and slay most of them except for a few stragglers who wouldn't

surrender. I saw one of them lying on the ground, bout ready to head on to the afterlife, so being the merciful sod I was, I decided to end his suffering. However, when I got close to him, the sneaky bastard lunged for my jugular. I thank both Gods, my reflexes were fast enough to save my life, but my naive kindness cost me an ear. Which, from what it sounds like, if it weren't for Brigid's bravery, little Freya here might not have been so lucky."

Freya was starting to feel sick, while Brigid seemed to enjoy the praise too much to notice.

"Oh, get off the stage. She's just a kid. She isn't gonna attack anyone." "Maybe, Tom. But are you going to bet your kid's life on it? I certainly won't."

"I'm not gonna let her hurt my friends!" Brigid exclaimed, but Freya was too nervous to say anything.

"I'm telling you two that she won't hurt anyone. She was probably scared or misunderstood what was going on. Give her a chance to fit in," Mister Conall pleaded.

Mister Conall and Mister Gallagher kept arguing back and forth when the two priestesses spoke with Missus Aibrean. Jacinta was there too. Her arms were being held by the priestess while she scowled at anyone who came too close to her. Freya tightly squeezed her father's arm, and he seemed to understand what she was trying to say. He took Freya's hand and tried to quietly leave their conversation.

They were able to get a little bit away before Mister Gallagher grabbed her father by the shoulder causing him to take a sharp breath. Mister Gallagher mustn't have noticed and asked, "Hey! You're Kal, right? Freya's older brother? You've lived here a while, but I don't think we've had a chance to really talk."

"He's her father, Fao," Mister Conall corrected.

Freya was not sure if Mister Gallagher was serious or just trying to mess with her father. It would explain where Ronan got it if he was. Freya wasn't going to let her father be bullied too. She gave Mister Gallagher the same scary stern look Missus Aibrean gave to anyone who was misbehaving.

"Awe, no need to fret, lass, I didn't mean anything by it. Yer Da looks very young, that's all."

"Why are people saying that?" Freya pondered. Before she could ask Mister Gallagher to explain, he continued.

"Anyway, I trust my boy can handle her, but would you want to risk little Freya's safety for a feral Elf kid who doesn't even want to be here?"

Her father shifted awkwardly before saying, "We need to buy herbs before they are sold out." And he walked away swiftly with Freya in tow, ignoring what Mister Gallagher wanted to say.

Her father waited until they were some distance away. He looked around before quietly telling her, "I trust Mister Conall would not do anything that

might get you or his own daughter hurt. But if she or anyone else even threatens you, let me know. I will deal with them." Freya slowly nodded, then grabbed his arm and clung to him the rest of the way home.

***

The constant rain had turned the dirt roads into a shallow river of mud, causing the already-busy marketplace to be congested with people, livestock, and caravans. Her father decided to take them through the back-alley shortcuts he liked to use whenever people were around. They made it home a little less drenched than when they left this morning. Her father placed a sign on his stand, telling any customers to knock on their door for business, and he placed his tray of potion vials on the dining table. Freya went inside, took off her boots, and started the fire on the stove to warm up their home. Her father joined her after he finished bringing everything inside.

After Freya was warm and dry, she asked her father if she could do some spell writing. He nodded, and Freya grabbed a pencil and a pile of papers from under her father's cot and began jotting down formulas. This was the closest thing to Magic Freya's father allowed her to do outside the woods. It helped her find ways to fix her errors, make the spells simpler to reduce the kick of the Rules of Reality, cut down multiple spell instances, and it was a fun way to pass the time.

Her father once told her he used to own a book full of formulas he used as a quick reference for spells, but had to get rid of it after the Crusade lest he was discovered.

"I wish we could have those now," Freya thought.

Her father told Freya if she was going to write spells down at home, he must be with her, and she must be near the stove with the fire going. Freya had to throw all of her work into their stove to burn it when she was finished and if anyone came to the house. Freya understood she couldn't risk getting caught, and she didn't have to burn them too often, but it still annoyed her to no end whenever she had to start all over.

Her father sat at the table organising his potion vials. Every so often, a customer would come and buy an everyday potion. Like a Phigs healing potion, potions for helping with sleep, or potions to tell if a baby was replaced with a pesky changeling.

As Freya worked on her spell, she couldn't help herself and took a few cursory glances at her father and thought, "Why do pe ople think he is my brother? They weren't the first ones to think that, but it was so much today. I guess none of Pappa's hair is grey like most parents. Is he really so young?"

After an hour and a half of forced concentration, Freya finished her entire spell, and she only had to burn her work twice today. The pages were sprawled with diagrams, algorithms, and formulas across them, covering every available space on the paper. It was designed for the mental control efficiency of the stones from the last practice. It would reduce the number of tasks she had to keep track of, freeing up her mind of redundant variables to worry about. Freya showed them to her father to get his opinion before another customer came and forced her to burn them again. Her father looked over each page carefully. Every so often, he would either nod to himself or make an approving hmm sound.

"You have here v is the x-axis causing a displacement x?" her father asked her.

"Ja, so for the constant force acting on a particle in the x-axis to be in the work done by then $K = \frac{1}{2} m v^2$," Freya explained. It was always strange speaking spell configurations out loud with him. As if she and her father were playfully swearing at each, not that he ever cared about swearing, but Freya tried not to get into the habit lest Missus Aibrean used her hickory stick on her.

Her explanation seemed well enough for her father, so he went back to reading it. As Freya waited, she wondered, "Would it be all right to ask him? No, what if he gets scared and shaky again? I don't want him to feel upset. He was all right talking about the Crusade. Maybe this won't bother him? And I should at least know how old he is … shouldn't I?"

Freya decided to force herself to ask, "Pappa, why do you look so young?" Her father, still looking at the pages, replied, "Because I am." He quietly laughed at Freya's unamused expression.

Freya asked, "Why are you so young then?" Hoping to get an actual answer this time.

Her father sat up straight and looked at her with a slightly more serious tone, "Because your mother and I had you when we were younger than most other parents would."

"Why?"

"It just sort of happened."

"I don't get it."

"You will when you're older."

Her father went back to the pages and asked Freya to explain why she believed it would be better to use existing momentum for turning the stone rather than to generate it herself manually. Freya answered it would reduce the amount of mental processing required to both rotate and stop it. Seemingly pleased with Freya's answer, her father nodded and continued through the pages.

"Do you even know how old you are?" Freya asked, starting to lose her patience.

"I think twenty-six or twenty-seven, maybe younger. I do not remember, and it is not important … I am sorry, vennen min, it is hard to focus on your spell while I am talking. So could you please give me a minute?"

Freya should have known her father was trying to tell her not to pry any further, and she mostly knew when to stop. Perhaps she was more upset that her father doesn't tell h er about himself more than she realised. How despite promising to tell each other everything, Freya has to tiptoe around every conversation about himself lest he gets scared. The few pieces of information she got were few and far between. Even finding out just yesterday he and her mother fought in one of the biggest wars in history.

"Are none of those 'important'?" Freya thought before angrily shouting out, "How do you forget your own age? Are you going to forget about Mamma or me? Are we not going to be important to remember?" Freya immediately regretted it when his hands began shaking. Her father was no longer there anymore. Freya didn't know where he went, but the man sitting at the table was someone else. Like a lifeless puppet that breathed.

Then

The scalpel slowly scraped scars across his soft skin. Tubes pumped putrid oily black fluids in and out of Kalby's stomach, like a new unwanted artery. He pulled his wrists, tore them till they bled, fought with every ounce of strength, and achieved nothing against the iron restraints. These men … these monsters in white robes and strange, inhuman masks poked, punctured, and prodded Kalby. One mask was half of a bone-white face which was sculpted, and the other half was a skull. Another was black with gold lines twirling around it. The third, who sounded younger, had a mask that looked like a simple flat brown board. It was like looking at a wall closing in.

They seemed to speak words, but it was all buzzing from pain and haze. Kalby would scream, but they clamped his mouth shut. It was tight enough to nearly grind his teeth. They said his voice was irritating. When the masked ones finished, they sewed him back together like a torn stuffed toy. Since they were done, he would be tossed aside to his cell. At least for a while, it will be another kid's turn.

Now

"I'm sorry, Pappa! Please don't get scared! Please!" He reached out and pulled Freya toward him. He wrapped his arms around her and hugged her as if she was going to float away. His arms were so tight it was getting hard for her to breathe. "I'll be quiet, I'll stop asking, I promise, please don't be scared!" Freya pleaded naively.

Her father's only responses were confusing, whispered rantings, mutterings, and apologies. Freya had no idea what to do as her stomach twisted and turned for a few moments. Her eyes began to sting and water

when all she could hear was her father's heart racing inside his chest. Freya noticed and tried to reach for the potion tray, hoping to find something which would get her father to relax or, at the least, make him fall asleep. But her fingertips could just barely reach the tray on the table.

There were a couple of knocks on the door. Freya's father jerked toward it, his eyes like that of a trapped animal. Freya feared her father might try to use Magic on whoever was on the other side of the door.

Her father was deathly silent for a moment. Then in a flash, the papers seemed to have disappeared from where he dropped them, and the stove cover opened and shut so fast it seemed to crack. Her father sharply inhaled and released Freya as he tried to spring to his feet, only to collapse back down. There were another couple of knocks. Freya tried to stand and run to the door, telling whoever was out there to go away. However, her father finally got up and grabbed her shoulder to stop her and keep himself standing. He took three slow deep breaths and rubbed his eyes. There was one more knock, and her father opened the door.

It was an older-looking man Freya didn't recognize, though he looked like a dockhand. He had long greenish-black hair that reached down to his shoulders and a thick moustache that trailed down to his jaw. "I came to get a potion, but I heard some quare noises inside. Is everything all right?" The dockhand asked.

Her father answered, "Ja, I …" but the dockhand cut him

off. "I was asking yer kid there."

Freya wiped her eyes quickly before saying, "I'm f-fine. Th-the knocking s-startled me while I was c-cooking and I accidentally s-slammed the stove cover. Da also tr-tr-tripped and fell over."

The dockhand took a careful look at Freya and her father. "Are you sure?" He asked, and Freya nodded. "If you say so." The dockhand turned back to her father. "Sorry about that, Mister. I have my own niece and nephew to look out for after losing my brother in the Crusade. You can never be too careful nowadays."

Her father nodded before coughing. "Potions?"

"Yes, I heard from Mister Conall that you sold those here. Truth be told, I didn't even know we had an apothecary in town. You should sell closer to the Port District."

Her father ignored the comment and allowed the dockhand inside, and they went through his tray of various potions. Freya busied herself cleaning the ashes that leaked on the floor from the stove. After a few minutes, the dockhand bought a potion Freya was unfamiliar with and then headed off. Once her father closed the door, he slumped down and leaned his back against it. Freya slowly walked over to her father. Tears started to well up in her eyes again. Shame and guilt covered her father's face, and Freya ran and hugged him.

It had been almost a year since her father panicked like that. He still had nightmares, but even Freya had those from time to time. Freya had been so careful to avoid saying or doing anything that could cause him to be scared. She had dared to hope she might stop it from ever happening again. But, Freya's curiosity overcomes her.

"I-I'm s-sorry, Pappa. I d-didn't mean to. I-I didn't know what to …"

Her father wrapped his long arms around her, gently this time, and she

buried her face in his chest. Her father's gloved hand gently stroked her long hair as he whispered, "I am okay now, vennen min. Please do not blame yourself. My fears should not be your burdens and I am sorry I have not been able to control them …"

***

Her father decided to close up early for the night and told her he needed to leave the house for a bit. Freya asked if she could come with him, both not wanting her father to be alone nor being alone herself. Her father didn't say anything, so Freya sprang outside after him, forgetting to bring anything to keep them both dry before leaving their house.

They walked around town for a while. Most of the shops in the marketplace were closing, and their lanterns had been blown out. Freya wasn't sure where her father was going or even if he was truly going anywhere. He sometimes just wandered after being scared. They walked on and on as the night was getting darker, as the air and rain grew colder, and as Freya could no longer stop herself from shivering.

Her father finally stopped and stared at Freya as if waking up from a dream. He looked like he had only now noticed Freya had been alongside him the entire time in the freezing rain. Her father quickly removed his jacket, wrapped it snugly around Freya, and took her straight home as fast as he could. As soon as they were inside, her father made Freya sit by the stove. He foraged around the house for warm blankets and clothes to pile on her.

After finding everything they had, encasing Freya in a tomb of blankets and coats, her father clasped his arms around Freya. He bombarded her with questions, "Do you still feel cold? Do you need another blanket? Do you want me to get …"

"Are you feeling better, Pappa?" Freya interrupted.

"What?" Her father asked.

"I'm fine. I was just worried you were still scared."

Her father winced for a second. "I should never worry you like that. It is … I." Her father closed his eyes and caught his breath before continuing. "I want you to know I love you beyond imagining. But I do not … must not remember my life before your mother. What little I do is … unpleasant, and I refuse to let it be a part of our life."

Freya wasn't sure how to feel as she contemplated. "Was there really nothing about Pappa's life from before that he wants to remember? His

childhood? Were his own Pappa and Mamma evil?"

Her father, practically reading Freya's confused and concerned expression like a book, said to her, "Nothing is more important to me than you and your mother."

***

When her father believed Freya was warm enough, he offered to read one of her favourite books before bed. It was a collection of stories about Knights from various kingdoms or keeps of Sanctus Venatores, saving people from evil villains and monsters. Though both she and her father would skip the parts that had Draois as the villain, which unfortunately there was plenty of. Before Freya had fallen asleep, her father kissed her cheek and told her goodnight.

CHAPTER 3
DAY OF CHOICES

"Are you awake?" Her father asked Freya as he carried her on his back through the woods again. Freya figured she was still tired from getting out of bed this morning and dozed off during the hike.

"Nooo," Freya said before she yawned and rested her head against his. "Would you prefer sleeping in instead of practicing today?"

"Nooooo."

"Heh, all right, vennen min."

Leaves fell all around Freya and her father as they headed toward their spot. Freya shivered from the cold air, watching her breath turn to fog. Her father reached into his belt, grabbed a metal canteen tied to it, and handed it to Freya. The canteen was warm against her fingers. Freya took a sip and tasted the hot soup. When Freya and her father reached their neck of the woods, everything had already been set up the day before. There were different stones, three buckets, and a short thick rope waiting to be used for practice. Her father lowered himself, and Freya climbed down his back. Her father went to one of the buckets and picked it up.

"For this exercise, I will pour whatever is in this bucket into the air, and I want you to catch it before it hits the ground."

"What is it?"

"It could be anything from a spoon, to a piece of cloth, or copper coins. The idea is that you would be able to identify it and configure the gravity on it fast enough to catch it before it hits the ground."

This seemed simple enough for Freya. She got herself prepared and in position, making sure she would have a clear view with little to distract her. The faint blue ring surrounded her father as the bucket rose rapidly. It stopped at six metres in the air, and when Freya nodded to her father, it began to tilt over. A pencil rolled out and started its descent to the ground. Although

she couldn't see them, she could mentally picture all the millions of instructions created by the Rules of Reality that caused the pencil to fall. It's mass, the force of gravity, and the exact angle of trajectory. She was aware of every minute change in velocity, acceleration, and kinetic energy.

Since it was so small, and all Freya was doing was catching the pencil, the Rules of Reality didn't mind the little amount of change Freya was making. If Freya wanted to lift dozens of pencils or a giant-sized one, then the Rules would fight her for control to return things back to normal as the Rules assigned it. This would require her to think of more configurations to get around it, which would cause her mind to fog and headaches if she kept going.

It took Freya a brief moment to think of all the different configurations to apply force. If Freya overestimated it and used too much opposing gravity, the pencil would collapse inward. The pencil was nearly halfway down before Freya had a hold on it. It was becoming clear Freya had underestimated it instead, as the pencil had only slowed its fall. Freya quickly came up with a new configuration accounting for this, increasing the pull on the pencil until it finally stopped only millimetres above the grass.

Freya could see her father's smile through the shadow of his big hat. The ring around Freya faded when she stopped focusing, and natural gravity took the pencil back to the ground.

"Ready for another one?" her father asked.

"Uh-huh."

Another bucket levitated in the air. It tilted over, and a dozen acorns fell out. Freya knew she couldn't catch all of them, so she only focused on three acorns. The first one she grabbed was closest to the bottom, and when it stopped falling, some of the other acorns bumped into it. They would only be slowed by half a second, but even that little extra time helped. Freya grabbed the second acorn when it was almost halfway down.

Levitating more than two objects was confusing to Freya. When she used Magic to grab things, Freya would use her hands to keep track, like counting with her fingers, but she can't do this if there were three or more objects. Despite that, Freya could hold and move around three things, albeit with far less grace and precision than she could with two. It was mentally straining to keep track and focus on several things at once. Freya had seen her father pull and move six objects at once, so Freya knew it was something she could learn if she practiced enough.

After a few attempts, she managed to pull the third acorn and have it suspended with the other two in mid-air while the rest of them fell to the ground.

"Good, you're getting faster!"

Freya dropped the acorns and did an overly dramatic bow to her father, similar to how the local bard, Mister Cadhla, would after he finished a song

or story, "Tusen Takks, Pappa."

"How are you feeling?"

Freya paused to make sure. When she didn't notice anything, she said, "I'm fine. No headaches or dizziness yet."

"Okay, here is one more."

The final bucket reached the sky. After Freya's previous successes, she was confident she could catch whatever this object was. The bucket tilted again, and water poured out. Freya had never attempted to alter the Rules of Reality on water before. In fact, she found it hard to recall whether her father had done so either. Freya tried her best anyway configuring in her head, "Water is $W = F x = m \ a \ x = m \ (\ (\ V - v \ ) / t \ ) \ (\ \frac{1}{2} \ (\ V + v \ ) / t \ ) \ (\ \frac{1}{2} \ (\ V - v \ ) \ ) t$ and uh and uh and and and …"

Anything beyond that was too much computation. Even after Freya had gone through thousands of configurations in her head, they all seemed to reach dead ends. Freya's brain was whirring and hurting as if she were going to have a mental overload with so much incomprehensible information. Her mind instantly went blank, and a sharp shock went through her head, causing her to yelp. The water splashed on the ground.

"Are you all right?" her father asked.

Freya's mind clouded, making it hard to think. "Ja? I uh … What just happened, Pappa?"

"I am sorry, I did not think you would have tried so hard. But hopefully, this will help you understand the next lesson," her father said.

Freya's head cleared up a bit, allowing her to at least pay attention to what he was saying.

"Vennen min, can you tell me how our Magic works?"

Freya took a moment to gather her thoughts. "Well, um … According to Missus Aibrean, it was the evil Angel Fraxineus's fault, but you said not to believe that story, so …"

"I did not mean that far back, vennen min," her father interrupted, trying not to laugh a little.

"Oh."

"Please tell me how Gravomancy works."

Freya thought back and recited what her father told her plenty of times, "Everything in the Known World runs off of the Rules of Reality. If an apple falls from a tree, it has to follow the instructions and formulas set in place by the Rules of Reality and fall to the ground. Magic Users can notice these instructions and alter them a little bit. By configuring the rules, we can make the apple fall upward or hover in place instead."

"Okay, but how do you alter the formula for every single drop of water in a bucket?"

Her father took another bucket of water and beckoned for Freya to come over to him. When Freya did, he took off one of his gloves and put his hand into the water. Her father clenched his hand into a fist and slowly pulled it out. Water leaked out between his fingers, and when he showed the palm of his hand to Freya, it was empty. "See? Almost all of the water has left my hand. So how do I pick this up and move it like I would with other objects?"

"We use a bucket?" Freya answered.

Her father tried to hide his amusement as he said, "Well … you are not wrong. How would you lift it if such a thing were not around?"

Freya put a great deal of thought into this problem; however, all possible answers seemed to require more mental processing than was possible for her, and she doubted anyone else would be able to either. "I don't know, Pappa. Everything I can think of won't work."

"This is because we think and see things as a gravity practitioner. So instead, we would have to use a different school of Magic called Hydromancy," her father said.

"Hydromancy?"

"It is a type of Magic focused on manipulating and controlling water and similar liquids," her father answered.

"How does it work?" Freya asked, eagerly hoping this is what the lesson would be about.

Her father shrugged, much to Freya's disappointment. "Trigonometry differs from calculus as calculus differs from statistics. They share the same principles but have to change aspects to solve specific problems. Same with Magic. They all have to follow the Rules of Reality, such as how we cannot create or destroy matter, or how the more we try to alter the rules, the more it tries to fight back to enforce normality," Her father said as if repeating something told to him.

"How many are there?" Freya asked.

"Not sure. I guess as much as we can think of."

"So what is Dark Magic? Missus Aibrean said almost all Draoi use it." "I do not think it is a different kind of Magic, but just a label locals give

to a type of Magic they do not like, such as Necromancy or Asthéneiamancy. In this country, practically all Magic is considered Dark Magic, but in others, they have different ones."

"Is there any Magic you dislike?" Freya asked.

"I do not know enough about any, other than Gravity, to have an opinion."

Freya began to feel overwhelmed yet excited at the same time. There was so much about Magic she didn't know, but that only meant she and her father could learn with each other forever.

Her father continued, "What I want you to understand is that I had an opportunity to expand what I knew during the Second Crusade. But I lost the chance due to my … difficulty with people." This did not surprise Freya. "If you can learn something that I cannot teach you, try to do so. I do not

want my lack of Magical knowledge to hold you back. But please be safe about it."

"Then I can teach you, Pappa!" Freya excitedly exclaimed.

Her father gave her head a soft pat as he said, "I look forward to your instruction, vennen min."

***

Her father did not have other lessons planned for today, so they spent the rest of their time playing games, such as quick throws and floating things around an obstacle course. The last game they played was tug -o-war. Her father suggested something else, but Freya wanted to perform a little test of her own.

Her father placed a thick piece of rope on the ground between them, and they both took ten paces away from it. Her father counted. One. Two. Three. The piece of rope was yanked into the air, cracking it like a whip.

Nearly all of Freya's concentration was on having gravity pull the rope in the opposite direction. She could tell the total tension force on the rope was well past fifty kilograms and slowly increasing as they both pulled harder.

Freya began to sweat, and her head was burning despite the cold air. She tried every configuration possible to make her pull more powerfully and efficiently. Yet the rope remained rooted in its place. The ringed lights around Freya and her father were so bright, had it been night, it would have illuminated the whole clearing. Freya knew she couldn't match her father in this pulling contest.

Freya's goal, however, was to see what his limit was. And right now, she wasn't finding it. Freya began to feel a throbbing headache as the game went on, and it became strenuous for her to keep a mental hold on the rope as her mind fogged. It was like trying to solve a math problem while looking at the equation from an ever-dirtying window. Freya tried one last time to pull using hundreds of configurations at once, but then her father called out her name. ***

Freya soon noticed she was lying in her father's arms, staring at the morning sky as it seemed to spin all around her. Her head was numb, and she couldn't form any thoughts. Freya could see her father was trying to say something to her, but all she could hear was a piercing ringing in her ear. Her father grabbed an azure vial from his pouch and slowly poured it into her mouth. It tasted like a copper coin on Freya's tongue.

Freya slowly began to awake from her stupor, and with that, her headache came back in full force. Her father wiped her tiny nose with his sleeve, and she noticed a streak of blood smeared on it.

Her father helped Freya to her feet, and as soon as she could stand on her own, he asked chokingly, "What were you thinking?"

Freya had no idea what to say other than she was sorry.

Her father took some time to calm down before saying, "Freya, our minds

can do incredible things, but they have limits. It can sometimes warn us if we strain ourselves, but it isn't perfect. You could get brain damage, memory loss, or even die. And I cannot lose you too."

***

Her father had brought Freya to the schoolhouse; Freya felt her stomach wretching and her chest tightening. She hadn't felt like this since causing her father to panic three days ago. Even though he tells her it wasn't her fault, she can never shake the guilt she felt. However, at least today, Freya had a bothersome headache to keep her distracted while she was back in class since her father ended Magic practice early. He gave her some Xatralt on their way to the schoolhouse to help alleviate most of the pain. But he didn't let Freya have anymore because he said it can be addicting if you have too much or in too high a potency.

Jacinta arrived in class before everyone else, aside from Freya. Jacinta sat at her assigned desk after the two priestesses, who escorted her, headed back to the Church. Freya didn't dare to try and speak with Jacinta since Brigid wasn't around to help yet. So instead, Freya closed her eyes and rested her sore head on her desk until class began.

This morning's lesson was geography, where they then learned about Truth, a city out east between the First and Second Third Rivers. It was once the capital of Bastiel. The old blood -thirsting Queen used to rule there until the Sanctus Venatores defeated her and turned her palace into the National Courthouse. The Sanctus Venatores also turned the city of Hope, where the Tower of Babel resided, into the new capital and their primary keep.

A few more lessons went by until it was time for lunch recess. Freya ate by herself while Brigid was busy proving to some boastful boys that girls can, in fact, play mob ball better than them. Jacinta went to a corner between the schoolhouse and the white fence where people couldn't see her.

Freya recalled the promise she and Brigid made to Mister Conall. They were supposed to be Jacinta's friends. It was starting to seem impossible as their attempts so far haven't gotten them anywhere. Such as two days ago when they brought Brigid's leftover candy to school and tried to share it with Jacinta. All she did was stare blankly at them with glazed, cat-like eyes and was going to say something; instead, she crouched and walked away from them, nearly tripping over herself along the way.

Jacinta had been doing some bizarre things lately, and Freya had no idea what to make of it. She started to wear a sun hat and a thick coat everywhere, even when indoors. She had often fallen asleep in the middle of class, forcing Missus Aibrean to stop her lecture and wake her up before continuing. Despite repeated punishments from Missus Aibrean, Jacinta would still break simple rules like not making her manners to Missus Aibrean before and after class.

Jacinta was also not making the best impression on the other students, as most were too afraid to be near her. Freya had asked a dozen of them yesterday what their thoughts were or if they knew anything about Jacinta when Brigid wasn't in school because of a cold, and Freya was too nervous to try to speak with Jacinta by herself.

"Why are you asking me?" Aidan asked, trying to keep his dark blue cowlick down.

"Brigid likes to tell me how smart you are and you raise your hand all the time in class."

"I don't …Wait sh-she talks about me?"

"Yeah, she started doing that lately. I guess because she needs help with math."

"O-oh," Aidan said, letting out a breath.

"But anyway, do you know anything about Aos Sí?"

"Not really, no. To be honest, Jacinta there freaks me out. I heard she nearly bit the hand off one of the priestesses."

"Did you hear that from Ronan? You know he likes to rile everyone up."

"Yeah, but his Da really did fight them in the Crusade. Maybe he actually knows something this time."

"Oh, forget it."

***

Since none of her classmates were of any help that day, she ate her lunch alone against the white fence. Something was skittering across Freya's back and she thought there was a creepy, crawling critter on her, and in Freya's mind, she wasn't too far off. She shuddered with horror and jumped from where she was sitting. Freya nearly screamed until she realised it was just Ronan with a blade of grass in his hand, and he thought it was the funniest thing in the Known World.

"W-what d-do you want, Ronan!" Freya demanded nervously.

"W-w-well," Ronan said mockingly in his cocky voice. "I heard you were
asking about the Elf today."

"I-I don't w-want to hear what you have to s-say."

"Well, my Da and I agree she isn't learning to be like us like she needs to."

"What are you talking about?" Freya asked, concerned about what he was planning.

"Don't be daft, Freya. You know as well as I do if Brigid wasn't around, that Elf would attack you like a wild animal."

Freya shuddered again as the memory came to her.

"My Da told me that if you must bring a wild animal into town, you ought to at least break it in before it wreaks havoc," Ronan said.

"You want to tame her?"

Ronan hopped over the fence to get back inside, "Kinda. Missus Aibrean is doing her best, but she's being softer than a boneless fish. The Elf needs

to learn the hard way that her shite won't cut it
here." "What are you telling me for?" Freya
asked.

"Because I want your help. Everyone here is too scared to confront her, but you and Brigid did. I need a plan for this to work, and you are the smartest person I know."

There wasn't a hint of sarcasm in what he said, which took Freya by surprise.

"I-I don't want to get into t-t-trouble," Freya stammered, hoping in vain Ronan would end his mischievous machinations.

Ronan moved toward Freya and said, "You can't let her scare you, Freya. As my Da always tells me, 'If you don't stand up for yourself, you might never be able to stand again.' Don't you at least want to get back at her?"

Freya knew she shouldn't and whatever he was planning is sure to cause someone grief. Yet Ronan, when he wasn't being mean, could persuade plenty of the other kids. Even Freya had been convinced before, just with his sheer confidence in how right he thought he was, which had often gotten them reprimanded. This time, Freya wasn't going to be tricked again and told him, "No, I am sorry, Ronan, but I don't want to."

"Freya, you can't let fear …"

"N-no, Ronan!"

The disappointment was visible on Ronan's face, but it soon turned to anger as he told her, "Fine, you milksop! Don't go crying to me when she attacks you again," before he left in a huff.

***

Nothing had happened since those two days, and Freya had hoped Ronan had given up his scheme. But then some strange sounds came from Jacinta's spot in the yard. Freya went over to investigate while keeping a safe distance, only to discover she was gone. Freya peered over the fence. Worried she might have tried to run away, from the corner of her eye, Freya caught Jacinta being dragged with her arms forced into the air by Ronan.

"Da told me you had to keep their arms up. Their legs are weaker," Ronan said as he and three other kids took Jacinta into the town alleys.

Freya ran to her friend.

"Brigid!"

"What is it, Freya? I'm about to win here."

"Ronan. He-he grabbed J-Jacinta and t-took her to the alleys!"

"Has that boy gone banjaxed? Come on then! We need to tell the older kids!"

The two of them ran to the nearest older boy they could find and told him what happened. He ran to the other older kids to figure out what to do.

"I don't think we should go after them. Missus Aibrean said no one is allowed past the fence," one of the older girls said.

"What? But they left the fence! What if she runs away or what if Ronan hurts her?" Brigid shouted.

"Perhaps either is for the best," an older boy said.

Brigid looked at him incredulously.

"I mean, she clearly doesn't want to be here. So she should leave for our sake or Ronan can actually teach her some manners."

Freya could see Brigid was about to call all of them some words that would have gotten her a few dozen lashes from Missus Aibrean, so Freya grabbed her by the shoulders and took her away.

"What are we going to do?" Freya asked.

"If they won't go save her, then we will," Brigid said before she ran toward the fence.

"W-wait!" Freya shouted, her legs shaking.

Brigid stopped with her hand on the fence ready to climb over, "What is it?"

"S-should we d -do a- anything? W-we did what Miss-sus Aibrean told us to do. T-telling the older k-kids."

"Yeah, and those dossers aren't doing anything."

"R-right, but w-why sh-should we risk getting in t-trouble when J-Jacinta doesn't e-even like us? S-she wouldn't h-help us i-if we were in trouble!"

"It doesn't matter. We made a promise to my Da and I am keeping it." And before Freya had a chance to say more, Brigid jumped over the fence and ran after them.

"This is a bad idea." Freya paced back and forth, thinking, "There's nothing we can do anyway." Freya pressed her hands against the fence before pushing herself back. "What am I thinking? This is stupid." Freya took a hesitant breath. Her mind was coming to dead ends as she tried to think of alternatives. "Was that what Mamma thought when Pappa was in trouble?"

Before she even had a plan, her shaking legs had climbed over the fence and caught up with Brigid in the alleys.

"About time you showed up," Brigid whispered.

"S-sorry."

"Don't worry about it. Come on, I think I can see a trail of where they dragged Jacinta."

The two stalked the trail and eventually found Ronan and his friends. They were dragging an exceptionally livid Jacinta through the alleys. Her mouth was covered by a piece of cloth. They had nearly lost them in a few of the twists and turns. Luckily, they didn't go too far when Ronan and his group stopped by some barrels next to a storehouse. Freya and Brigid hid behind a nearby crate of old fish and got a better look at the whole group.

Freya recognized them from school but didn't know them by name. Two of the kids were fairly tall, one had short red hair and the other curly black hair. They were both around Brigid's age, if not older, and were the ones holding Jacinta upside down by her legs. The other one seemed to be a

freckled little boy of around six with bright red hair whom Freya figured Ronan had either tricked or threatened to come with him for a reason Freya didn't know.

Jacinta tried clawing at them, but they held her too high and far for her to reach.

Ronan made a show of slowly walking toward Jacinta, swaying his shoulders and having one of his hands resting on something Freya couldn't see on his belt. "A bit of a minus craic facing someone who knows how to fight, huh?" Ronan gloated. "Da was right. We let you Demi-Humans live in our towns, and until we run you out, all you do is cause trouble for our friends."

Freya was flummoxed. "Was he referring to Brigid and me?"

Ronan continued, "Everyone else may ignore what you did and what your kind always do, but we won't." Ronan turned to the little kid nearby and asked, "What should we do to make sure she won't attack our friends again?" The little boy took a moment to think of an answer then said, "Use a hickory stick like Missus Aibrean?"

Ronan ruffled the little boy's hair as he said, "I like your thinking, but it's not quite enough. I have an idea." Then Ronan pulled out a knife from his pocket.

"Woah! Where did you get that?" the curly haired big kid asked.

"My Da gave it to me. He used it during the Second Grand Crusade to beat up bad guys like Jacinta here who don't belong."

Jacinta's eyes contracted into a narrow line.

Brigid rushed out of her hiding spot, "What are you doing, you eejit?"

Ronan looked at her and said, "Don't worry. I won't use it unless she gives me a reason to."

"Y-you n-need t-to s-stop, R-Ronan!" Freya said, no longer hiding behind the crate.

"I stop and do what? Wait till she bites someone's hand off with her animal teeth? Wait for her to scratch someone's eyes out with her claws? Wait for her to bury someone alive with her diggingness? People like you waited and my Da's hometown of Temperance was destroyed by this lot." Ronan moved toward Jacinta, placing the knife against her ear before he said, "And we won't let it happen again here."

In a flash of movement, Jacinta shoved Ronan, causing the knife to slide across the tip of her ear. The way Ronan was knocked back, Freya would have thought he was kicked by a donkey. Brigid, without hesitation, tried to wrestle Ronan to the ground, while Freya and the other boys were too scared to move.

"Freya, get the knife!"

"Get off of me!"

Freya approached cautiously. Hoping Ronan wouldn't notice, but as soon as she could reach, he started swinging the knife around wildly hoping to scare her off. But the knife slid across her face.

Freya fell backward, and everyone else froze in place staring at her. Ronan turned his head and looked at Freya in horror. Freya's fear turned to blind fury at Ronan.

"How Ronan could be so stupid to bring a knife to school and such an arsehole to try and use it on Jacinta? If he wants to show what it was like to face someone stronger, I can gladly demonstrate."

She could use Magic, altering the Rules of Reality to toss him around like a doll.

"Or I could dangle him upside down in the air until his face became redder than an apple just so he could see what it was like."

Freya could do whatever she wanted to him. It would be so simple. It's just a tiny problem she could simply solve. But then she remembered if she did, then the Sanctus Venatores would come and take her away from her father forever.

All of a sudden, a searing pain burned on her face, and she began to cry.

Ronan quickly tried to apologise, but Freya ran deeper into the alleys.

"Freya!" Brigid called, but tears and blood covered her eyes and made it impossible to see where she was going. When Freya finally stopped, she curled herself against a nearby wall and patted around blindly for a washbasin to clean her face.

Freya thought she would never want to go back to school while Ronan and Jacinta were still there. Ronan had always been a jerk, but now he was going too far. And Jacinta? If she hadn't been so angry and mean to everyone, then Ronan wouldn't have had an excuse for what he did, and even if he did it anyway, the older kids wouldn't have been too scared to do anything. Freya hoped if she asked her father, he might let her stay at home. Perhaps he can teach her how to make and sell potions, and they could run the shop together. Freya started to panic and get dizzy as she could not find a washbasin. If she couldn't see, then what if she accidentally wandered into one of the bad parts of town her father warned her about? What if someone tried to hurt her, kidnap her, or worse?

"Where are you going? Get back here!" Freya could hear Brigid shouting. "She'sh thish way!"

"What? Oh, thank Gods. Good job, Jacinta. Are you all right, Freya?" Freya shook her head while choking back tears.

"It's going to be all right. Let's wash off your face first."

The two of them guided her. There were dripping sounds of water and soon cold, wet hands wiped her eyes. Freya opened them. Jacinta and Brigid were wiping their shivering hands dry on their skirts near a washbasin. One of Brigid's knuckles was bruised and Jacinta had wrapping on the tip of her ear. Freya went to the washbasin and used the water on the rest of her face.

When Freya was all clean, she looked at her reflection in the water and was horrified upon seeing the red gash across her face.

"Hold still," Jacinta said, slowly enunciating every word. She used her claws and ripped a strip off her own dress like it was paper and wrapped it around the cut on Freya's face. Brigid winced, but Freya was unsure if it was because of the wound on Freya's face or the tearing of a dress.

"Th-Thank you, Brigid and Jacin-mmm," Freya said, stopping herself short as soon as Jacinta's eyes contracted sharply.

Jacinta closed her eyes and let out a breath before slowly asking, "Why did you two help me? What do you want out of me?"

"Well, cutting out the attitude would be a good start. We want to be your friends, but you're making it damn hard."

"Why do you want to be friendsh sho badly? Just sho you can try to turn me into a human like everyone elshe here?" Jacinta asked, slipping back to her normal accent.

"Hey, what's wrong with being a human?"

"I don't think that's what she meant, Brigid," Freya said, trying to calm everyone down.

"You want to be a blacksmith, but imagine if all the adults were trying to get you to be something else like a farmer or a nanny."

"I … I guess… Sorry. That's not why. Like we know you lost your family, Freya and I lost our Mammas and I hate seeing people getting bullied, so I couldn't just let Ronan get away with it, and uh, yeah."

Jacinta crouched and started scratching one of her clawed fingers on the ground for a minute before saying, "Fine. I shuposhe you sheem nishe enough. I'll try to do sho too."

"Well glad we got that settled. Come on now. We ought to head back to the schoolhouse before Missus Aibrean can finish tying up our nooses."

***

The three managed to find their way out of the needlessly confusing labyrinth, otherwise known as the alleys, and back to the schoolhouse. Half an hour later, the bleeding stopped, and they threw the blood-stained face wrap away before they were greeted by a couple of angry and panicking older kids. The two were brought before Missus Aibrean with Ronan. Who, for some reason, had a broken nose. His group was already there, standing in wait like criminals brought before the gallows. Freya, Brigid, and Jacinta were told to stand next to them and face the rest of the class as they watched it all happen.

Missus Aibrean stood in front of them with a hickory stick in hand. She said in a tone that could make an innocent man plead guilty, "I am going to ask each of you what happened, and you will answer politely and honestly. Do you all understand?" They all nodded. Missus Aibrean started with the two bigger kids.

The red- haired one said he didn't remember what happened, and the black-haired one said he wasn't with them. Even though everyone saw them all come back together. It was plain to see Missus Aibrean wasn't buying it, though she let them finish their stories.

Then it was the little kid's turn, it sounded like he was trying to confess, but he was crying too much for anyone to understand him. Missus Aibrean let him wait outside with one of the older girls accompanying him to help him calm down.

Missus Aibrean noticed the cut on Freya's face and started her questions about that. The other students tried to look at Freya from their desks, causing Freya to bashfully hide her face with her long hair. Freya was worried about how much trouble she would be in for going over the fence and out of school grounds. Still, she decided to tell the truth. Partially to make sure Ronan got what he deserved. Also, despite how strict Missus Aibrean can be, Freya still respected her and didn't like lying to her.

"And do you disagree with anything Freya said, Brigid and Jacinta?" Missus Aibrean asked. They shook their heads no. Missus Aibrean asked Ronan the same question.

He didn't confirm nor deny it, simply saying, "I did what I know is right, but I didn't mean for Freya to get hurt."

"Well, you will make it up to Freya and Jacinta on your own time. What I don't understand is how you broke your nose?" Missus Aibrean asked.

Freya noticed Brigid looking at something on the ceiling as Ronan glared at her.

"I tripped," Ronan answered as he turned his head away from her.

"You tripped and broke your nose?" Missus Aibrean asked, unconvinced.

"Yes …" Ronan affirmed.

It was hard for everyone to watch what happened next for their punishments. The two bigger kids received five lashes to their knuckles for fighting, seven for lying, four for leaving school without her permission, and ten for misbehaving to girls. They would also have to come into class early for a week to bring firewood. The younger kid was only given two lashes and a stern word in front of the class. It was his first offence, and he was too little to know much better. Ronan was given four for leaving school without her permission, five for fighting, ten for misbehaving to girls, ten for leading a younger peer into trouble, twelve for bringing a knife, fifteen for attempting to injure a fellow schoolmate, and twenty for causing injury to a fellow schoolmate.

Suffice it to say, Freya would be surprised if Ronan could hold anything properly for the next month. He would also have to write and present a full-page apology to Freya and Jacinta on Monday. Jacinta didn't have to worry about punishment since she didn't have a choice in all this, but Freya and Brigid did, and they broke the rules by leaving and wrestling down Ronan.

However, Missus Aibrean told her she would deal with their punishment after class.

***

When the dreaded time came, everyone went outside except for Freya and Brigid. They stood before Missus Aibrean. Freya stuck out her hands and closed her eyes. Freya anticipated the stinging pain of the hickory stick. Instead, Missus Aibrean's hands held hers as she told them, "I am proud of the two of you for standing up for Jacinta."

"Th-Thank you, ma'am?" Freya said nervously, keeping her eyes closed if it was meant to lower her guard.

"Does this mean we're not in trouble?" Brigid asked.

"Not this time, but if either of you leaves the schoolyard without my permission again, you will be. Understood?"

"Yes, ma'am!" They both said excitedly, they made their manners to Missus Aibrean and ran outside.

As they walked home, Freya tried to cover the cut on her face with her hair, and when Brigid noticed, she told her, "Don't fret about it so much, Freya. If anything, it makes you look deadly! People would think twice before messing with you." Freya was turning red as she imagined herself looking like a cutthroat bandit. Once Brigid laughed and hugged Freya before saying, "Aww, I take it back. You're too adorable to scare anybody."

"I could be scary if I wanted to," Freya mumbled as she hid her mouth in her dark purple robe. When they were close to Brigid's home, Freya asked her if she knew what really happened to Ronan's nose, out of both curiosity and catharsis.

"Oh, when that ill-set arseface hurt you, Jacinta went to look for you. He and his goons tried to stop her and were getting me all hepped up saying some gobshite like Jacinta was going to eat you or something. So I busted his nose, and that set them all straight." Brigid answered proudly.

"Aren't you worried he'll tell on you?"

"As if that cocky bloke would admit to getting his arse kicked by a girl?" Brigid chuckled.

Mister Conall waved to the two of them. Brigid said goodbye to Freya before heading in the smithery to help her father. Freya walked the rest of the way home by herself.

***

When Freya reached the foot of their hill, she raced up it to see her father. Her father went around his stand to meet Freya. Upon seeing her face, he immediately rushed over to her.

"What happened? Are you all right? Who did this?" Her father asked in raspy trepidation as he examined every inch of her face.

Freya assured her father she was all right but hesitated when trying to find a way to tell him what happened without her father panicking even further.

45

"I know I have had trouble keeping it lately, but remember our promise to tell each other everything, vennen min," her father said in a calmer tone. And so Freya did, and her father listened intently and patiently. When she was done, her father hugged her and said, "I am happy beyond words that you are so brave and kind as your mother. But I never want you to do that again."

"What?" Freya asked, not sure what her father was saying.

"Your well-being is the only thing in the world that matters to me, vennen min. I better let Mister Gallagher know of this as well." And her father began marching into town after giving her a small, web orange, Phigs potion. Freya chugged it down and followed him in increasing concern about what might happen. It tasted like a copper coin covered in cinnamon and the cut on her face faded as she caught up to him.

They went all the way across the Starboard District toward the Port District. Along the way, Freya told her father how Ronan was punished at school hoping that would end things, yet it seemed he was still determined to have a word with him. They reached Mister Gallagher's house, and Freya could see Ronan and his father about to head out on a hunt while his mother was inside cooking.

It was a one-story wooden house, similar to Freya's, but was at least double the size in length, and they lived close to the docks, so the salty sea scent was strong here.

As soon as Freya and her father approached, Ronan averted his eyes while Mister Gallagher headed toward them. "Look, my son told me what happened. It was unfortunate but an accident."

Freya's father remained silent.

Mister Gallagher continued, "I gave him the knife so he can remind the Elf girl of the fear of Umba's Justice. But little Freya here was probably scared and confused, and unintentionally got caught in the crossfire. We never meant for anyone to get hurt. Can you both find it in your hearts to forgive us?"

Mister Gallagher extended his hand out to her father and grasped it.

"That's quite a grip you have there. Uh, o-okay now. That's a little too much. Ow, all right, it's starting to hurt now. ARGH, I -let go of me, Kal!" Then Mister Gallagher fell to his knees, his hand still in her father's grip, as he let out a scream that almost hid the sounds of the bones in his hand cracking. Freya's whole body shuddered uncontrollably. Meanwhile, it appeared as if her father was barely applying any pressure. Ronan froze in fear and Missus Gallagher did the same when she went outside.

Freya's father had let Mister Gallagher go once he noticed they were drawing attention. He lowered himself to whisper to Mister Gallagher. Freya couldn't hear it, but whatever it was caused Mister Gallagher to look back at Ronan. Her father took Freya's hand, and they left on their way back home.

Freya looked back to see Ronan and his mother trying to help Mister Gallagher get inside.

The sky was bright pink from the sunset when Freya and her father arrived home. Freya should have been uneasy about what her father did. But she was too curious to think of anything else.

"What did you say? To Mister Gallagher back there."

"That if you get caught in their 'crossfire' again, I would let them both relive the Crusades as it was not how he fantasises."

CHAPTER 4
FIRST SÀBAID, DAY OF GILLIAN

"What do you do if you think you're in danger and I'm not around?"

"I try to find you," Freya answered instinctively and correctly, as she does every morning. After all that and breakfast, Freya and her father went off for their hike through the woods.

This time they weren't alone. The Clurichauns were heading to their homes in the woods early. It was the Day of Gillian, so their night shift at the local taverns ended early. They kept Freya and her father company for half of the journey despite her father's insistence that they would rather be alone. Normally, her father could simply lose them by walking with a longer stride. Their tiny eight-inch bodies wouldn't be able to keep up. This time, however, the Clurichauns were riding on sheep as if they were horses.

Freya had no idea where they got the sheep since Valour didn't have any farms. This, however, did not make the situation any less hilarious for Freya. She couldn't stop giggling as she rode on her father's back as he tried to get away from them.

One of the Clurichauns, whose head was swaying like a ship at sea, hiccupped before asking, "Ey you lads know that Gallagher bloke?"

Freya tried to turn her head to see the Clurichaun but could only get him in her peripheral vision. "You mean Mister Gallagher or Ronan?"

"The one that's tall."

Freya wasn't sure what standard he meant by tall, so she asked, "How much taller?"

The Clurichaun leaned his head back and squinted at Freya. Most likely thinking Freya was mocking him. "The one with the brown hair."

"They both have brown hair," Freya said.

"Gods dammit," the Clurichaun said in a defeated tone before taking a drink from his bottle.

Freya, remembering what happened yesterday, asked, "Did his hand look hurt?"

He pointed a finger at Freya until he finished off his bottle, then said, "Aye, that's the one. Thanks a million, good lass. Hear what happened to his hand?"

Freya didn't know what to say, and her father didn't seem to pay them any attention.

"Well, he was in the Starboard Tavern last night with his hand in a sling boasting how he got it from punching a bear or some other tall tale."

"I heard he got into a fight with the potion seller in town," another Clurichaun chimed in.

"We have a potion seller in town? Why don't we get healing stuff from him then?" the green-hatted Clurichaun asked.

"Because this is all the healing we need." The other Clurichaun said before laughing and tossing the green-hatted Clurichaun another bottle. They then proceeded to sing what Freya believed to be four different songs at once and completely off -key. They went on until it was time for them to leave Freya and her father and to their tiny homes. Her father sighed with relief when they could no longer hear their singing.

They didn't have to walk much further to their practice spot, and when they were there, four rocks, which appeared to be from the mountains at the other end of the woods, were placed in a row of increasing size. The smallest was about the size of her hand, and the largest of them was half a metre in height and similar width.

When her father let her down, he told her, "This is just a power exercise, vennen min. All I want you to do is lift each one three metres in the air, hold it for five seconds, and then bring it back down slowly. Keep the spell simple and the Rules of Reality will not fight you as hard."

It sounded easy enough for Freya. She went to the smallest rock, which was the size of her fist. Freya began configuring the Rules of Reality in such a way as to make gravity pull in the opposite direction. Soon it was three metres in the air with little resistance. After five seconds, she slowly brought the stone back to the ground. Freya looked at her father, and he gave her an approving nod, so she went on to the next. This one took more concentration because the Rules of Reality put up more of a fight. It seemed to weigh almost as much as she did. Regardless, she was able to accomplish this as well. On the third rock, the Rules fought her like getting a stubborn cow back in a barn. The stone must have been heavier than herself for the Rules to fight her so much. After having it in the air for two seconds, Freya's mental grip loosened to the point of slipping, and the rock fell diagonally toward her but stopped nearly halfway down. Freya looked back to her father as he had his hand reached out, but there was no glowing ring around him as if he wasn't using Magic. Freya knew for sure this time.

"When will I learn how to do that?" Freya asked.

Her father gently brought the rock to the ground. "Do what?"

"What you're doing right now, Pappa. I wouldn't have to worry so much if I could hide my Magic like that."

Her father looked at what he was doing then looked back at Freya, "Oh … this … I do not think you can, vennen min."

"Is it because of what happened with the rock?" Freya asked.

"Nei, I do not think using Magic this way is natural." Her father said, starting to look unsettled.

"What?"

"It's like this one Rule of Reality does not apply to me. Imagine singing at the top of your lungs while not allowing yourself to utter a sound."

"What does that even mean?" Freya thought to herself.

"Perhaps it is a Rule itself you are altering?"

"That is an interesting theory, but it does not feel like casting a spell to me. Or I suppose it could be a school of Magic in itself that I have never heard of. I do not think I am imaginative enough to come up with a brand-new school though."

"How did you learn to do it then?" She asked.

"I do not …" Her father said as his voice trailed off and his eyes stared at something Freya knew wasn't there.

Freya noticed what was happening and quickly changed the subject. "What did Mamma look like?"

Her father managed to walk away from his original thoughts. After taking time to slowly breathe, he said, "Look at your own reflection and imagine your eyes were as green as the hill under our home, vennen min." At that moment, Freya wished they could afford a mirror.

***

The sun was well over the horizon, but the practice was still going because it was Freya's favourite day of the week. The First Sàbaid, the Day of Gillian. From what Freya had learned in school, since Gillian is the Goddess of Life, she wanted all her creatures to experience life to its fullest.

For Freya, this meant not having school today. Her father and other adults were expected to go to work later and leave earlier. This meant Freya could spend almost the entire morning with her father and the afternoon with her friends. Freya was using Magic to play with the practice dummies like dolls, while her father used the nearby tree stump as a desk to write on some papers. After a little less than half an hour, her father called Freya over.

"I have something for you, vennen min." Her father said after handing the papers to her.

Freya carefully and curiously looked through all the different configurations and diagrams. "A constant acceleration of a body. If we suppose the resultant acceleration of a body and x = ½ m v². We have force,

acting on target," ran through her head as it seemed relatively straightforward for a spell.

"What would I use this for?"

"After what happened yesterday, it reminded me that you could be in danger at any moment. I want you to be prepared in case something worse happens, and I am not around."

Her father took one of the training dummies Freya was using and had it set into the ground in a standing position. He walked behind Freya and put his hands on her shoulders. Freya ran through the configurations in her head, and after a bit of concentration, Freya cast the spell.

The dummy was motionless, but all the blades of grass around it began to point at it like a line of spearmen facing a giant beast. Then nearby sticks and twigs gradually accelerated toward the dummy until they started flying at it like arrows, piercing the dummy's straw body. Rocks and pebbles joined in and pelted what remained into a mushy pulp in the dewy grass. The thought of what this could do to a person made Freya feel nauseous.

"I don't want to use this spell, Pappa."

Her father patted her head as he said, "And I do not want you to ever need to use it, vennen min. But I am not going to risk someone having a chance to harm you."

***

They switched to a more light-hearted Magic practice for the remaining hours before Freya and her father made the journey back home from the woods. Her father began his setup of the potion shop stand. Freya could see black plumy smoke coming from the forge at Brigid's house.

Freya asked her father if she could go over to ask if Brigid could play. He told Freya she could, on the condition that if Ronan, Mister Gallagher, or anyone gave Freya any trouble at all, then she needed to come straight home and tell him. Freya was more than fine with the arrangement and, after a quick hug, she headed straight for Brigid's.

The roads were strangely relaxed to Freya on this day of the week. It was wide open and nearly empty, much like when she walked to school in the morning. Today everyone was awake and at work, only without the usual crazy busyness. It reminded Freya of the woods when she thought about it.

Once Freya reached their house, she could see Brigid helping Mister Conall hammer down a glowing red-hot sword fresh out of the furnace.

"Good afternoon, Freya," Mister Conall greeted. "What's the craic?"

Freya waved and said, "Good afternoon to you too, Mister Conall. The craic's been mighty today."

"Glad to hear it." After giving the sword a final few blows of the hammer, Mister Conall placed it in a bucket of water where the intense heat of the sword caused the water to boil and rapidly cool the blade. He put the nearly finished sword on a nearby table. Brigid would polish and help with the final

51

touches later.

Afterward, Mister Conall sat on a stool near Freya and pointed to her head.

"Brigid told me how you got that scratch there." Freya's face started to turn as red as the heated sword did. Freya tried to hide the scratch with her hair. Mister Conall let out a hearty chuckle and patted Freya on the back before saying, "Hey, no need to worry, it's hardly noticeable. And what I really wanted to tell you is that you two did good. It's hard to find people who would stand up for strangers these days." Hearing this made Freya feel better about the event, but she was still unsure of herself after what her father told her.

Brigid, after getting her work smock off, which covered a vibrant purple dress of hers, chimed, "Oh, Freya! What happened with that bout between your Da and Mister Gallagher?"

"You heard about that?" Freya asked, feeling the red coming back on her face.

"Me, Da, and pretty much the whole town. Mister Brian told us what happened. Said your Da panned him good."

Mister Conall looked at Brigid when he said, "What did I tell you about listening to rumours, lass?"

"You heard it too, Da."

"That's not what I meant, and you know it. But, now we're in the thick of it, c'mere to me, Freya."

After Freya gave them a quick explanation, Mister Conall let out a roar of laughter. "What's so funny?" Freya asked.

Mister Conall caught his breath and said, "It's just about time he had a good arse-kicking."

"Aren't you and Mister Gallagher friends?" Freya asked.

"Aye, he's a good tavern buddy, but it doesn't mean I don't know when that eejit needs to be taught a lesson. Gods save them. You lasses promise me you won't grow up and be as gobdaw as him or his pup." Freya and Brigid laughed as they promised him. "So I'm guessin' you and Brigid want to go out and play?"

"Yes, please!" Freya and Brigid said in almost unison.

"Okay, off with you two then. Brigid, I want you to help me read some of the new orders when you get back," Mister Conall told them. Brigid nodded before the two girls headed out on the road.

They wandered around aimlessly for a bit until Brigid found a nearby bench for them to sit on so she could fix Freya's messy hair.

"So, what should we do today?" Freya eagerly asked, trying her best not to bounce around with excitement.

"Welp. After I get this three-foot knotted catastrophe dealt with, I think we should see if Jacinta would want to play with us."

Freya looked down at her feet. "I don't think she likes us much."

"Well, Jacinta said she'll try to be nice to us. Figure if she plays with us, she'll come around to liking us."

"I suppose," Freya said meekly.

"Then let's go!" Brigid exclaimed, and as soon as she finished Freya's ponytail, they were off.

***

The Church of Valour was close to Brigid's house, with only one building toward the Starboard District and two buildings toward the Bow District. The church was the only building in town to have its walls painted white, and it reminded Freya of the colour of a seagull's feather. It was also the tallest building in Valour, being at least half a story taller than Brigid's house and four times as wide. The roof had a sharp pronounced angle, which made it appear even more out of place in Valour since most of the other houses and buildings had more of a curve. The back of the church held a large bell tower that would ring every Second Sàbaid or for events like a wedding or funeral.

The doors were both large and made from dark green-stained wood. A carving of Gillian was on the left door, a beautiful young woman with long curly hair and the gentlest smile Freya had ever seen. The right side had a carving of Umba on it, an older but muscular man carrying a shield on his back to defend others. When the door was closed, the Gods would hold hands. Just above the door, there was a sign which read, "May neighbours respect you, trouble neglect you, the angels protect you, and the Gods embrace you."

Brigid knocked on the door, and after a few seconds, Saint Orlaith opened the door to greet them. She had turquoise-coloured hair, which she usually kept in a bun. Her eyes were blue with flecks of green. Her face had a mature and soft appearance yet still had a presence that made it hard to forget her. She wore what most considered street clothes, which was strange for an official of the Church but not unusual for her.

"Hello dere, lile oness!" Saint Orlaith greeted. Freya had been told her accent was how they spoke in Eastern Bastiel since Saint Orlaith grew up in Liberality. This made every 's' sound longer and replaced the 'th' with 'd', and every 't' at the end of her words simply didn't exist. "How can we help you?"

"We wanted to know if Jacinta could play with us today?" Brigid asked. "You wish to sspend time with Jacinta? Fasscinating. Please, tell me wha interactionss did you have to feel dis way?" Saint Orlaith said as she lowered herself to their height and fixed her eyes on them. Saint Orlaith wasn't how Freya imagined Saints to be like. Eccentric instead of stoic and regal like the drawings and statues depicted.

Brigid stumbled on her words, trying to respond. "I, uh … I guess we met her at school and thought it would be fun to have her play with us?"

"But was da interaction you had at sschool with her differen dan with a

Human?" Saint Orlaith asked as she appeared to be mentally taking note of everything they said.

"I mean, she was a bit grumpy at first."

"And how did dat make you wanna have her as a playmate?"

Brigid looked at Freya in such a way as to silently ask, "I'm not the crazy one, right?" But Freya was too shy to respond.

"I don't know?" Brigid said, likely hoping it was the correct answer.

Seemingly disappointed with Brigid's response. Saint Orlaith sighed and

said, "Alrigh, well, I'm ssorry she'ss assleep righ now, but I'll le her know you were asking for her when she wakess up."

"She's asleep? It's noon!"

"Yes, Aoss Ssí are a type of nocturnal Elf. We had her conform to the Human ssleeping sschedule sso dat she may be more like uss. Ssince sschool is ou for the Ssàbaidss, we decided to le her ssleep in to help her with the transition," Saint Orlaith answered.

Hearing this made Freya wonder if Jacinta's grumpiness was because she was tired. Freya knew how upset she felt whenever she got tired.

"I'm sure she will be up in four hourss," Saint Orlaith added.

"Oh, but that's too close to dinner time," Brigid moaned.

"I'll be easier once she getss ussed to her new ssleep sschedule."

"I suppose. Well, thank you anyways, Saint Orlaith," Brigid said before curtsying to her. Once Freya remembered, she stumbled doing so herself. The two headed back out into the main road again and went around looking for something to do.

They spent time playing tag in the areas between Freya's house and Brigid's. It was harder for Freya to tag Brigid since she was slightly older and faster than her. Freya still enjoyed the rush of it. There were other games Freya was better at than Brigid, such as card games like spoil five. Brigid didn't like those after playing with Freya. They switched between a couple of games for about an hour before they both started to get hungry.

They agreed to meet back at the Oak Tree between the Stern and Starboard Districts as soon as they grabbed some food and ate lunch there. When Freya made it back to her house, she could see her father working at his stand just as usual, and after grabbing some fruit, bread, and water, she was off to the tree.

It was the only tree inside the town of Valour and had its own space of grass while being surrounded by houses. The tree itself was massive enough to see over most of the homes around it and was tons of kids' favourite place to play. Luckily, it was empty for the moment, and Brigid was already there with a mat for them to eat on. A few minutes in, Freya had already inhaled most of her food while Brigid had barely eaten half.

Brigid looked at the far-off mountains, then back to Freya, "Only ten more days."

"Wha?" Freya could barely manage to ask with the food in her mouth. Brigid gawked at Freya, "Ten more days! Until Souls of Saints Day!" Freya nearly jumped at the realisation. "What's today?" "November twentieth."

Freya laid her head against the tree, trying to wrap her head around how fast time was moving for her and the excitement for Souls of Saints Day; the only thing she could say was, "Wow!"

"Ah. I figured you two would be here." Freya and Brigid looked around the tree to find out where the voice came from and realised it was Saint Orlaith with Jacinta in tow wearing a coat so thick it made her look like a wooden barrel. It was hard for Freya and Brigid to keep a straight face, but Jacinta wasn't looking so sulky or grumpy today, and they didn't want to ruin it.

"I thought you said she wouldn't be out for another two hours?" Brigid asked out loud what Freya was thinking.

Jacinta looked up at Saint Orlaith then slowly said, "They told me you asked for me as soon as I woke up. I wanted to be out of the Church and schoolhouse for once, so I hurried over here."

Before leaving, Saint Orlaith told them, "Pleasse, make sure to keep Jacinta in your sight and have her back ah the Church before you head home. Have fun."

As soon as Saint Orlaith was no longer in earshot, Brigid asked, "So what's with the big coat?"

Freya looked at Brigid in disbelief. However, Jacinta simply answered, "Aosh Sí don't like the cold or wind. And you have a lot of both on the shurfash thish eshpecially sho far north." Reverting back to her natural, albeit strange and fast, way of speaking.

Brigid shrugged and headed straight over to Jacinta. Jacinta started to tense and moved away from her.

"Come on. If you're not going to do your hair, at least let me."

Jacinta looked at Freya and after seeing Freya happily roll her eyes at Brigid, she relaxed a bit.

Once Brigid got into the thick of untangling, she muttered, "Why is it so hard for you two to do your own damn hair?"

"You volunteered!" Freya said bursting into laughter.

"Yeah sure," Brigid said dismissively.

"What were you talking about earlier?" Jacinta asked, wincing when Brigid had to give one knot a tug.

"Oh, just talking about how Souls of Saints Day is coming up," Freya replied.

"Whatsh that?"

"You never heard of it?" Brigid asked loudly.

Jacinta nervously nodded her head as if worried about giving a wrong answer.

Freya took a minute to find the best way to describe it and then said, "On the last day of November, we celebrate every deed of every Saint by wearing masks of their faces, playing games, singing songs, listening to stories, and watching plays about them. It's so, so fun! It's the best holiday!"

"I don't know, there's Night of Saint Clement it has to compete with," Brigid said.

"Don't listen to her, Jacinta! She's just saying that because she wants to be a blacksmith."

"I guess Souls of Saints does have candy," Brigid conceded.

Freya nearly jumped as she said, "Oh, yeah! People are supposed to do good deeds for each other, and the best way is to give kids like us candy!"

"You should come with us, Jacinta! We can show you all the best spots," Brigid said.

"I don't want to promise that."

Freya and Brigid asked, "How come?" in unison.

"I don't plan on staying in Valour. I don't belong here and I want to go back home."

Freya and Brigid looked back at each other, and then a moment of awkward silence passed between them. Neither of them seemed to know what to say for a while. Brigid chimed in, "Hey, why don't me and Freya show you around town? It will be fun, and it will help you from getting lost." Jacinta didn't protest, so off they went. Their first stop was to the cold and hard sandy beaches past the Stern District and on the shores of the First Third River. Freya and Brigid would sometimes play with the sand during summer, and since kids weren't allowed on the docks, it was one of the few ways to see all the ships coming in and out of Valour.

"Oh crap!" Brigid said, stopping them on the road.

"What is—Oh no …" Freya said when she realised who Brigid spotted.

"I can't see, what's going on?" Jacinta asked, squinting her eyes.

"You can't see? He's right there!" Brigid said.

"I lived in tunnels! We don't see far!" Jacinta said defensively.

"Shut it, will you!" Ronan whisper-shouted from his hiding spot behind a crate near the alleys.

"Excuse me? Did you suddenly hate smelling again?" Brigid said.

Ronan instinctively covered his bruised nose, "Be quiet! There's a couple of gombeens over there."

"What are you on about?" Brigid asked.

"He's just trying to mess with us again!" Freya said, refusing to even look at him while noticing Jacinta was ready to lunge at him.

"I'm not lying! Their ship came in the morning and they've been snooping around here like crows on a dying man."

"So what? They're visitors. Probably just touring around," Freya said,

trying to end the interaction as soon as possible.

"Don't be daft. Who tours back alleys? Only thing interesting there is the sme … Wait shut—please be quiet."

Brigid and Jacinta ducked around the same crate Ronan was hiding behind and even Freya's curiosity got the better of her and joined in.

There were two men in the alleys. One of them looked slightly older than Freya's father with a shaggy brown beard and matching short hair. He had ruddy sunburnt skin, bloodshot grey eyes, and a bit of a gut. The other one was younger looking like he might have just graduated from their schoolhouse. His skin was even more sunburnt than the first and had long white hair, which he kept in a ponytail. It appeared he was trying to grow out a moustache, but could barely get peach fuzz.

"How long do tese usually take, Silas?" The white -haired young man asked. His accent was nasally like something was caught in his throat. It was not one Freya had ever heard of before.

"Will you relax? You're making my throat dry with all your worrying," the other man named Silas said before taking a swig out of a bottle he was holding. He had a trade tongue accent meant to be understood by almost anyone he would meet around the Known World. It was most often used by sailors with a nasal tone and hard 'R' sounds.

"Ow am I supposed to relax when I can see the Venatores' tower looming over us?"

"Because no one would be crazy enough to bring someone like you so close to the capital of Bastiel, which means no one would ever think to look."

"Well, we're ere, so what does that make us?" "Bold, as my old admiral used to say."

Two more men showed up, both looking around the white-haired man's age; one of them was a Demi-Human Freya was unfamiliar with. His clothes and cloak hid most of his body, but Freya could see he had oily deep blue skin and exceptionally wavy green hair, almost like strips of paper. He must have been from another country since Freya had never even read of such a Demi-Human before.

"What did you find out?" Silas asked.

"Well Captain, the granary's to the far southeast away from the ports," the Demi-Human answered in a clicking and bubbly accent.

"Well, that makes it a no-go. No quick escape there."

"The dock guards appear to be a volunteer system so I expect very little training, but they are fairly equipped. Smithy gets a decent bit of business from them. Their armoury is in the southwest."

"We can secure it if things get … complicated."

Even Freya was willing to admit this was all sounding awfully suspicious.

Ronan might have been on to something here.

"I believe there is an apothecary in this town, but not many people seem

to know where it is at."

"I'm surprised these bumpkins would drink anything that wasn't water or communal wine," Silas said, rolling his eyes.

"Who's this sap calling us bumpkins!" Brigid said, forgetting to whisper in rage.

"You can come out now," Silas said, sounding not at all surprised.

"Run!" Ronan shouted before leaving before them.

Amidst the panic, instead of running in the opposite direction to make it hard to find all of them, Freya followed wherever Brigid was running, and Jacinta, not knowing anything about this town, struggled to follow them, hindered by all the thick clothing, and her weaker legs.

"Wait up! If … I am… caught running around … by myshelf … they won't … let me out … again …" Jacinta said, gasping with each word.

"Sorry, I was caught off guard," Brigid said. "We-
we-we need t-to tell s-someone!" Freya stuttered.

"Will they … believe you though?" Jacinta asked.

"Th-they have t-to!"

"They won't," Brigid said. "Wh-why?
Yo-you heard what th-they said!"

"Right and I'm sure Ronan has already told dozens of people by now. Which means people will assume what we heard was an exaggeration at best." "They didn't directly shay what they were going to do either."
Jacinta
pointed out.

"Exactly. No one is going to listen to us unless we have proof."

"Pappa would!" Freya thought, but then realised if her father knew being with her friends could have her accidentally run into criminals, he might not let her see them again. But she did promise to tell him everything.

"Oh why did they have to cause trouble here of all places?"

"What do we do? What do we do?" Freya moaned.

"Just give me some time to think. In the meantime, let's just clear our heads with a walk and stay in the busy areas in case any of them saw us," Brigid suggested.

***

Going up the Stern District through the main road, they passed Valour's Woodcutter & Carpentry building on their right side. Further ahead to their left was Alaina's Bath House. It was hot and cosy to go there to warm up when it was mid-winter, and Miss Alaina herself was sweet, but both Freya's and Brigid's fathers told them not to go inside without them.

Once the three made it toward the centre, they went inside Cassidy's Bakery. It was filled with the sweetest smells of sugar bread and made all of their mouths water. They watched as Mister Cassidy brought out a fresh batch and were shooed out after they hungrily stared at the food for almost ten minutes. None of them had enough money for one.

Then they began to head off to one of Freya's favourite places. Along the way, Freya asked Jacinta what the Fay Forest was like and she seemed so excited to talk about it. The more she went on, the faster she spoke and the less she could hide her accent. It got to the point where Freya and Brigid had little to no idea what Jacinta was saying. The only thing Freya could pick out of it was that it was dark. Which Jacinta seemed to enjoy. Swampy and warm, which explained why she felt so cold here, and it may or may not have a bunch of trees. Jacinta seemed unsure of this part herself since she lived underground.

After a few more minutes of walking, they arrived. Some may argue the Grand Cathedrals in Faith was the most sacred place, others may say it is the Tower of Babel in Hope, but for Freya, it is Sadhbh's Sweet Store. A small store stockpiled with sweets and sporting sea-green colours on its structure as a shrine to all the tastes Freya desired. Freya believed the Gods must have seen this store and proclaimed it was good.

Freya rushed them inside to show Jacinta all of its splendour. Candy dispensers of every colour lined the walls behind the apple-red wooden counter. Shelves full of dried fruits and gummies were at the centre and stood next to a barrel of honey for coating or to grab a jar full to take home. Right after the bell over the door rang, Miss Sadhbh herself popped her head over the counter, revealing her young freckled face and hair, which nearly blended in with the counter.

"Oh, if it isn't my favourites! Good afternoon, lasses! What are you craving today?" Miss Sadhbh said. Then after doing a double-take on Jacinta, Miss Sadhbh asked, "Wha-what's your name, lass?"

Jacinta seemed too focused on the sweets to hear her.

"Well, even if she doesn't like Valour, she certainly knows our sweets are pure class," Freya thought with an amused smile.

"Care to introduce your friend?"

"This is our new classmate, Jacinta," Brigid said.

"Oh, right, I heard about her. Seems like you're the talk of the town, Miss Jacinta."

Jacinta still had her eyes glued to the sweets.

"Perhaps a little bribe is needed to loosen the tongue. Okay, Jacinta, grab a handful, but I want to hear your voice before you leave," Miss Sadhbh said.

"Oooh, you should get the peach gummies; they're the best!"

"Freya, you are biased! Everyone knows you can't go wrong with honey chips," Brigid countered.

After twenty minutes of arguing, Jacinta decided to get half of each, and proper introductions were made.

Jacinta took a bite and wiggled with delight. "Sho shweet! Theshe are better than wax wormsh!"

"Wait, you eat worms?" Freya asked in horror.

"Yeah, they're jusht hard to find in the moundsh and tunnelsh." "That's gross!" Brigid said.

"Well, what do you moshtly eat?" Jacinta asked defensively.

"I guess fish is pretty common," Freya answered.

Jacinta gagged before saying, "How can you not vomit from the shmell?" "Fish have a smell?" Freya and Brigid both asked in unison.

"Not everyone is used to it like we are," Miss Sadhbh answered.

"What does it smell like?" Freya asked.

"Eehh, fishy?" Jacinta said.

"What? What does that even mean?" Brigid asked.

"I don't know. There ishn't a good way to deshscribe it."

"You can have this conversation outside. Make way for other customers, please. Oh, but do bring your brother next time, Freya! I miss his alluring silence."

"I don't have a brother," Freya said, getting annoyed at everyone's confusion and slamming the door.

"Sho … you known eash other for a while?" Jacinta asked. Though if it was already hard to understand her, it was doubly so while she was eating.

"What?" Brigid asked.

"You and Freya?"

Freya smiled and said, "Yep, since I was four! We met on my first day of school, and I was so scared of everything, but Brigid helped me through it all."

"Nope," Brigid said dismissively.

"Nope?" Freya asked. Not sure what part Brigid was disagreeing with, and Jacinta was equally confused.

"We met earlier."

"What? We did?"

"Yeah."

"When?"

"When you first moved here."

"When I moved here?"

"Yeah, you and your Da came here from somewhere when we were both wee little. I don't remember much, but it was before my Ma passed and she wet-nursed you when your Da brought you to our house."

"Janey Mack! I wasn't even born here?" "You didn't know?" Jacinta asked.

"I guess I just thought—I mean I don't remember being anywhere else. Do you know where I was born?"

"I don't know. Probably wherever your Da got his strange way of speaking from? Why don't you ask him?" Brigid said.

Freya tried to hide her grimace as they walked back to the big tree.

***

Upon a thick branch on the tree, the three sat silently staring at the spire of the Tower of Babel. The massive ivory tower split any cloud that floated toward it and stood in opposition to the setting sun.

"Welp. Looks like it's time to head home now," Brigid said while stretching.

Jacinta looked out a little longer before slowly saying, "All right. Today was … fun. Thanks."

"Ah, don't mention it," Brigid said before leaping off the branch. "Come on, I'll take you two home."

"Go ahead, the church isn't far, and I think I know where to go from here."

Freya quickly opened her mouth and just as quickly closed it as she couldn't think of what to say. They were having a fun day with Jacinta, and she didn't want to ruin it by saying they couldn't trust her with this. At best, if Jacinta does go to the church alone, they would get in trouble for not obeying Saint Orlaith. At worst, she would try to leave Valour and could get seriously hurt or worse.

Freya looked over to Brigid, hoping she would know what to say, "Didn't you say you would get in trouble if you were caught by yourself?"

"That'sh only if it'sh in the middle of town. If I head right back, they won't care." Jacinta answered, not looking at either of them.

"Well just to be safe …"

"Shafe from what?"

"Uh ... um, Ronan! Ronan and any of his goons might still hold a grudge for getting in trouble and might try to ambush you if you are by yourself."

Jacinta gave out a sigh and conceded.

Freya gave out a sigh and was relieved.

***

When they took Jacinta back to the church, they said their goodbyes, and Freya began to head home.

Brigid followed her pensively, and after a while, Freya asked, "What's the story?"

"I know I made up the Ronan ex cuse, but thinking of either him or those strangers earlier got me spooked. I doubt either would be so stupid to do something like that with you being so close to home, but Ronan has at least proven me wrong before."

CHAPTER 5
SECOND SÀBAID, DAY OF UMBA

THEN

Kalby was awake again in his big sister's arms. His frail, thin body was too weak to even shiver from the cold air on his naked skin. He tried to speak to her, but all that came out was a meek moan followed by violent vomiting. Kalby was glad he didn't eat earlier. His big sister stroked the back of his shaved head and whispered about all the beautiful things outside, the fuzzy green ground she called grass, food that had a taste, and clothes that felt warm and soft. Soon after, the pain set in. It quaked in Kalby's stomach. It was like being ripped apart. He tried to claw whatever it was out of him, but his big sister stopped him before he tore out his stitches again.

Two of the masked ones from outside ran to their cell. The man in the half -skull mask yelled at him to stop his screaming. He had a short temper and would often vent his frustration on the subjects like them. His big sister wanted to tell them to leave Kalby alone, but even she was too scared of him. The best she could do was cover her little brother, but it was meaningless to their power A green light came from underneath half-skull, and then the air from Kalby's lungs was sucked out, and it was dark again.

Now

Freya tried to snuggle herself back into her covers, hoping to catch more sleep, but it seemed that her mind was off thinking on its own going back and forth on whether or not to tell her father what happened yesterday. She still couldn't decide, but she knew she was not going to be able to get back to sleep. Freya let out a big yawn, stretched her back, and looked around her room. It was a comfy, cosy cubbyhole just for her. Her bed lay snuggly in the far end, with the walls pressed tightly on both sides. Hanging from a string above her were some of her best doodles. They were covered full of scenes from her favourite storybook, with Freya and her father sometimes added in.

Freya started to smell breakfast just outside her room and had to decide if getting up to eat was worth getting out of her warm blankets. Her stomach decided for her, so Freya slowly inched her way off the foot of her bed. She poked her toes around to find her slippers but instead touched the wooden floor, which was cold like ice. She peered over her bed and thanked the Gods her slippers were within her reach.

Out in the main room, their stove burned as much wood as her father could stuff in it to keep the house warm. He sat by the table, staring intensely at a book of his. She walked toward him and poked her head around his shoulder.

"Which one are you stuck on?"

"Um …" He moved his finger back where it was on the page. "Here. Under Aplite potion."

"Oh. It says, 'Not reco-mmen-ded for single-dose intra-ven-ous, intra-mus-cular or sub-cut-aneous ad-mini-stra-tion,'" Freya sounded out.

"Ah. Tusen Takks, vennen min. Sorry, I forgot to get a bowl out for you. Breakfast is ready in the pot."

"No problem, Pappa," Freya said as she poured herself a bowl of porridge.

***

During their morning meal, Freya's father decided to give up reading his book for now. Then he went over the daily questions with Freya, which she passed as usual. When it was all finished, they packed up and began to head out for Magic practice but stopped as soon as they opened the door. Everywhere outside was covered in a thin layer of snow, and it didn't look like it was going to stop there. Freya rushed out to look at the whole town, and she began to giggle with excitement as snow fell all around them. Freya was just about to dive in and make snow angels when her father called her inside to get a warmer coat. After being thoroughly bundled up, they finally headed off to the woods.

They began their practice with a simple exercise of her keeping as many coins balanced on their edges as she could. A dozen copper coins laid out on a flat tree stump. Freya thought of a couple of ways to go about it. By artificially shifting the centre of mass of each coin, she could make the coins balance on their edges. Although on the grand scale of things, this would have been a minor change to the Rules of Reality. With each coin, she would have to fight each instance of the rules for control at the same time, straining her focus to a quick breaking point.

If she tried the same spell with one coin at a time, she risked a light breeze knocking over any coin she released. If Freya tried to alter the rules to increase the tree stump's gravitational pull, she would have no way to guarantee they would stand on their edges.

Freya spent the next ten minutes thinking about this puzzle, and then a solution came to her. Freya couldn't stop grinning, and her father gave her a curious smile. With all the configurations already done in her head, all she had to do was execute the spell.

Freya extended her arms and pinched her fingers as if the coin was between them. The pale blue ring formed under her feet as she cast her spell. She shifted the centre of mass to orient the coin on its edge. Then she rapidly increased the pull of gravity on the coin until it was how she wanted it and then released it. After it was over, she went to the next one then the next one until all of them were standing on their edges.

Freya had to try her best not to start dancing as the spell left her light-headed. This was the first time she managed to get all of them to stand up like so.

Her father walked a few laps around her and the coins examining and trying to understand what exactly she was doing. It didn't take him long to figure it out. Once he did, he let out a laugh that was unusually loud for him, which, by any other metric, was still quiet for most people.

"Did you just jam it into the stump?" he asked, catching his breath.

Freya nodded as sweat from the strain formed on her forehead.

He gave her a jovial hug, "You are lucky the wood was wet. That could have cost us twelve coppers. My silly, clever venn!"

Their next practice was more focused on defence. Freya needed to use Magic to keep herself steady while her father would use Magic to knock her off her feet or make her too tripped up for her to focus on a spell. Freya had gotten into a braced stance, and her feet sank deeper into the snow while she waited for her father to make his first move.

A soft blue ring surrounded her father and Freya was about to fall sideways. Freya made her own configuration, so her gravity was in the opposite direction. This put her back at zero net force, nullifying her father's spell; however, it still caused her to slide half a foot before she stopped it. Her father then tried pulling her from one angle to another in rapid succession. Freya nullified those too, but it was like being on a boat during a storm, and Freya had nearly stumbled a couple of times. After a few rounds of those, her father stopped for a few seconds. Freya was sure he was going to use a big one next.

The ring around her father had flared up once more. Freya prepared herself. She was confident even a pull with the force of an adult pushing her couldn't knock her down. Then came her father's pull. Or perhaps pluck was more accurate. By the time Freya realised she had overcompensated and altered more than she needed, she had already been face-first in the snow.

Her father helped Freya to her feet, dusted the snow off her face, and said, "It is good to try and prepare for what your opponent might do, but you need to keep yourself flexible."

"How am I supposed to know how hard you are going to push or pull me? It's not like we can see gravity," Freya moaned.

"Since you are a gravity practitioner, if you read the equations in my ring, you could get an early idea of what I am changing in the Rules of Reality. This works both ways, however, and unless you at least know the fundamentals of the type of Magic being used, the equations might as well be gibberish."

"Or if my opponent can hide his Magic."

"Well … Ja, but I doubt you will encounter
another." "How would you know if they could hide
it too?"

Her father thought for a moment, "I suppose if someone else could, I might have heard about it, but I guess that does not make much sense either."

"Do you even know any other Draoi?"

"I have met dozens during the Crusade, but did not get to know
them." "Because of your difficulty with people?"

"That was certainly part of it. But also, I just … I do not know … I … I would rather not think about it."

***

After a quick lunch break and a sip of Xatralt for Freya's headache, her father started to set up a dummy for the next practice. A delightfully devious design dawned on Freya when her father's back was turned. She scooped up a handful of snow as quietly as she could. She tiptoed her way toward him, and when the moment looked right, Freya threw the snowball at his back. Freya giggled for a bit until she noticed her father was still and hadn't said anything.

"Oh no, no, no, please don't be scared again, Pappa," Freya thought, too afraid to make a sound. She was about to head over to check on him, but seemingly out of nowhere, a snowball hit the side of her face. Freya looked around in every direction, trying to figure out where it came from, but then her father chuckled, and it all became clear to her.

Realising the rules of this battle had changed, Freya used her Magic to roll up a snowball of her own. Her father turned and jumped over a tiny hill for cover just before the massive snowball crashed into him.

This was no issue for Freya as she made the snowball gravitate toward and above him. Her father popped his head over with six little snowballs floating around him. Freya started to run before her father launched each one after another. She thought she had avoided them all, but the two that missed her turned mid-flight and got Freya in the back.

The surprise made Freya lose control of her snowball, and it dropped

right on top of her father, burying him in the snow. Freya grabbed another handful of snow and ran to her father so she could get him while he was down. As soon as her father turned, Freya fell toward him and soon found herself scooped up in her father's arms.

Freya spurted out a laugh contagious enough to spread to her father as they lay in the soft snow. It took them a while, but when they finally caught their breath, Freya asked her father, "Did you and Mamma have fun like this?"

After coughing out the last bit of laughter left in him, her father said, "Nei, not really. Your mother was not afraid of Magic like most people. But she ... She was not ... comfortable with it. She didn't say it herself, though I think she felt uneasy, so I tried not to use Magic around her often."

"Would I make Mamma uneasy? Would she think I was unnatural or scary? Would she believe I was a freak like the rest of the town would if they knew?" Freya wondered.

"Is that why Mamma never came
back?" "What?"

"Did she know I would be a Draoi and that's why she left us?"

"No! Your mother loved you, and being a Draoi like me would never have changed that. You are the best thing to happen in our lives. Do not ever think differently."

Freya hugged her father tighter.

***

They resumed training shortly after. Practice consisted of exercises such as knocking a play sword from her father's hand. Or redirecting mock arrows her father would launch at her; standard stuff when her father ran out of ideas. They finished around mid-afternoon and went on their way to do Sunday errands. Unlike the First Sàbaid, where everyone is expected to work less, the Second Sàbaid is dedicated to Umba. And he wanted people not to work at all and instead commune in church for most of the day. This means even if her father were to open his shop today, no one would come. Sometimes the other townspeople would get mad at him for trying. So her father decided to dedicate this day to Magic practice, errands, and chores they didn't have time for during the week. Freya had asked her father before why they never went to church. He told her he didn't understand the teachings despite her mother's efforts and was uncomfortable with all the crowding. Freya had been curious about it, but Brigid told her it was 'dry-shite,' so she didn't mind not going.

Their first task today was to collect potion ingredients by the stream. They were looking for frosted feverfew, mountain basil, and lavender. Since winter was here, her father wanted to get all the ingredients he could before they all wilt for the season.

The stream had a far gap from where they stood to the other side and was

deep enough that Freya's feet would no longer touch before she was even halfway there. On both sides, some flowers and herbs liked to grow and dangle toward the water. Farther north, the stream led to a lake. While down south, it was fed by the First Third River. In most parts of the woods, the stream was quiet, but up close, it had a constant growl, making it hard to hear her father unless he was nearby.

This made it easy for Freya to think, and her thoughts had wandered toward the coming Souls of Saints Day. Freya's stance on her current predicament seemed to change with each petal she plucked. She wanted to ask her father to come with her to the Souls of Saints festival, but she couldn't decide if she should.

"It would be so much fun with him. But what if something like last time happens? It won't!" Freya argued back and forth to herself. Despite recent events, her father had been getting much better. He didn't flinch when Freya touched his wrists anymore.

"Perhaps if I tell him how great it is, he might want to come,." Freya decided.

"Pappa?" Freya asked, loud enough to be heard over the stream.

"Ja, vennen min?" her father replied as he handed Freya another herb to put in the bag.

"I hear Mister Brian is thinking about playing his flute alongside Mister Cadhla. He's great at the fiddle if you haven't heard him play before."

"Uh-huh …"

"Yeah, and there will be lots of free food, oh and super fun games and amazing plays, and at the end they—"

"Vennen min." Her father interrupted, "You know I cannot. I am sure Mister Conall would be okay taking you with his daughter."

"But I want you to come too."

"I would like to, but I canno—" her father stopped, and both he and Freya turned to see a brown rabbit rushing toward them. It came close enough for Freya to pet, but then without notice, an arrow flew from the woods and pierced the rabbit in the back of its small leg. It fumbled to a halt, and Freya started to scream as her father covered himself over her.

***

Kal darted his eyes around trying to find the source of the arrow and to prepare. His daughter was in his arms, but she wouldn't be safe if another arrow managed to hit him before he could catch it. It was like being back in the Crusades again, old instincts and adrenaline kicking in. Not like an old gear left to rust, but one that had only stopped for a moment. It was one of the last places he wanted Freya to be in.

A strong heavyset man with shaggy brown hair and beard came out of the woods with his hand and bow raised trying to show peaceful intentions. It took Kal a great amount of discipline not to kill him right away in case there

were more in hiding, but he still kept configurations of the Rules of Reality to discreetly snap his neck in the back of his mind.

"Iss anybody hurt?" The man asked, his speech slightly slurring in a trade-tongue accent. If the man was simply a drunk hunter, being able to shoot at a rabbit through woods at this distance was impressive. Perhaps naval training would explain his ability to shoot while off balance.

The man slowly approached him and the smell enforced Kal's initial suspicions of being drunk, but he kept a lookout just in case it was an act.

"Y-you al-almost hi-hit us!" Freya stuttered and screamed.

"Hey, look, oh Gods, I'm really ssorry about that. I was out here hunting, which is not something I can do often, especially if the place has a King or Queen, sso this place was nice, and I, uh … Good thing no one wass hurt, right?" The man was about to reach for something on his belt and Kal looked at a nearby tree, ready to use Magic to snap it and crush him. While hiding his Magic, it could easily be blamed on an accident.

The man took his hand away from the flask on his belt and instead reached it toward Kal and said, "The name's Silas Akerman."

Freya tried to hide her face deeper in Kal's coat. Kal didn't shake his hand, keeping his focus on the tree just behind Silas, but he did give him his first name to keep him distracted.

The rabbit in front of them was screaming in pain and Freya couldn't help but peek in horror.

"What's your name, Miss?" Silas said with a grin of missing teeth and swollen gums. Either from being punched or scurvy, Kal couldn't tell. Silas looked down at the rabbit, grabbed it, and turned around so Freya couldn't see it. There was a loud pop and the rabbit stopped screaming. All the colour left Freya's face.

"Oh hey, haven't I sseen you round town before?" Silas asked. Freya quickly shook her head.

"I think I *hic you remind me of my little ssister before she … well, she would be around if she had a big brother as good as yourss." The tree behind Silas cracked so loud to be heard over the stream. Silas turned and noticed a tree just about ready to give out on top of him. He ducked out of the way, "I'd watch out *hic there if I were you. Accidentss like that could ha-happen to anyone esspecially if you take a *hic wrong step into something … or somebody. Welp, ssorry for all the trouble. I should get going. Gotta show off the, uh, trophy down at the tavern."

"I don't like him, Pappa," Freya said when Silas was out of sight.

"Neither do I … Remind me to go over to Mister Conall's when we are
done here." Her father said gravely. Freya nodded, beginning to regret not telling her father what happened yesterday. When they finished, they dropped off their ingredients at their house and went into town. Since the only people working were the essentials like dockhands, doctors, and innkeepers, the

town was quiet. Freya and her father were able to get to Mister Conall's moderately quick. Her father knocked on the door next to the metal fence, and after a few seconds, Brigid answered it with a broom in hand.

"Hi, Freya! Hello, Mister Pantar. What's the story?" Brigid said, surprised to see the two of them.

"Can I speak to your father?" Freya's father asked.

"What? Oh, sure. Da! Mister Pantar wants to chat with you."

"Mister Pantar?" The sound of clinking dishes came before Mister Conall arrived, drying his hands on his pants.

"Everything all right?"

"Can we speak inside?" Freya's father asked.

"Sure, come right in."

The inside of Mister Conall's house was far roomier than their own, but with the amount of furniture, tools, and works in progress lying around, it was hard to tell. Mister Conall had his forge furnace connected to his home so it would keep it warm during winter, and unbearable during summer. The stairs divided the den and the kitchen and led to the second floor to their bedrooms. Brigid went back to sweeping the kitchen floor, Freya followed her as her father and Mister Conall sat at the armchairs in the den.

"What's going on, Freya?" Brigid whispered.

"We met Silas in the woods." Freya tried not to think of the poor rabbit he killed.

"Of course, you did. Creepy blokes always seem to lurk in the woods. There are hundreds of stories about that for a reason."

"Should we tell them? Please?"

"I don't know, maybe they'll be able to believe us."

Before Freya could respond, they both overheard Mister Conall, as he said, "Aren't you being a bit paranoid, Kal?"

Freya had to keep quiet and strain to hear her father. Brigid could barely comprehend what Freya's father says in the best circumstances. Brigid wasn't used to the way her father spoke like Freya was.

"I have seen things like this before in the Second Crusade."

There was a short pause before Mister Conall spoke again, "Things have changed since the Crusades. But I'll keep an eye out and a few swords from stock nearby just in case … I'll also teach those girls of ours a lesson about spying on people."

Brigid quickly went back to sweeping as Freya ran around the kitchen, looking for something which could make her appear innocent. Nothing came about of the threat, though, as Freya's father took her back home.

Nothing else was planned for today. Freya and her father did chores like collecting the water, cleaning the stoves, and washing dishes. As well as decide whose turn it was to empty and clean the chamber pots and take turns bathing. After all the chores were finished, the two played card games until

dinner. Freya tossed and turned in bed, battling with what to do. She couldn't take it anymore. She went to the living room and tried her best to wake her father up as gently as possible, "Pappa?"

CHAPTER 6
DAY OF CHANGES

Almost a week had passed since Freya and her father met Silas in the woods. Rumours both in class and around town have been spreading like wildfires. Apparently, some property was mysteriously damaged, cargo from the ships had been going missing, and a few wealthy folks had been injured from unexplained accidents. There was even another rumour people were going missing too. What bothered Freya most with these rumours was no one could agree who or what was causing all this. From overly learned ruffian kids to faithlessness spreading and most commonly blaming Demi-Humans. Freya believed Ronan started the last one as their classmates have been worse than usual to Jacinta despite Brigid's efforts to get them to lay off her. It was so obvious Silas and his friends were the cause of all the problems, but everyone just wanted to blame someone else.

Every kid was escorted to class by their parents, not just Freya, and the younger kids. This meant everyone was coming to class earlier, which meant more people were on the road. This caused Freya's father to decide they should take a different, far, out-of- the-way route for a while, which meant Freya was late for class a few times.

"I'm sorry again, Missus Aibrean. My Pappa—"

"It's all right, Freya. Please take your seat," Missus Aibrean interrupted.

Freya quickly curtsied and made her way to her desk.

As Brigid began fixing Freya's hair, she whispered, "Jacinta was worried something had happened to you."

"I'm sorry."

"Ah, don't be. I knew you were fine. Ronan has been turning the class into nervous nellies with all his horror stories about kids going missing."

It seemed the punishment Missus Aibrean had given him at the beginning of the week that left his hands a red, swollen mess for some time had lost its

effect on Ronan. As he was right back to torment them. Freya's
face paled as she asked, "Tha-that's not true, right?"
"I don't think so. Looks like everyone made it to class just
fine." Freya let herself breathe again.

Missus Aibrean started today off with history, which began with a reading of the Libri ex Dii, "Umba, sickened by his creation, wanted to unleash his wrath on the would-be tyrants and warlords. Gillian begged him to show mercy, for they were still their children as all life were. He capitulated to her and managed to trap them in an eternal prison. They were scattered across and deep beneath the Known World, but Fraxineus was sent into the stars. Humanity was safe and was now aware of the Gods' laws. Umba had ordered the remaining loyal Angels to aid us, humans, in the construction of the divine Tower of Babel before they were called back to the heavens. As both a reward for their deeds and to prevent them from following in Fraxineus's footsteps. This allowed Venatores who made the weeks-long pilgrimage to the top to speak with Angels before taking a leap of faith …" - Partus Vitae 1:34-41

"Who can tell me how our country is governed?" Missus Aibrean asked after they finished reading.
Aidan Corith raised his hand.
"Go ahead."
"Bastiel is a theocracy, ma'am."
"And why is that?"
"Because only servants of the Gods should lead us. Right?"
"That's correct. After we learned the truth about our former Queen thirty-one years ago, the Grand Masters of the Sanctus Venatore Order took charge to guide us through troubling times. As mandated by Umba and Gillian."

After a few more lessons, lunch recess came, and Freya noticed some of the older kids didn't come out till a little after everyone else. She thought it was strange but was more focused on thinking about what to do with Brigid and Jacinta. Freya and Brigid had been trying to hang out with Jacinta as much as they could, especially since the other kids were avoiding her more and more. Jacinta was no longer pushing them away like she used to. But she still tried to keep herself at a distance.

This hasn't stopped Freya from noticing some of Jacinta's unique quirks. Apparently, Jacinta loved to dig holes and tunnels with her nail claws. Freya wasn't sure how deep or how far she could dig, but it was enough to make the adults decide to dull out her claws. Jacinta was not at all happy with this. Only one rumour was true about her and she actually did bite into one of the priestesses's hands when they tried to restrain her to dull her claws. This forced them to dull out her sharp teeth as well. Jacinta had not gotten used to this either as she struggled to eat her food.

"Well, isn't this quare," Brigid said, pointing to each of the three older kids who were at the corners of the fence and staring toward the town. Freya wasn't sure if Brigid meant this as a means to distract Jacinta from her eating troubles, but it was awfully strange.

"Whatsh quare about it? Jacinta asked.

"The older kids are supposed to keep an eye on the rest of us. Making sure we don't get into trouble. So why are they looking away from us? Let's find out!" Brigid said.

"Wait, what?" Freya asked.

"Come on, Freya! Don't tell me you're not curious too."

"I- I mean I am, b-but I don't want us to get in trouble. Right?" Freya asked, looking at Jacinta, she just shrugged.

"We're not going to get in trouble for asking. Look, I see Aidan! I'm sure I can get him to talk." Brigid headed toward him while Freya and Jacinta followed. Freya wasn't sure how to subtly ask him, but Brigid had a plan.

"Hey, what are you looking at?" Brigid asked loudly behind Aidan. Seeing his reaction, one would think he just barely survived a heart attack.

"Ah! Nothing!" Aidan said, as his voice was indecisive about which pitch to take.

"Nothing? Oh, you must be a deep thinker. You are so smart after all." "Well, I um." Aidan stammered.

"Is that why Missus Aibrean sent you out here?" "What? No! No one sent me."

Brigid swayed her dress back and forth as she gave him a disappointed look.

"I don't like it when people lie to me, Aidan. It hurts my feelings. Do you know what happened to Ronan when he hurt my feelings a week ago?"

"I thought he ... Oh!"

Freya at first thought Brigid was bullying Aidan and if she had kept this up, Freya would have told her to stop, but this seemed different to Freya.

"It would be a shame if it happened to your cute little nose." "Are you threatening me?"

"It's only a threat if you feel threatened. You aren't threatened by a young lady, are you?"

"Eh uh … I'll tell you. Just please, don't tell anyone else." "Not a soul," Brigid said with a cheery smile.

Aidan looked back over the fence and then back to his fellow older classmates. He whispered, "Missus Aibrean asked us to keep an eye out for anyone who looks like trouble during lunch recess for a couple of weeks. In return, we don't have to take any tests for the time being."

"Is this because of those rumours Ronan has been spreading around?" Freya asked.

"I-I mean, it's happened before. Remember what Missus Aibrean taught

73

"I-I mean, it's happened before. Remember what Missus Aibrean taught us about the town of Temperance?"

Freya could see Jacinta curling her claws into her palm and Aiden took a step back.

"Oh, shut it, will you," Brigid said. "You're too smart to be this dumb. Honestly, how many more Demi-Humans have you actually seen staying around town? One? Maybe two?"

"L-look I know Ronan can exaggerate stuff, but—"

"But nothing. We saw them ourselves. They're just some bandit thugs, not Demi-Human rioters. They were mostly human too."

"You saw them? When?"

"Same time as Ronan."

"Ronan didn't say you were there."

"Of course, he didn't," Brigid said, rolling her eyes.

"Why didn't any of you say anything sooner? Told Missus Aibrean?"

"We didn't want to spread rumours without knowing more," Freya said sheepishly.

"And Ronan shtarted making shtuff up," Jacinta added.

"I suppose that makes sense. I don't know if the others will believe you though."

"At least you're willing to. Thank you," Freya said.

"Yeah, keep your pretty head on right," Brigid said.

"W-well, I uh … please don't let Missus Aibrean know I told you about us keeping watch! She'll make us all take tests and the others will have my hide for sure."

"Of course! Thank you for keeping us safe, Aidan." Before the thr ee left, Brigid blew a kiss to Aidan. His pale face turned red like a sunburnt sailor. Which left Freya to think, "What was all that about?"

***

"So, does that mean things are getting worse?" Freya asked.

"I don't know, but we'll keep each other safe. Make sure nothing bad happens to any of us."

Freya stopped in her tracks and asked, "How can you be so brave all the time?"

Brigid smiled and said, "Well, someone's got to set an example for you two. Aaand this is a golden opportunity for all of us."

Jacinta cocked her head, and Freya thought the same.

"Now that we know, we can ask Missus Aibrean to let us be lookouts too. We can help keep the schoolhouse safe and skip those damn maths tests!"

Freya tried to object, for although not having to take a grammar test was tempting, she wanted as little to do with Silas as possible.

"I can't shee far like humansh can," Jacinta said before Freya could say anything coherent.

Freya's curious mind demanded answers and she would argue this was

not just an excuse to distract Brigid from her plan. Freya grabbed Jacinta by the shoulders and led her to the schoolhouse wall. Freya turned her around and looked intensely at Jacinta's cat-like eyes, which turned from small slits to black orbs.

"F-Freya, what are you doing?" Jacinta asked with a nervous smile.

Brigid was barely able to contain her laughter as she said, "I'm sure Freya had something different in mind."

Realising they didn't understand her experiment, Freya explained, "I'm going to walk farther and farther back. I want you to tell me when I start to look blurry."

Jacinta looked over to Brigid for a better explanation, but all Brigid gave her was a smile and a roll of her eyes. Freya was not even ten steps back before she was knocked over by the other kids playing.

Jacinta tried to rush over to Freya, but Freya stopped her to ask, "Do I look blurry from here?"

"You look daft," Brigid said.

"Yesh, you look blurry."

"You can't even see this far? That means you need to be at least one foot away to see what we can at two and nine-eighths metres!"

"How did eyeball something so specific?" Brigid asked.

"Eh-I'm just guessing," Freya answered quickly, realising she hadn't rounded the numbers enough.

Jacinta's face scrunched up before she said, "Well, you don't need to shee that far underground, unlike humansh, we Aos Sí can shee in the dark!"

"G'way outta that! No, you can't. Oh, look at what you did. Now you got Freya all excited," Brigid said, or at least what Freya thought she said.

She was too busy thinking how fascinating it would be to discover how Jacinta's eyes work to pay attention. "Is that how they see underground? Can she see in the forest at night? I don't think Pappa would let me outside so late. I don't think I want to be outside either if Silas is—"

Her thoughts left just as soon as they came when a ball flew mere inches past Freya's face and knocked Jacinta over and on the ground by Freya.

As Jacinta tried to get back to her feet, Freya could hear a smug voice say, "Give us the ball back, wagon."

"First, say you're sorry to them," Brigid growled at Ronan. "Why? I already apologised for the knife thing."

"Barely. This is for being a plain arsehole."

Ronan was creepily quiet for some time. Freya was unnerved, and his friends looked at him, curious to know what he would do. Ronan said, "I'm sorry, Freya. Are you all right?"

Before Freya could answer, Brigid said, "Hey, aren't you going to apologise to Jacinta too?"

Ronan looked at them, puffed out his chest, and said, "Never mind, keep it. It's probably covered in worms and dirt because of her anyway," before he walked away.

Jacinta started to march toward him, but Ronan turned around and put his hand in his pocket. Freya was sure Missus Aibrean had confiscated his knife, but it didn't mean Ronan couldn't have gotten another one from his father.

"Come on, prove me right!" Ronan barely whispered.

Freya had hoped one of the older kids would intervene, but they were all looking outside the fence.

"Remember what happened to Freya last time? Don't risk it, Jacinta," Brigid pleaded.

Jacinta's breathing was loud and hissing through her fanged teeth, but she managed to force herself to turn away from Ronan.

"I knew it! Just going to wait till you outnumber us, just like Da says—" Ronan was saying until a fistful of mud splattered on his face.

Freya cackled in nervous laughter as Brigid quickly got between them. Freya had never seen Ronan so mad, but before he could retaliate, lunch recess ended and everyone was called inside. Missus Aibrean gave Ronan a bucket to wash his face off and Jacinta was given five lashes on her knuckles for fighting. Even with Ronan looking smug seeing Jacinta punished, Freya could imagine it was worth it and wished she was brave enough to throw a handful at him too.

***

Once Jacinta got back to her seat, Missus Aibrean wrote the words, "Souls of Saints Day" in big, spaced-out letters. Missus Aibrean read the words slowly and had the younger children do the same.

After a few repetitions, Missus Aibrean went on to say, "This holiday is to remember the great deeds of Saints past and present and has been a tradition of Bastiel for nine hundred years. Many of you are surely excited, especially since it is fast approaching, so I decided this would be the focus of the lesson. Who can tell me the most famous Saint in Bastiel?"

Freya's hand couldn't have shot up faster without the aid of Magic. "Well, I should probably pick you before your arm falls off." "Oh, sorry."

"No need to apologise. Who do you think it is?"

"Saint Patrick. Because he defeated the mother of our demons, Caoránach, and the great Wyrm Oilliphéist."

"He is also the reason why Bastiel doesn't have any snakes," Missus Aibrean added.

"What's a snake?" Freya asked.

"It's like a big worm with fangs."

"So, a giant worm vampire!" Ronan shouted, and Freya nearly fainted at the horrifying thought.

Missus Aibrean continued, "So, who can tell me why we wear masks for the festival?"

A younger girl raised her hand and said, "Because the best deeds are done in secret."

Before Missus Aibrean could say anything, a sharp CRACK sound rang out. The window shattered, and the little girl who spoke fell over with her head covered in blood. All the kids started to scream and cry, and the other window cracked and shattered. Missus Aibrean tried to head over to all of them, but then loud, vicious laughter came from outside.

***

"Good afternoon!" Saint Orlaith greeted Kal.

Kal nodded a silent greeting of his own behind his potion stand. He rarely interacted with the Saint herself around town and this was the first time she ever came to his shop. He didn't know what to think about this but treated her as he would any other customer.

"Been bussy laely?" she asked, and he shrugged in response.

"And how'ss your lil one been?"

"She is well, I think," he answered, feeling a little awkward with the small talk.

"You did righ when raisin her. Been a fantasstic friend to Noirín. Oh ssorry, I meand Jacinta. Been tryin to get her to adop a human name to help her assimilate, but even I ssometimess sslip now and den. She'ss sstill pretty resistan, wanting to go back to her home. I imagine you can relate with dat. But hopefully, she'll learn like you did dat dere is no better place to live. Ah, here I'll take a Ruswil potion, pleasse. This can help Jacinta ssleep during nigh time. How poten iss it?"

"Fifty-five percent potency, but for a child, I would water it down to twenty-five. Not sure how Aos Sí metabolises though."

"Tank you. How much for a vial?"

"Forty silver."

"You uh … know how to price your produc." "Price is not negotiable."

"Of coursse," Saint Orlaith said as she reached into her backpack and started to pull out various items from it so she could find her coin pouch. One of those items caught Kal's eye and it was a mask with a circle carved on it, covered with dozens of painted eyes.

"Oh, dat old ting. Hadn worn it in yearss. Figured I could ssave a penny getting ih repained."

As Kal stared into the dark eye slits. His hands trembled and his heart raced. He wanted to catch his breath, but his throat was closing. His head was pounding and the world was spinning. Everything in his body was screaming to him, "You Are In Danger!," but he couldn't see from where or what. He needed to escape, but he didn't know where to go. He wasn't even

at his shop anymore, he was …

Then

Released into the big room with his sister. At least they believed it was a big room. It seemed more open than their cell, but every wall was dark black stone, so they had no sense of depth. Others were released into the big room; human and Demi -Human kids of varying ages and varying scars and deformities. Kalby could recognize a few from the other times they were in the big room. Though he never spoke to them. The masked ones did this when everyone had their turn. Or when they had to replace the ones who didn't survive their turn.

Kalby's sister quickly looked around for the goal while Kalby had to lie on the floor. His stomach was in searing pain. The scars didn't heal fast enough for the masked ones, so they burned them shut with their hands. At least he couldn't tear it open again.

The masked ones always had a goal in this room, even though it wasn't always obvious. Last time they left extra food in the centre so everyone would fight over them. The time before, they restrained all of them except one and allowed him to do whatever they wanted to those helpless. Kalby vowed to kill the older boy if he got the chance for what he did to his sister. Kalby's sister believed the masked ones were watching them somehow; this room made her paranoid. Kalby always assumed he was being watched. He never knew what it was like to have privacy.

The floor began to grow colder and wet. Increasingly wet. Kalby had to sit up as the water was getting into his mouth, and it was rising. Some of the kids, mostly the newer ones, ran to the doors screaming to be let out. Some tried to fight on top of each other for higher ground. Most were resigned to whatever would happen to them.

"You need to get up, Kalby. Quickly!" his sister said, as she held him up, but the water was getting higher. Soon the water was over their feet, then their knees, then their waist. Kalby's sister looked around desperately one last time before looking back at him with a face of love and sorrow. She told Kalby he needed to get on her back. Her parents had taught her how to swim before she was taken here. She would keep his head above water for as long as she could.

Kalby refused at first. There had to be some way out, some trick or test. They wouldn't just kill them now after everything they had done to them. Would they? As the water reached up to his neck, he did as she said, and soon her toes hovered above the floor as she tried swimming in the rising water.

Only a rare few other kids knew how to swim. The rest flailed until their weak little bodies could no longer hold them, and they sank into the

blackness. Kalby's sister floated for as long as she could. Even when their heads hit the ceiling, she kept treading, but she could only do so much for herself, let alone carry the weight of Kalby. The water had stopped rising, and Kalby dared to hope this was the end of it, but his sister's kicks and paddling grew weaker with each minute. Her body could no longer take it.

Kalby soon followed, as not only could he not swim, but the ripping ache from his scar stabbed at him each time he tried. Kalby tried to reach for his sister. His lungs burned much like his scar. His ears popped as he fell deeper. He breathed in water, and what little he could see of his sister's faint glow started to dim. Kalby blinked, but his eyes didn't open for a long time.

Now

Kal grabbed his side as he keeled over coughing and barely breathing. "Are you all righ?" Saint Orlaith asked as she tried to help him up. Kal

shoved her away reflexively and ran down his hill. He was finally able to get some trembling breaths of cold air after focusing on the grey sky. Then from a distance, a mob of townsfolk started to gather around and rush toward the Port District. It would be a distraction at the very least.

***

Missus Aibrean quickly picked up the little girl and cleaned some of the blood off of her. "Someone take Riley and the others away from the windows!" Missus Aibrean shouted.

Freya's muscles were stiff yet weak. A chill crawled down her spine and heat burned in her head. She couldn't breathe but was gasping so fast she was getting lightheaded. Brigid and Jacinta huddled Freya, and she could feel her sweat mixed in with her tears. They took her back with the others and wrapped their arms around her.

"WHAT ARE YOU DOING? THERE ARE CHILDREN HERE!" Missus Aibrean barked.

"Sso what?" One of the vandals asked before throwing something else at one of the schoolhouse windows. "Plenty of *hic plenty of uss were out marching over corpses when we were their age."

"Yeah! Bout time they learn what the world's really like!" Another one shouted.

Some passersby tried to stop them, but nearly got cut down when they started wildly swinging their swords. Others went to get help, but others kept their distance.

Tears started pooling from Freya's eyes. She wanted this to stop. She should make it stop. With her power, she could scare whoever they were away. It would have been so simple. Just a tiny problem she could simply solve. And then what? The Sanctus Venatores would come and take her away

79

and no one would care if she saved them. "Why isn't Pappa here? What do I do?" Freya thought.

Missus Aibrean ran to the supply closet by her desk and tossed a set of bandages from inside.

"Brigid, apply that on Riley! Make sure it's tied on tight!" she commanded. Brigid grabbed them and quickly went to work as Ronan started to run toward the window shouting, "Who do you eejits—"

"Get your arse back here, Ronan!" One of the older kids shouted as they dragged him back.

Missus Aibrean came out carrying a crossbow and a round metal object with a crank in the centre and a flat, notched metal stick that stood out of the centre. She attached the drawstring to the end notch of the stick and turned the crank. A fist-sized rock had broken through, hitting the stove and spraying embers. Missus Aibrean finished her cranking, rested the crossbow on the now-empty windowsill, placed the bolt in the groove, took a breath, then exhaled. She pulled the trigger, and a loud thwack reverberated throughout the classroom. This was soon ignored as a piercing, agonised scream followed from outside. Freya covered her ears and wished all of this would stop.

"IF YOU COME NEAR MY STUDENTS AGAIN, FERGUS AND I WILL SEND THE NEXT ONE RIGHT THROUGH YOUR THICK SKULL!" Missus Aibrean roared. She made sure all the vandals ran off before she stowed the crossbow back in the supply closet and rushed over to the students. Before Missus Aibrean could take a headcount, a large mob of men and women burst through the door. They all crammed themselves inside the tiny classroom as they each tried to make sure their own children were all right. Mister Conall had nearly fallen over as he was shoved into Freya's view.

"Are you lasses all right?"

"Th-th-the wi-windows b-broke and Ri-Riley—" Freya tried so hard to say.

Brigid interrupted, "Someone or some people were attacking the school!" Her voice nearly trembling. Freya tried peering through the crowd, hoping that her father would finally be here. He soon was, as he moved the mob unnaturally effortlessly as if it was a thin door, knocking over and nearly crushing anyone in his way. Once her father could see Freya, he grabbed her hand and strode through the opening and to the streets. He took her through winding corners of the alleys making sure to not take a predictable path.

A flood of emotions washed into Freya as her mind raced with thoughts, "It has to be Silas or his friends, but why are they bullying us? What if they try to hurt me again? Why wasn't Pappa there to stop them? Pappa should let me use Magic on people like them! NO! I can't think that. I don't want to lose Pappa."

"What's going to happen, Pappa?"

80

Her father was about to drag her through another corner, but he yanked her toward himself all of a sudden as he pressed his back to a wall and covered her mouth.

Freya had almost forgotten how to breathe when she heard his voice.

"What did you idiots do? You leave our sight for barely twenty minutes

and now the town's out for our blood!" Silas said, sounding more sober than usual.

"Why are they making such a big deal out of this? They're just a bunch of spoiled kids!"

"Dumbass! You don't think people might get a little protective of kids after millions of them died in the Crusade?" Freya could hear Silas's heavy boots pace back and forth in the mud.

"Did you hurt any of the kids?"

"Wh-what?"

"What if we did? Getting soft on us, Captain? Thinking about your dead little sis—" another young man said before a gross crunching noise came followed by a curse that would have gotten twenty lashes by Missus Aibrean.

"Captain, you could have killed him! Caymen's bleeding out!"

"I'm starting to care about that less and less the more the three of you talk."

"Cover 'iz mouth. I'll cauterise ze wound."

A red light leaked out of the alley, and then there was a muffled scream followed by a sweet putrid scent.

"Now drag im back to ze ship. Quel bordel!"

Freya's father quietly carried Freya further back from the wall and behind some crates as the two of the young men carried an unconscious third one with a black mark on his shoulder.

"Who told them about her?"

"You did, mon chér. You tend to get very … personal when you drink." "Gods dammit … might have to hurry things up after this stunt." "Won't zat be dangerous?"

"Just got to pick the right moment and create a little chaos. Then it's in and out, Jean. Worst-case scenario, we got you as our ace in the hole."

"What does he mean 'chaos?' Are they going to attack again?" Freya thought, panicking as she tried and failed to catch her breath. Her stomach bubbled and gnarled when Silas and Jean walked past them. After they were gone, her father tried to rub her back as Freya was dry-heaving but Freya pushed his hand aside, saying "What's go-going on? W-why are these p-people t-trying to ruin everything?"

"I am sorry, vennen min. I do not know."

"Y-you're lying!" Freya shouted as she stomped her foot. "Y-you and Mist-ter Conall were t-talking about this!"

Her father was silent. He lowered himself to see eye to eye with her. His

dusty brown eyes looked into hers with indecision. Freya wanted to shout at him to say something, but then she remembered.

"We pr -promised to t-tell each other everything! We p-promised! I t-told you what I saw, now p-please t-tell me what's going on!"

"I really do not know for sure and I would not frighten you unnecessarily if I was not correct or cause you to think wrong if it was worse, but I sense owls in the moss."

Her father put his gloved hand on Freya's back and gently rubbed it as he said, "During the Second Grand Crusade, I had seen groups that looked like this, though much larger back then. Bad people learned to work together to do … worse things in subtle and sometimes lawful ways."

"How can they do crimes lawfully?" Freya asked.

"Sometimes they worked with or were the very people making the laws. This is why the Crusade had to force … drastic changes."

"What are they?"

"Pirates, criminal enterprises, Camorra, Yakuza, warlords, so, so many names. These groups would quietly come to a trading centre like Valour one by one and have some cargo misplaced. They would have enough of them mixed in with the dock workers to make it hard to tell which one is real and threaten anyone who tried to let everyone else know. Smart ones would leave before their thieving was caught on."

"Just like the lessons of the Second Grand Crusade Missus Aibrean taught us!" Freya realised.

"So they will leave on their own?" Freya asked optimistically.

"I do not know. This is strange. Why stay for so long? Why stay after causing so much trouble already? The only thing I can think of is that they have some reason to believe they won't get caught. And it might have something to do with their 'ace' Jean."

"D-do you think he is a Draoi?"

"It certainly seems like it."

"Let's get the Venatores to c-catch them then!" Freya said excitedly, hoping they could make things back to normal.

"No! I'm not even going to think of risking that with you."

"Then what do we do?" Freya moaned as she turned to press her head against the wall. The cool touch eased her stomach.

"What we have been doing. Keeping our heads down and keeping ourselves out of the way. Although I will be more careful and always have you within my sight until they leave."

"If you don't want to do anything, then why did you tell Mister Conall?" Freya asked.

"I thought about not telling him, and I probably should not have. But Mister Conall helped us before. I chose to let him have a choice."

"If you're going to vomit, could you aim at that building there?" A voice

came from behind. Freya's father reflexively spun on his heels only to have to look down to face the mysterious voice coming from the familiar Leprechaun.

"Miss Moira still hasn't paid me back for those boots I made, which she likes to flaunt around," Mister Brian said before pretending to take a puff from his smokeless, carved wooden pipe. Freya let out a chuckle despite her anxiety.

"You two want to wait inside? It's fierce weather today, and I have a nice clean pot if Freya is feeling sick," Mister Brian asked, stroking his greying brown goatee.

Her father only needed to look at Freya to decide.

***

Mister Brian's cobblery was unlike most of the stores in town, especially one so far from the main road. It was vibrantly colourful, with a bright apple-red-stained floor and equally vibrant yellow wooden tables holding beautiful, well-crafted shoes and boots made of all sorts of fine materials. Freya and her father bought all their shoes and boots from Mister Brian for as long as she could remember, and Mister Brian made each visit a trip. Freya remembered how she would measure herself to him and how excited she was when she was five and finally grew taller than him.

Freya was slowly breathing into the pot Mister Brian had lent her. Her father gently rubbed her back.

"Be sure to have your Da clean that pot once you're done. I'm gonna need it if I ever get any gold out of this place."

"Why is it so empty in the middle of the day?" Freya asked as her voice echoed from the pot.

"Business gets slow for people like us during troubled
times." "It's because of Ronan isn't it?"

"I would like to blame it all on one person or even a handful of people, but after living a hundred and eleven years and having to move from town to town, it's just something to expect with humans. At least there are good folks like you and yer Da. But enough about that. What's the story? I figured I would wait until someone inevitably gossiped about it, but it seems you will be the first."

Freya looked up at her father, and he merely shrugged. So Freya tried her best to recount everything that happened at the schoolhouse. When she got to the scary moments, she found herself trying her hardest not to choke up again.

"Well before you go staining up my nice floors with yer tears, listen to this," Mister Brian had grabbed his flute from a shelf, away from its case, causing Freya to ask, "Why don't you keep your flute in the case?"

"Because that's where I keep my money."

This, in turn, begged Freya to ask, "Well why do you keep your money in

there?"

"Because no thief would want to steal it. You want to keep asking questions, or do you want to hear me play?"

"Play, please!" Freya quickly pleaded.

Mister Brian took a breath, and once the notes began to flow freely from the flute, Freya's frets and fears faded away with the melody.

CHAPTER 7
NIGHT OF TERRORS

THEN

Kalby jolted uncontrollably as if someone had kicked his chest in. He looked up and there was a masked one with sharp orange-and-yellow light between his fingers that made the hair on Kalby's arms stand up. His mask was plain white with two eye slits.

Kalby lay on a cold metal table surrounded by other kids laying on similar tables. His arms and legs were restrained. His sister had been laid on one next to him. The same masked man went to another table, and Kalby could see a dark blue waving ring surrounding the man as the water was ripped out of the boy's throat. The ring then changed to a crackling orangish-yellow, and he placed his hands on the boy's chest, and then he started jolting as Kalby did.

He was talking to another masked man who Kalby could recognize. He had a half-skull mask and was there when Kalby was last cut open.

"How many expired?" Asked the man in the half-skull mask in cold frustration.

"Only three this time. Two of the childr—I mean subjects suffered irreparable brain damage, so I would suggest disposal. Unless …?"

Half-skull waved his hand dismissively, so the white mask continued, "Their adrenaline hormones seem lower than I thought they would."

"We have to account for the fact that many of the subjects either didn't believe they would expire or wanted to expire. ... We should only use half now and save the others as a control group."

Kalby closed his eyes. He hoped if they thought he was still unconscious, they might pass over him. With each sound of the masked man's footsteps, Kalby could hear his heart thud. A shadow passed along his eyelids, and his heart nearly stopped.

"How is subject J16-30 recovering?" Hot
breath inched near his face. "Remarkably.
What shall we call this potion?"
"Our most generous donor requested this one be named after
him." "Barnaby Phigs? Has he even ever stepped foot in the
laboratory?" "For all you know, I could be him." "Are you?"

"Do you not understand the purpose of these masks?"
There was no response and one of the tables squeaked while it was
being wheeled off. Kalby squinted his eyes just a bit to see who it was.
"Which half?" White mask asked.
"Let's try the older ones like the Ljósálfar specimen there."
They were talking about his sister. She was chosen. They were going
to make her go through that again, this time without him. Force her back
into the big room and experience the torment all over. Not even giving
her a little moment of reprieve.

Kalby begged and pleaded for them to take him instead. But to them, he
was less than a noisy animal. None of it would stop them. Kalby tried prying
himself violently from the table. He could feel each of his shoulders pop and
dislocate, yet he could not stop them. He screamed, cried, and roared, and
none of it would stop them. He was utterly powerless to stop them.

The two masked ones were too close to the door with his sister, and
all at once, Kalby felt something. He felt what pulled him to the table and
what pulled the table to the floor. He felt what made a quill fall off a
nearby table. He felt everything as it was, every rule which made reality
as it was. He could bend it, control it, weaponize it. With a mental
alteration of a few hundred digits, every quill nearby acted as though the
man in the white mask's neck was the correct direction of gravity. They
soared toward him like a barrage of arrows.

Cutting, slashing, and stabbing the masked man, drawing blood. But
they did not kill him. The man in the white mask turned to see a faint
bright blue light beneath Kalby. They weren't going to give Kalby tim e
to try again. The man in the white mask pointed his finger. A line of
orange light struck Kalby over and over again, causing his body to
contort and his jaw clenched so hard he could barely shout his sister's
name.

Now

"FREJA!"
Freya shot up from her bed and rushed into the other room. They lost
track of time and got back late at night from Mister Brian's. Freya was
already

sure what was happening. Her father sat on his cot, breathing heavily and dripping with sweat, and this all but confirmed it.

Freya wanted to go over to him, to hug him, to calm him, to let him know she was here and there was nothing to be afraid of like he would have —as he has done for her, but what if it was not over? What if he was still panicking? If she touched her father, would he be startled? Would he accidentally hurt her in a panic? Freya hated herself for being too cowardly to do anything.

Did she cause this panic too because of yesterday, Freya wondered. She had been so concerned about how scared she was, how worried and angry she was, and she didn't consider how her father was feeling during all this.

"How could I have been so selfish when Pappa needed me most?" Freya thought and mustered every bit of courage she had to take a step toward her father. The moment she put weight on her bare foot, the wooden floor creaked. Her father's head snapped toward her. Freya stayed dead still.

Her father stared unblinkingly at Freya with watery red eyes. His hands shook as they gripped the bars of his cot so tightly his knuckles had gone white. He wasn't wearing his worn-out gloves, and his undershirt didn't have sleeves long enough to hide his torn and gnarled wrists.

Freya didn't see them often, and she began to wonder if they were caused by some horrible torture her father suffered during the Second Grand Crusade.

Freya slowly imagined darker, scarier images in her head, but then her father asked, "Freya?"

She looked back at him. Instead of seeing a dangerous, scared, snivelling man, he was her father again as he looked at her with a loving concern that broke Freya's heart. Tears trailed behind her as Freya bounded toward him and collapsed into his arms repeating, "I'm sorry. I'm so, so sorry, Pappa." Over and over again.

Her father tried to stop her and told her in choked words, "This is not your fault, vennen min, and it was never your fault."

She didn't argue with him. But despite all of his efforts, Freya would not be convinced otherwise.

"I think it is late, vennen min. You should go back to

sleep." "I don't want you to be alone," Freya said.

Her father moved the pillows and blankets around his cot, and Freya jumped right on. There wasn't much room for her father, let alone the two of them. Yet she slept better knowing she kept her father safe.

***

A smell of cinnamon filled Freya's nose as she awoke to see her father making breakfast. Freya stretched and realised she was feeling a little too well-rested. She sprang out of the cot, sprinted back to her room, and threw on any clothes she could find. Freya was just about to charge out the door before

her father grabbed her shoulder and puzzledly asked, "What is wrong vennen min?"

"I slept in! Missus Aibrean is going to be soo mad!"

"Freya, do you not remember?" her father asked and Freya stared at him like he just asked her how to spell hippopotomonstrosesquippedaliophobia.

"You will not leave my side until I believe it is safe." Freya slumped to the floor. "So, no school?"

Her father nodded.

"Huh ..."

"I made you some breakfast."

Freya took a minute to collect her thoughts, then stood up and slowly sat at the table, "Ja ... Tusen Takks, Pappa. So are we still going to practice Magic?"

"I do not think that is a good idea. I do not know if Silas has anybody hiding in the woods and do not want to risk finding out."

"Why do they have to ruin everything?" Freya moaned as she grabbed a spoon and fed her sadness with food.

"I am sorry I worried you again last night, vennen min." Her father said. "No, I'm sorry I—"

"You have nothing to be sorry about, vennen min." Her father interrupted. Freya still could not believe those words.

***

After they finished eating, her father went ahead and grabbed his tray of potions and a blanket.

"What should I do?" Freya asked.

"I guess just keep yourself entertained for the time being. I will come back inside once it is time to close the shop." He went outside and would be out there for hours and hours, so Freya needed to find something to do lest boredom take away her sanity.

On her list of activities she could do, re-reading some of her storybooks was first. She had read them so much as to reach well past double digits. Still, it was certainly more fun than any of her father's apothecary books. They were old and dusty with words so big that her father often needed her help to read them.

***

While his daughter was safe inside, Kal could focus on a contingency plan until a customer eventually came. It had been almost a decade since Kal had to fight someone, he had kept his Magical abilities from rusting with his training of Freya, but it was not the same as battlefield experience. To be able to keep a level-enough head to alter the complex Rules of Reality while someone, something, or many things were trying to kill you was difficult. If and when violence is needed to keep Freya safe, will he still be able to commit it as effectively as he had during the Crusades? Would he be able to handle

the aftermath and reactions? It was an uncomfortable dilemma. Anywhere they could live that could keep him combat-ready would not have been safe enough for Freya. But by keeping Freya as safe as he had, he was bound to have gotten weaker. Though he couldn't deny he enjoyed the unusual peace Valour had.

Then there was the issue of Silas's Draoi, Jean. Kal did not like how little he knew of what Jean could do. A Draoi's abilities could vary drastically per person. If Jean had gained his powers at an exceptionally young age like Freya, then he might have had more time to develop them, especially as an impressionable child. If Jean was a late bloomer and gained his power at eighteen, then even Freya would have more experience and training. Training and experience itself was a major variable to consider. Kal didn't remember who trained him or how he was trained. From his own observations during the Crusades, he considered himself at the time to be above average as a combative Magic user, but he majorly lacked diversity in other Magical fields. His one and only real advantage was being able to hide his Magic and a deeper understanding of Gravomancy.

"And it is not just Magic that can make someone dangerous," Kal had to remind himself. Plenty of Non-Magical people can be just as if not more dangerous as the Sanctus Venatores had proven. Silas and his crew must be competent enough to be able to hide Jean, and also keep the general authorities from taking action. Kal could use his Magic to discreetly kill them, but unless he could get them all in the same room at once, he risked any survivors retaliating. And there was no way he was going to leave Freya alone while any of them were in town.

A customer came by, tried and failed to haggle Kal's non-negotiable prices, and bought the potion she was looking for. Once the interaction was over, Kal would go back to thinking and planning.

***

After the storybook knight had once again saved the day, Freya was still left with too much time to spend, so she thought how thinking about things would help. Freya had to stop doing this after a few minutes, as she began overthinking about herself, and how she looked, with Brigid always needing to straighten her hair, her changing moods, and how others in her class think about her. She became self-conscious, and it was making her embarrassed and uncomfortable.

Freya remembered her few toys and was embarrassed as soon as she tried to play with them. None of the other girls her age did. Brigid had stopped playing toys with her a few years ago. Ronan would love to make fun of her for it. But she was also sad because her father bought them when she was little, and they didn't exactly have much money to spend.

With nothing else to do, Freya decided to go outside to see if her father was just as bored as she was, only to catch him in the middle of dealing with

a customer. Freya realised that she still didn't know what she wanted to do when she grew up. Considering how young her father must have been when he started working, Freya needed to think of something soon.

The moment the customer left. Freya ran up to her father with the fear of future poverty chasing behind her.

"How do I do your job?"

"What?"

"If I don't learn, I'll become a beggar!"

"What?" Kal asked again, ceasing his previous thoughts to understand this panic.

"I don't want to be poor and homeless!"

"Freya, I do not understand," Kal said, wondering if Freya was seeing a Bean Sidhe right behind him or something.

"How do you do your potion stuff?" Freya asked more specifically.

"Oh, vennen min." Her father said with a sigh of relief as he moved the

blanket from his lap. Freya climbed on, and her father made sure they were both wrapped up tight.

"So, what first?" Freya asked eagerly.

"I guess I should show you where I keep all the potions." He then pulled open the sliding door at the bottom of his side of the stand and brought out his potion tray. He pointed at a row of pale orange vials and said, "I always make Phigs potion because someone always needs it."

"That one heals people, right?"

"It hastens people's natural healing, though it did save a lot of people's lives during the Crusade." He pointed to a smaller row of clear vials and said, "This is an Aplite potion. Surgeons use these on patients since it makes people numb." He grabbed one out of the three azure vials and brought it closer for Freya to see. "I am sure you know what this is."

"Liquid Xatralt!" Freya answered excitedly.

"Correct, although some call it Magic water because of how often people like us use them. Unfortunately, I cannot make many of these. Otherwise, some may get suspicious."

"Can other people drink it?"

"Ja, from what I understand, it helps them to focus better. I guess it does the same for us just … better."

"What are those?" Freya asked, pointing at the small row of midnight blue vials.

"Those are Ruswil potions. Saint John's wort is a major ingredient and it helps people fall asleep. I use them now and then when it gets too hot in the summer."

"How did you learn how to make all of them?" Freya asked. "You don't have to answer if you don't remember!" she quickly added.

Her father wrapped his arms around Freya and stared at the cloudy sky.

90

"During the Second Grand Crusade, your mother would get hurt from protecting others and quite often myself. The divine militia had limited medical supplies. Even giving her all of mine was not enough. I had blood on my tooth to help her any way I could, so when I was allowed to rest, I instead went to the apothecaries in our camp and learned from watching how to make potions to help her."

Her father looked back down at her and said, "The business side of things I had to learn from trial and error. The most important things I learned were to be patient and thank them when they buy something. Oh, and to let them know very clearly and sometimes repeatedly that the price is not negotiable." Her father went over a standard greeting and did a pretend sale with Freya. After twenty minutes of waiting, her first customer came, and she put all of his lessons to practice. It went off without a hitch, and Freya could not have been more excited for her next.

"If potion selling was this much fun, I wouldn't mind doing this with Pappa when I'm done with school," Freya thought before she realised her eyes were opening again and her head was resting on her father's chest.

"Wha-what happened?" Freya asked with a yawn.

"You were probably still tired from the night before, and there were not any customers for a while, so you must have gotten sleepy."

"Oh no, did I miss any?"

"Nei, you have not missed anything."

"Oh. How long was I asleep for?"

Her father looked at where the sun was before saying, "Two or three hours, I think."

"What?" Freya shouted. "How do you make enough money if no customers are showing up for so long?"

"Because everyone will always need potions. I am the only one in town selling them, so even if they do not like how much I sell my potions for or how far I am from them, they will eventually have to buy them at whatever price I set. I am sure we would be better off if I set up the stand in town, and I will probably have to make changes eventually as more of your classmates graduate from the schoolhouse. But until then …"

Freya didn't understand the nuisance of business, but she did know that she was getting tired of just sitting around. "Don't you get bored from just sitting here all day, every day?" She asked impatiently.

"Sometimes. I enjoy making the potions more than selling them and I have caught myself napping here once or twice as well. But it keeps us fed and ... it is peaceful at least."

Freya looked over the stand and, from their hill view, she could see most of the town. Every roof was blanketed with white snow, the roads were filled with people, and the docks had boats coming in and out. Over there, it was anything but peaceful. But from here, she could practically watch everything

going on in town and only hear the sounds of nature around her.

It seemed odd to Freya that her father does so much to avoid crowds and most people in general, while also hiding himself and Freya's powers with such dedicated care. He decided to live in Bastiel, let alone Valour, one of its largest, if not the largest, port towns of all places.

"Pappa?"

"Ja, vennen min?"

"Why do we live here?"

"Well, because the house was out of the way and it was really cheap."

Freya smirked, not knowing if he was making a bad joke or was serious.

Either way, both were definitely her father. "Nei, silly. I meant why do we live in Bastiel?"

"Ah. Well, when you were born, and your mother was gone, I was so … I carried you around wandering, trying to find someplace safe. Away from the chaos of the Crusades, away from the Sanctus Venatores, away from— but such places were scarce and far. Your mother used to tell me how she loved this country so much. I hoped perhaps by living here, you might have some of her goodness. And I think it is working."

Freya tried to hide her smile in the blankets. "Mamma lived in Valour?" "No, she grew up in Charity."

"The orphanage city? Wait, Mamma was an orphan?"

"Ja. I was told the civil war before was … violent."

"Right. The one where the blood-thirsting queen was defeated by Saint Joan and the Grand Masters."

Before Freya could ask more, she noticed some familiar faces.

"Where the heck have you been?" Brigid asked as she ran up the hill with Jacinta following behind her, wrapped in an oversized, thick coat.

"What are you doing here?" Freya excitedly asked.

"What do you think? We haven't seen you all bleedin' day." "Sorry," Freya said.

"Wash it becaushe of yeshterday?"

Freya nodded to Jacinta.

"Don't say sorry. I'm just in a shite mood. They did a shoddy job boarding the school windows, so we were freezing our arses off the entire class."

"They were just worried about you, lass," Mister Conall said, breathing harder as he finally made it up the hill.

"I'm all right. I've been working the shop with Da."

"That's good. Means you'll be able to do all the classwork you missed. Don't want you to miss your education, after all," Brigid said with a wicked smile as she put a big stack of papers on the stand.

"Gee. Thanks …" Freya said through a fake smile and gritted teeth. She had hoped she would not have to work on it.

"So what Saint are you going as tomorrow?"

92

All of a sudden, the world had stopped for Freya. Her father had said he would not let her leave his side, and he made it clear he would not go to the festival.

"Pappa?" Freya pleaded.

"It is too dangerous."

Before Freya could beg, Mister Conall asked, "Could you three let me speak to Mister Pantar in private, please?"

Freya's father nodded.

Not wanting to make things worse, Freya took Brigid and Jacinta inside. Jacinta ran from corner to corner and looked at Freya with what used to

be a sharp toothy grin, "Your home ish sho

wonderful!" "Oh, thank you. It's a little small, but

I like it."

"A little shmall? That'sh what makes it amazing! What'sh that picture there?" Jacinta asked.

"Oh, that's a map of Valour. Da uses it to find shortcuts around town." "So what're the markings—"

"What's the story at the schoolhouse?" Freya interrupted.

"Not much. Rumours are getting worse. Though strangely Ronan was asking about you."

Freya didn't care, but she was curious, "What does he want?"

"Don't know. He said he was going to get a posse with the older kids to 'run Silas and his Demi-Human gang out of town.'"

"What? He's going to get everyone killed!"

"I doubt it. Don't think he'll actually do it. Just full of hot air. I hope."

The door creaked open and Mister Conall and her father walked in.

"All right lasses, Mister Pantar and I have come up with a little plan." Mister Conall pulled his belt up before continuing, "Freya, your Da said it would be all right for you to come with us on Souls of Saints Day on two conditions. First, you must never leave my sight. Second, we all have to stay within sight of my house, where Mister Pantar will be staying for the festivities so he can get to Freya quickly if he feels worried about her. Sounds good?"

Freya nodded so fast she gave herself a headache. She didn't realise how relieved she was until her legs wobbled. She wouldn't be able to visit most of the attractions or stores, but Freya didn't care. The centre of town was where the best stuff was anyway.

"Glad to hear it. I'll see you two tomorrow then. Come on, lasses, let's get you back home."

"Oh, before you go, Mister Conall, do you want to buy a potion?"

"Oh? Learning your Da's trade, aye? All right, let me have a look."

"Right this way, Mister Conall!" Freya took them back to the stand and she explained each potion to Mister Conall as her father explained to her. Mister Conall pointed at the Ruswil potion, "Figure I'll need a good sleep tonight if I'm going to keep up with you three crazies tomorrow night." "That will be fifty silver, Mister Conall."

Mister Conall coughed, "Fifty silver? That's almost as much as a Phigs outside of Valour."

"We sell those at one gold."

"Go way outta that! You serious?"

"Price is not negotiable," Freya said, smiling at how well she had remembered her father's lesson.

Mister Conall mumbled, "Your Da should consider himself a lucky man. Few can say no to a smile like that. Here you go."

"Oi, Freya," Brigid whispered, "Can you teach me to smile like that? I want to get a new dress from Da before the festival," before she ran off with Mister Conall and Jacinta.

Today's work ended in a few hours with three more customers. Freya's father thought it was a busy day and together they made a total of one hundred and twelve silver. While her father was cooking dinner, he beckoned Freya to come over to the stove with him.

"I am going to show you how to make a Phigs potion. It is quite useful for emergencies."

Her father grabbed a pestle and mortar and then filled it with mountain basil, frosted feverfew, and lavender from their labelled jars. He ground them into a fine powder and poured it into a pot of water he had boiling on the stove.

"It has to be salty seawater or else it will be overactive and cause side effects like tiredness or dangerous digestion rate."

"Dangerous digestion rate?"

"Uh, you starve to death in a matter of hours. Even if you had already eaten."

"Oh," was all Freya could say, promptly making extra sure to pay attention.

They had dinner while it boiled and when it finished, he poured it into a strainer and dumped what remained in a cup of fresh water. He stirred the cup a bit before saying, "Now to demonstrate, vennen min."

Her father grabbed a kitchen knife and gave himself a tiny cut, drawing a little bit of blood. He took a few sips, and within a minute, the skin scabbed and faded away as if it was never there. Freya was amazed. Such power and yet no Magic was involved.

"Alright, vennen min, it is time for bed."

Freya was about to head into her room, but stopped, "Can I sleep on the cot with you again?"

Her father looked so sad as he said, "I am so sorry, vennen min. You should not have to worry about me like this. Please sleep in your own bed tonight. I will do as Mister Conall and take a bit of Ruswil. It should make

me have a quieter night.”

“Al-all right, sweet dreams, Pappa.”

Freya headed into her room and wondered how she will sleep when she knew tomorrow will be so much fun.

CHAPTER 8
SOULS OF SAINTS DAY

THEN

"Let kθk = −∞. In [12], the main result was the derivation of one-to-one substrings F=GMmr2 log(distance). Extend the results of [1] to quasi-countably ordered random variables. A right- Eratosthenes set is a path if it is complete. We can't create or destroy matter, only alter it."

Cram, memorise, practice, punish, test, master, repeat. They separated Kalby from his sister once they learned about his new power. Since he was like them now, he became important. He was still a subject and not a sapient, of course. A few masked ones showed him the symbols and forced him to learn and recite them.

Kalby's only rest was when his migraines were unbearable. His nose would bleed so much he had trouble not choking on it, and they left him alone in his cell. So alone. They had to restrain Kalby from himself when it got worse. Didn't want to lose a valuable subject after all. Tests replaced most of the surgeries. Test after test.

They tried to make Kalby use his new power on the other subjects. They were given herbs and potions to make their shrivelled, pathetic, malformed bodies into something dangerous. He defended himself, but they were trapped here like him. Kalby never knew a life outside of this, but some of them had lost whatever they had before the masked ones had taken them, like his sister. If any of them were like her, how could he kill them?

They tried beating him, but he suffered worse. They tried lying to him, but he never trusted them. They couldn't use the herbs or potions, or else his mind couldn't calculate. They locked him in his cell. Kalby had hoped they had given up or forgotten about him. Then he was scared they had forgotten about him as days went by and he was not given any food or water. Kalby resorted to drinking the dew droplets from the cave ceiling as days turned to a   week. The man in the half-face/half-skull mask gave an amused chuckle when he threw a strange animal inside Kalby's cell. Kal tried to use Magic on him before the cell door closed, but he couldn't think through the hunger and dehydration. The animal was furry with a long tail, floppy ears, and a tongue that liked to stick out. No one came for another few days. When they did, Kalby's mouth and hands were stained with blood, but his hunger finally ceased.

The masked ones made Kalby fight them. He tried to kill them, but they had their power for much longer, and they clearly didn't teach him the powers they considered a threat. Kalby would try to slam, grab, and launch anything and everything he could at them, but they would simply burn him, drown him, shock him, blind him, deafen him, and everything else he couldn't do to them.

They had Kalby face another masked person. Her mask looked simple compared to the others. Freshly carved wood with no paint or markings. It didn't matter. Before she could get out the door, Kalby used his power to alter the Rules of Reality so the wall had a stronger pull of gravity, slamming her against it. She didn't make a sound, but she was still breathing. He dragged her across the jagged stone floor.

She didn't fight back, but she still was breathing. Kalby was more deprived by her silence than any starvation or isolation. He could finally hurt one, inflict pain on one of them, but even now, she remained silent. With his power, he made her spine bend to a new gravity that pulled back her upper half as far back as it would go and beyond. She was silent, but her spine popped and cracked. He went even further until it broke and snapped. Kalby ended his configuration, and she fell hard to the floor. Kalby couldn't believe it. Did he kill her? No one had tried to stop him. She didn't even counter any of his spells. What was going on? He needed to know what these masked people were. He carefully approached the fallen woman. This had to be a trap, but he had to find out. He lifted the mask and it was his big sister, unconscious, with her mouth gagged. She would never walk again, but she was still breathing.

Now

"Come on! Hurry! Hurry! Hurry, Pappa!"

"It is not like today will be over anytime soon," her father mumbled as he was closing up the potion shop. Her excitement was dampened, but not extinguished. The festival was so close Freya could practically taste all the sweets in the air, even from their house.

As soon as her father put the last tray of vials inside and locked the house,

Freya dragged him by the hand all the way down their hill. Even before they reached the town sign, Freya could see Valour was getting full. Merchants from all over were selling their wares. Townsfolk and tourists walked around, wearing costumes and thick wooden masks of all shapes, sizes, and colours. Bastiel's greens and purples were the most popular.

As Freya and her father walked past the Starboard Inn and Tavern, a man wearing a mask of Saint Amand of Barkeepers, who looked like a jolly man with a long beard, nearly fell. The man wrapped his arms around her father for support and asked, "Where'ss your massk, ssonny? Can't celebrate the Saintss proper without one."

Her father squeezed her hand tighter. She dragged him away from the masked stranger by pretending to be excited to see something far away from the man. She could see her father was practically shaking.

"Do you want to stop for a bit, Pappa?" He shook his head and picked up his pace.

***

Freya was four the last time her father went to Souls of Saints Day. It was her first time and could very well have been his too as far as Freya knew. She didn't remember much of that night. She was too young to form any memories beyond abstract feelings and images. Happiness, wonder, and a hazy memory of colourful confetti and candy rising up into the air and falling back down. Though she would never forget the end of that night. It was getting late, and her father decided to head home. The streets were too crowded to get around. He carried her on his back everywhere, back then, and took her to the alleys.

They wandered around for some time. Thinking back, Freya was fairly sure her father hadn't memorised the town layout then. It was perhaps that night that made him decide to do so. They ended up in a dead-end. When her father turned around, there was a man in a Saint mask. It appeared to be cracked, and the darkness of the alleys made it impossible to tell who it was supposed to be. The man in the mask held a chipped dagger and brought it close to her father.

"Empty your pockets, or I will drown your little sister in your own blood!"

Her father's breathing was all over the place. Going from rapid to sharp, sudden stops. He was panicking and was starting to shake. The mugger might have thought her father was about to resist and lunged the dagger toward her father's chest. If Freya had done nothing, the dagger would have killed her father. If Freya had done nothing, her father would have been lying on the ground as blood would rapidly pour out of him. If Freya had done nothing, they would have been too far in the alley, too quiet to be heard to call for help. If Freya had done nothing, her father would have died six years ago,

and it was unlikely the mugger would have left her alive either.

Freya had to do something back then, and she had plenty of time to think.

Or perhaps it would be better to say she could think fast enough in the microseconds. For the first time, Freya could see everything as it was. She could feel the Rules of Reality and she could change them. Freya knew the instructions that allowed things to rise up in the air and come back down. She knew what she needed to change to make it happen. A soft blue ring circled below her as she changed the properties of the dagger to rise up out of the mugger's hand and fall back down away from him.

Her father snapped out of his panic. Both he and the mugger looked up at Freya in shock.

"DRAO- !" The mugger was about to scream, but abruptly he fell sideways and crashed into a brick wall of a nearby house. Her father ran off before Freya could see what happened to the mugger, but she remembered the crunching sound he made.

The world was becoming too complicated. Numbers and symbols forced themselves into her mind. Closing her eyes helped only a little as she could feel the numbers of every sound of every imagined location of objects in the black room of her vision. It was becoming too much, overloading her. A confusing cacophony of white noise and cluttered unintelligibility. Freya started to scream. Hoping it would at least drown some of it out, her father covered her mouth and held her close to his chest.

"Hush, vennen lille min. Keep your eyes closed and listen to my heart," Her father whispered.

Freya listened as her father's heart slowed to match his now walking pace. Thump -thump. Thump-thump. Thump-thump. Thump. Thump. Thump. Thump … Thump … Thump … She listened and made her whole world into those soothing sounds. There were numbers around his heart, but they seemed familiar and it was far more manageable.

They made it back home late and all Freya wanted to do was sleep with her father reading to her, but he needed to tell her, to explain to her, "You are a Draoi."

Freya had heard the word before. It was one of the first things she was taught to fear in class.

"I don't want to be a Draoi! I want to be me!" She was so upset but didn't know how to say it. This made her more angry and sad, and it was just so frustrating she started crying because nothing else made sense.

"It is all right, vennen lille min. You are not alone. I am one too. I did not tell you before because I did not know if you would be like me and you are so young, but now that we know… I promise to tell you everything from now on, and I need you to do the same. Can you promise me this, vennen lille min?"

Freya nodded. From then on, her father taught her about Magic almost every day. He tried his best to teach her not to be afraid of herself and to keep what they knew a secret, no matter what.

***

That night brought Kal equal parts joy and terror he lacked the vocabulary to express, but since then, he could never bring himself to come to Souls of Saints Day. It wasn't until Freya and Brigid became friends that she could go with her and Mister Conall to each one after.

Tonight was the closest her father had been to the festival since that night. Freya could tell the only part he enjoyed was getting to Mister Conall's house as he took a breath of relief. He knocked on the door and impatiently tapped his feet as Mister Conall was taking a bit to open the door.

When he did, Freya had to stifle a laugh after getting a look at his groomed beard. His red curls were twisted, tied, and held in fancy shiny rings like a hair braid. It looked dapper, but Freya had never seen Mister Conall look dapper, so it took her by surprise.

"You all right, Kal?"

He nodded and asked, "Can we please come in?"

"Yeah, please do. There's a seat inside if you need it."

Jacinta ran up to Freya and took her by both her hands and looked a little too intensely into Freya's eyes, but perhaps this was just something people who live underground do, "I'm sho happy you could make it Freya, I wash worried I wouldn't be able to shee you before … I mean for the feshtival." Freya noticed she was wearing a more boyish outfit. A thick wool shirt, a dark tanned jacket with several pockets, and a pair of plain trousers instead of the usual dress outfit the priestess would make her wear. Even more shocking she had been in Brigid's house for some time now, and her hair was only in a simple ponytail.

"Has Brigid been replaced with a changeling? How did she let you get away without spending at least two hours on your hair and clothes?" Freya asked with semi-joking amazement.

"I jusht wanted to wear shomething comfortable. And I told both of them if they tried to get me into another dressh again, I was going to tear it apart no matter how much it coshtsh."

"She threatened to do the same thing to her hair if I tried to style it. The ponytail was a compromise," Brigid said as she came out wearing a purple-and-green dress with a longer hem that almost dragged behind her and a sparkling silver sash twisting all around her. It was all slightly fancier than her usual dresses, which Freya didn't think was possible.

Her father had taken the chair Mister Conall mentioned, and Freya could see he was trying to slow down his heavy breathing.

Brigid dragged Freya and Jacinta away to her room saying, "Come on. If I have to suffer Jacinta's plainness, then I'm going to have to make you at least double beautiful or I'm going to have to kick someone's arse to feel better."

Brigid presented the dress Freya would be wearing. It was a pearl white

blouse, covered in a grape purple bodice and a matching skirt that was a tad long on her. As Brigid began helping Freya with her hair she asked, "So what's wrong with your Da?"

"Nothing's wrong with him!" Freya said a little too defensively.

"No, I mean he looks like he saw the old Queen back from the dead … Again."

Freya gazed through the crack in Brigid's door to see her father lost in worrying thoughts. "Oh. The masks just creep him out."

"Right! Which Saint are you two going as?"

"Saint Magnus of science!" Freya answered as he was her favourite Saint. "Of course, you would, you bookworm. I, however, will be going as the great craftsman Saint Clement."

"This would be the third time in a row she has gone as him," Freya thought to herself.

Freya and Brigid turned to Jacinta expectantly.

"I didn't know of your human Shaints, sho I picked at random."

"They are not all human," Brigid argued, but both she and Freya struggled to remember their names. Those Saints weren't taught as much in class.

"Can we see it?" Freya asked and Jacinta grabbed it from where she left it and showed it to them. It was an older man with a long white and groomed beard with short white hair.

"Oh, that's Saint Brendan of sailors. He's fairly common in Valour because, you know, ports and stuff."

"It was between him or a large man with long ears."

"Oh, I think his name is Saint Buddha. Though I believe he is supposed to be skinny."

"Which one ish mosht popular in Bashtiel?"

"Saint Patrick," both Freya and Brigid said in unison, prepared for the question.

"Why him?"

"Don't you remember what Missus Aibrean said in class?" Freya asked. "No, I think I wash-was asleep."

Freya was flabbergasted anyone could fall asleep when they talked about such exciting heroes. She was ready to jabber Jacinta's pointy ears off about him. But before Freya could even exhale a single word, Brigid cut her off saying, "You'll definitely learn about him during the festival … And done."

"Isn't this a bit much?" Freya asked.

"Not at all. Just look at your reflection."

Freya walked over toward an unfinished yet polished shield hanging on a nearby wall. Her hair was in one large braid going down her back with multiple small braids circling it. A medium braid overlapped them all from left to right of her hair and was woven with a white ribbon. Freya would never admit it lest Brigid made this look into a habit, but this was the prettiest

101

she had ever felt. Freya ran to her father to show him.

"How do I look? Isn't it beautiful?" Freya asked him with a twirl.

Her father smiled at her past his anxiety and told her, "You are always beautiful to me. Try to have as much fun as you can. I love you, vennen min." After being told that, how could she not give him the biggest hug? Her father relaxed a bit and reminded Freya of the same things he reminded her of every morning. Stay warm and follow their plan if she got into trouble.

"Don't worry, Kal. I'll have her back to you before you know it. Just keep an eye on us upstairs." Mister Conall said as he sheathed his arming sword and opened the door for Freya and the others. Her father nodded, and Freya was off with them to the festival.

***

It was slightly past dusk, but the entire town was lit up with lanterns of every colour hanging on every door and numerous paper ones flying in the sky. White, green, and purple ribbons were strewn across buildings like rope bridges. The green -and-purple Bastiel flags flapped in the chilly wind, showing the famous armoured horse head with a sword and woodcutter's axe crossed together behind it. Music played in every corner. The smell of various delicious foods floated in the air like the sweet cakes and hot cinnamon rolls from the bakery, the savoury scents of juicy, sizzling bacon and spiced beef, or the rich, roasted smell of hot chocolate from the brewery.

This was perhaps the most packed Souls of Saints Day Freya had ever seen. Performances were going on in any place that had room. A play was performed about Saint Joan holding off a major siege during the civil war against the foul Queen. The actress playing the Queen wore a grey wig and painted her lips crimson red. She also wore comically large fake fangs, almost like bucked teeth, and nails so long as to touch her feet without bending over.

Freya first watched this one in the front row when she was six. The actress playing her before stuck her face near Freya, hissing and cackling. Freya had nightmares for a week after the play and Brigid teased her for years after. It was why she is still afraid of monsters like her.

They walked through the stores and stands, seeing all sorts of toys, tomes, and treats. Townsfolk and visitors all wore masks and handed out small gifts. One lady in particular gave Freya a small wooden puzzle toy with sliding pieces. Freya would have betted silver it was Missus Aibrean.

"Before we buy anything, why don't we see how much money we all got?" Brigid suggested.

"I got three silvers."

"Umm, I was given two silvers and a copper," Freya said, making absolutely sure not to drop any of them.

"One shilver and two copper coinsh," Jacinta said, hesitant to even look in her pocket.

“All right, then we should plan how we should spend or if we should pool

102

“All right, then we should plan how we should spend or if we should pool our money together to get something big that we can share. And I hope you don't spend all your money on peach items like last year, Freya. You should get something that will last you longer than two seconds."

"Fine," Freya agreed though she was slightly disappointed.

"We should just use our own money," Jacinta said slowly, trying extra hard to be clear.

"Got something in mind?" Brigid asked.

"No, I just think you should keep your money." Freya and Brigid didn't object.

After another lap around the stores, Freya bought herself the second volume of the stories about Knights so she could finally have new stories to read with her father. Brigid had purchased a necklace and a treatise on smithing techniques. Freya and Brigid didn't know what Jacinta got, and she told them it would be a surprise. Freya was excited to find out what it was. She was even more excited when the faint familiar fiddle of the Gancanagh Mister Cadhla played in the wind. Wearing his white puffy shirt and his long black hair dancing after him and the eyes of older girls were entranced by him. Then there was the fleeting flute of the Leprechaun Mister Brian and the surprisingly sweet and soft singing of Saint Orlaith as the three delivered the tale of Saint Patrick.

"Oh, our Saint of saviours."

"You jumping in, Freya?" Brigid suggested with a sly smile.

"No, no, no! I can't! There are so many people here."

"No one will know it's you if you're wearing your mask." Mister Conall added.

"I mean that's a good idea, but I don't—I mean there's—uhh …" "Dance with me," Jacinta slowly said. "W-what?"

"A slave nevermore,"

"Sho-so you won't be with only strangers."

"Oh, okay," Freya said. She tried to think of a way out of this, but Jacinta had put Freya's mask on her, grabbed her hand and took her to the crowd. Freya's legs shook nervously with each step. She was close to collapsing, but Brigid gave her a helpful push. Jacinta was in the thick of it. She kept her arms rigid by her sides and kicked her feet in the air, and when they came back down, it made a rhythmic click-clack following the beat of the music.

Freya was amazed at the artistry of it. Her heels and toes moved with such precision in tight movements all timed perfectly to the music. It was similar in style to how the townsfolk danced but was most likely adapted to the tightly cramped mounds.

"He will tell you the good words, all day 'n' night along."

Freya decided to tap her feet. Then without warning, her legs started following suit and soon there was no one around to watch Freya. They were

merely part of the scenery at this moment. Her arms swayed on their own, no longer following any rhythm but her own. Until a boy, slightly taller than her in a mask with the young face, strong jaw, and curly hair of Saint George approached her.

"Drowner of Caoránach, may her name be long gone."

He didn't say anything and extended his hand to Freya. Freya's chest tightened, her heart pounded, and her face reddened behind the mask. Everyone else stopped their dance and watched the two of them as they clapped along. They were no longer scenery, they were an audience and Freya was centre stage. Freya looked around for Jacinta or Brigid, but the crowd had overtaken them. Freya tried guessing who this boy was, but for the first time without Magic, her mind was like mush. She could only see he had bright blue eyes. Freya had to remember how to breathe. She had never been excited like this before.

"He had carved the rivers through, with Oilliphéist's bones."

"Come on! Don't leave the poor lad hanging!" Someone from the crowd shouted.

Freya was still stuck, but the boy's legs were trembling. He was just as nervous as she was and for some reason this made Freya feel safer. She slowly gave him her hand, he grabbed the other, and they spun and swayed to the music.

***

When the outro faded, the trio band left to party. The boy reached into his pocket and presented her with a beautiful, drooping, pale blue Harebell flower with a tiny white clapper. He held it out for Freya, and she just stood dumbfounded. What was she supposed to do? She had just found out that she liked boys, and it's not like she was taught how to act around them. The boy was no doubt just as awkward as her, as he delicately placed the flower in her hand and ran off. The crowd's cheering followed him for a bit before going back to the rest of the festival.

Freya, light-headed and trying her hardest not to sway, headed back to Jacinta and the others, who were all looking at Freya with concern.

"We couldn't find you, what happened?" Brigid asked, slightly annoyed. Freya tried to answer, but found herself too giddy and could only giggle at the memory.

"If you can't use that mouth for talking, you might as well use it for eating."

To get to the food stalls and stores, they had to walk across the road near the centre of town. It was where they held the plays on stage. Brigid had them stop to watch since this one was her favourite.

The actors dressed as three Draoi. A short and stout Demi-Human with pitch-black skin, a human with maniacal features like wild eyes and an evil

grin, and a human-shaped talking cat. Freya was unfamiliar with those
Demi-

grin, and a human-shaped talking cat. Freya was unfamiliar with those
Demi-

Humans, and she wasn't sure how accurate the costumes were.

"With thine Magic, thou shalt turn the meek, weak, simpering humans into thy playthings for merry amusement. Thou shalt bend their bones and chew on their marrow as poultry!" the cat said before someone behind the curtain cracked something like walnuts to sound like bones.

"With thine Magic, thou shalt mould steel and metal to lock all hereafter in cages like birds!" the short Demi-Human said before she bent a silver-painted rubber stick.

"With thine Magic, thou shalt boil their blood from thine innards! HAHAHA!" the crazy human said as red- dyed water splashed around and the crowd booed and hissed at them. Freya couldn't help but imagine herself and her father being on stage being jeered just like them.

"I think I see food this way," Freya whispered to Brigid trying to walk away.

"Hold on! This is my favourite part," Brigid said and quickly found a seat second from the back.

A man in brown armoured robes entered the stage and proclaimed, "Anon! Anon! I, Saint George, Praetorian and vanquisher of the scaly dragons, shall slayeth thee for thy malice and Magic! Thine transgression shall only be forgiven once thine blood is spilled and your corpses bringeth about new life!"

"Gods almighty! Did they let a two-year-old write this?" Someone whispered from behind Freya. Freya looked over to Brigid and Jacinta and their faces confirmed her suspicions. Mister Conall, never having met him before, was none the wiser.

"Didn't know you were into plays, Captain."

"I'm not. I just needed space away from Jean. I would have gone to a tavern, but then he would know where to find me."

The two couldn't have been more than a metre from them. The three kept silent and still, hoping somehow Silas wouldn't recognize any of them.

"A little lovers' quarrel?"

"Nah. We're not actually lovers. I prefer women."

"Well, you ought to tell Jean. Poor boy seems to have that impression."

"Yeah, well. He's more willing to work for cheap this way." "That's rough, Captain. Even for you."

"Better than where he was! I'm doing him a favour! Once we're done with it all, he'll learn to be smarter next time without learning the hard way. Someone else would have taken worse advantage of him."

"You're a real Saint, Captain."

"Very funny. Heard that from a jester, did you?" Silas said before he and his crewmate walked away.

Freya let out a sigh and Brigid groaned, "Gods dammit! They made

me miss the fight scene!"

***

Brigid's frustration was soon quelled after they got toasted soda bread with smoked salmon to eat, but Jacinta wasn't eating. She stared at her shoes until she noticed Freya looking at her.

"What's wrong, Jacinta?" Freya asked.

"Itsh, uh … I want… I can't—"

"What are you acting all nervous for? You spot Ronan or his gang or something?"

"No! I …" Jacinta looked to Mister Conall, "Is there a privy nearby?" "Uh, sure just across the road."

Jacinta smoothly made her way across the large crowd, more than used to navigating tight spaces. But instead of going into the outhouse, Jacinta veered toward the alleys.

"Gods dammit! You two stay there!" Mister Conall shouted, dropping his food and getting stuck trying to push his way through all the people.

Freya wanted to go after her. But Mister Conall had told her to stay put. But her father told her to stay with Mister Conall. But he also told her to stay within sight of the house.

But Jacinta was her friend. But if she was truly her friend, why was she trying to leave her? Freya didn't know what to do.

"Come on, Freya!" Brigid said.

"But your Da told us to stay put."

"He did. And we said we were going to be her best friends and best friends don't let each other do stupid shite."

"She is trying to leave us."

"She is not an adult and she will get hurt or worse if she leaves Valour," Brigid said calmly.

All of Freya's muscles were rigid. She was sweating, yet freezing. She didn't know what to do.

Brigid did, though, and ran after their friend.

***

Freya's legs quivered and gave way, collapsing her to her knees. Her chest was tight, and she was sick to her stomach. She was alone in the crowded streets. Her mind could think faster than everyone in this town, save her father, and she didn't know what to do. Why was she such a terrible friend? Why was it so hard for her to know the right thing to do? Why can't everything be simple, just a little problem she could easily solve.

Jacinta came running back from the neighbouring alley with her mask on. Freya figured she gave Brigid and her father the slip by going backward. She must have expected Freya to be with them as she didn't seem to notice Freya sitting and staring right at her as she crossed the road again and took the alley, right of Freya.

106

There was no choice now. Mister Conall would not be able to stop Jacinta from running away. Freya was the only one who could. And so she went after her, going through the alleyway to the left of her.

It was a straight path through the section. Freya remembered it from all the times her father made her study their map. If Freya's estimations were accurate, Jacinta would be heading deeper down the Stern District. All the other Districts would be full of people, and the Bow District was too far away from the great bridge over the First Third River. Freya was correct, and Jacinta ran right across from her, giving her the chance to leap at her, and knocked her to the cold dirt ground. Freya ripped off her mask and climbed on top of her, pinning her arms so she couldn't escape.

"Why are you leaving? Why didn't you at least say goodbye? Are we no longer friends!" Freya nearly screamed at Jacinta as her eyes began to burn and the tears chilled on her cheeks.

"Don't shay-sh -say that, Freya. Please, I'm begging you, Freya, don't say that," Jacinta said, sniffling and tremoring.

"You and Brigid saved me. I felt so lonely and scared and angry before. And you made everything better. I just couldn't … I need to go back to my family."

"You have no family! Mister Conall said your parents were killed!" Freya shouted more angrily than she had ever before.

"Mister Conall lied! Or maybe he was confused, I don't know anymore. They keep forcing me to be a human like all of you. Hitting me for talking or acting different from you, cutting my claws, forcing me to live above ground! I'm not a human! And if your people force me to be like all of you, then my people might not recognize me anymore. I need to leave! Please, Freya."

Freya's hands trembled with how tightly she was gripping Jacinta, and she was finally seeing it was hurting her. Freya quickly got off before she did worse. Jacinta picked herself up and pulled out a wooden brooch with an arm holding a shiny green rock from her bag.

"Please give this to Brigid and I want you ..." And Jacinta put her hand in Freya's palm.

"To have this ..." And revealed a copper ring.

"B-but these are yours," Freya said.

"I bought these as a goodbye gift for you two, but it was too hard to say. I promise to write letters to you every day! And perhaps we can visit each other often!"

Freya was silent.

"I'll miss you ..." Jacinta tried to say, but Freya grabbed her again. "Y-you can't leave! I don't want you t-to get hurt out there!"

"I can hide underground if there is any danger. Please, Freya! Wouldn't you do the same if you were taken from your Da?"

Freya released her, knowing she would. Her hand ached as though she

pried open a bear trap. Jacinta hugged her tightly and Freya had to fight every urge in her body not to grab her again. Jacinta gave Freya a kiss on the cheek and told her, "Thank you," before running deeper into the alleys, disappearing from Freya's sight.

***

Freya tried to head back to the Stern District, but her eyes were so raw it was hard to see. She focused on retracing her steps, but a couple of voices came from one of the corners. She didn't recognize any of them except one. They had the same accent as Silas. She peeked out a nearby corner and a group of adults pushed Ronan to the ground.

"Back off! One of my friends is around here and I need to find her," Ronan shouted.

Freya thought it would have been just desserts seeing Ronan on the other side bullying, but not with Silas and his crew. This was scary.

When they wouldn't move out of his way, Ronan pulled out his knife and said, "I'm not going to let you thugs terrorise this town anymore!"

"Well, Captain, does this count as self-defence?" one of his crew asked before kicking Ronan in the stomach. Ronan was gasping for breath, and Freya could see he had the wind knocked out of him. But they didn't seem to care as they stepped on him. Freya tried to think of something she could do. There was no way she could stand up to them in a fight, and there were no adults she could get to help in time.

Freya looked around and noticed a loose brick on the wall behind them. Freya quickly devised a plan, but she was in the middle of town. She could easily be spotted using Magic if someone came around the corner as she did. And if she got caught, the Sanctus Venatores would be after her. She needed to think of a different plan, but Silas's men kept hitting Ronan.

Freya couldn't let this go on. She tried her best to look around and make sure no one could see her. When it seemed safe, she got herself to a corner where she could see the brick and no one could see her. Freya memorised the positions of the stranger and used Magic. The ring surrounded her again as she altered the Rules of Reality, changing the gravitational pull on the brick to be twice as strong. Using her hands as a focus, Freya mimicked the action of ripping it from the wall at a sixty -degree angle. There was a sharp clink, followed by a loud moan and thud from one of the crewmen, then quick footsteps, followed by a shout to chase after Ronan.

Freya tried to break her thought process as fast as possible to get the ring to disappear. It was a jarring feeling to forcefully distract herself. She took another look around. The alley was empty aside from the few tall crates and barrels. She walked halfway toward the exit and back to the main road when she noticed Ronan had dropped something. A mask of Saint George.

Freya's cold face began to blaze. Her breath became harsh as she was seething at the thought of, "Why? Why did he have to spoil this? Why does

he have to spoil everything with his stupid pranks? Was he laughing the whole time? Were his Godsdamn friends laughing somewhere as they watched him make a fool out of me? It was such a special moment and it was a lie. I can't believe I felt… I should have left him to Silas and his crew!" Her eyes burned as she tried so hard not to let any more tears fall. That would be just what Ronan wanted; she was sure of it.

She wanted to cave Ronan's face in, but instead, she settled for his mask. The blue ring around her flared once more. His mask began to collapse in on itself, groaning and creaking until it crushed. Freya's ears were pounding, but she wasn't sure if it was from anger or strain, nor did she care.

"Niccee trick, missss." A voice came from behind one of the crates.

***

Kal had to look away from the window again. Something about the masks deeply unnerved him and he couldn't watch too long without feeling ill. Being stuck in Mister Conall's house wasn't helping. Not that there was anything wrong with his house. It just wasn't Kal's. He didn't know it very well.

Kal adjusted himself on the wooden chair hoping in vain he could get himself comfortable. He had to look back out the window because every moment he wasn't keeping a watchful eye on Freya made him anxious. Kal needed her to be safe. The whole Known World could burn to cinders if that was what it took. If Freya were ever taken from him … Well, Kal doubted he could live without her. Ever since her mother had left them, Freya had been the only thing he lived for.

"If only she were here now," Kal often wondered to himself. "No doubt we would go to Church every Second Sàbaid. Poor Freya would have had to somehow m emorise the hymns with her spell work." Kal smiled, remembering how she sang to herself when she rode her horse or sharpened her blade.

"She would have had fun at the festival, I think. I could see her dancing with the crowd, or competing with Freya in the games."

Kal could see Freya, her friends, and Mister Conall eating until the Elf girl ran into the alleyways. Mister Conall followed after her, leaving Freya alone with his daughter. Kal immediately sprang up from the chair, went downstairs, and out the door. He understood why Mister Conall had to go after the Elf girl. He promised Saint Orlaith to watch over her as he did for Freya. But Kal didn't care. The only thing that mattered to him was Freya, and while Silas and his crew were in town, Kal wasn't going to leave Freya alone. He needed to take her back to their home, where he could keep her safe.

When Kal reached the section of the road where Freya was before, he looked around frantically and shoved his way through crowds. Kal couldn't find her and he was terrified.

"Did she get lost? Where's Brigid? Were they kidnapped?" Kal thought

as his heart raced. He tried to find someone familiar to ask for help, but everyone was wearing those damn masks.

"Please let her be safe," Kal begged whoever was out there to listen. "I don't know what to do. How do I protect her? How do I do what's best for her? I can't do this on my own!"

***

"No use hiding it. I saw you use Magic, Freya," Silas said, making his speech clear and making sure to let her know he knew her name.

Freya quickly glanced out of the alley, hoping her father would show up out of nowhere.

"Dad not around?" Silas asked slowly, getting closer and guessing what she was about to do.

Freya did not realise he was within arm's reach. She tried to run, but Silas had her by her long hair. She tried to use Magic any way she could think of, but she was too terrified to keep her head straight.

"L-let m-me go! Or I'll-I'll scream!" Freya said, failing to stop herself from shaking.

"You do that and I tell them all what you are. Mage

…" "A w-what?"

"Mage, Sorcerer, Onmyo, Draoi, whatever you dumb yokels call it here. You scream, I talk, and the Venatores will be after you."

"Th-they w-won't believe you. Y-you're just a crook!" Freya stuttered. "Doesn't matter. According to the Doctrine they wrote after the

Crusades, they have to check out any Magic accusations. They won't care from who. Think you'll be able to outrun them?"

"Wh-why can't you l-leave us alone." Freya whimpered.

"Hey kid, it's not our fault. We aren't the bad guys. As soon as the Crusades were over, everyone just tossed us aside. We're trying to survive like everyone else using the only skills they taught us."

"What d-do you w-want with me?"

"Well, we've been quietly 'commandeering' some valuable cargo from the ports, but it's high time we move on. Before we do that though, we could certainly use those weapons and armour your dock guards leave rusting around. Of course, we don't want to be chased after, so you and our personal Mage will set fire to their sails using your Magic. Then we will never have to see each other again. How does it sound?"

"I-I don't want t-to steal from my t-town."

"Why do you give a crap? They'll sick the Venatores on you in a heartbeat if they find out what you are."

"Get your hands off her before I kick your arse!" Brigid shouted, standing tall, but Freya could see she was shaking.

"She doesn't even know, does she?" Silas asked Freya, not even looking at Brigid. "Think she'll still be your friend if she found out?"

110

"I don't give a crap what a creep like you has to say, let her go now!"

"Or what? You'll oof—!" Silas said as Brigid tackled him from behind, knocking over Freya as well. She tried to brace herself, but as her hands touched the ground, Silas tripped and all of his heavy weight crashed right on top of h er. Freya's wrists made a loud pop and she screamed as the pain shot through her arms.

Silas scrambled to his feet and yanked Freya up by her hair. Freya could see a crowd forming around them and was trying to close in.

"Let her go, you craven!" one of the crowd shouted.

"Lazy hole parasite! Get out of our town!"

"Too minus craic to have anything better to do than hurt little girls?" More kept shouting and were getting hawkish.

Luckily for Silas, Jean and some of the crew showed up with their cutlasses out and their Saints masks still on. The crowd was swiftly silent and Brigid stopped before she tried another tackle.

"Please pardon the Capitaine. I should have kept his coin purse after the first few drinks. How about you leave us be and we'll leave you be. Does that sound bien?" Jean announced to the crowd as he made his way toward Silas. More people were gathering, but the swords were keeping them at bay.

"Give me a break," Silas snarled.

"Mon chéri, please! You are drunk. Let the girl go and let's get back to ze ship," Jean tried to whisper to him.

"You all can rot!" Silas shouted, his voice dripping with venom as he dragged Freya in front of the crowd while she sobbed in pain. "All of you with your vile crap! How dare you call me—any of us—cowards!" His voice started cracking, "How many of you fought in the Crusade, huh? How many of you had to wash off your friend's blood after an arrow or cannonball hit them? Or had to burn their bodies after smallpox started to spread? I still can't get their Godsdamn smell off of me!"

"I-I'm s-sorry," Freya wept.

"No, you're not! None of you are ever sorry or thankful beyond lip service. You people only cared about me when I was killing for you. Slapped a fancy- ass uniform on me so you could forget I was another poor peasant boy on the streets you ignored, ripped it right off my back, and stopped feeding me the second you no longer needed me to be your on-call murderer. What did you expect I would do? 'You should just be proud to have served.' Screw you! I'm just trying to survive using the very skills you all gave me."

He took another step toward the crowd.

"But knowing folks like you need something to hate. Can't go a minute without something to violently fear. Need it like air in your lungs. Well, look no further than your own!" He tried to take another step and present Freya, but once his foot touched the ground, Silas had a sudden intense pressure on his neck, and everything went black and he fell.

***

Jean blinked, a little surprised, then announced, "See what I mean? Our Capitaine just needs to sober up a little. Go enjoy the festival. There's no need to escalate things. Come on, Capitaine. I'll help you up."

Some of the crowd chuckled, some whispered amongst themselves, and others started to walk away, disregarding Silas for a clumsy drunk.

Someone had lifted Freya up. Her tears made it hard to see who it was in the dim light. Instinctively she wanted to push them away, but her wrists were in too much pain. Freya began to panic when she noticed she couldn't move her fingers and her wrist bones were in the wrong spot.

"Shh, vennen min. It will be all right. I have some Phigs to give you when it's safe," her father said as he cradled her.

He carried her through the crowd. They started quieting down again as they began to notice Silas wasn't moving. Jean shook Silas. His head dangled like a broken doll.

"Capitaine, come on, get up. We need to leave, Capitaine ... Silas? Please? Oh, Gods! Oh Gods, please wake up! Don't you dare leave me!"

Jean pointed at her father and yelled, "What have you done to him?"

Both crew and crowd stared at them. Her father stopped. He turned his

head slightly, not looking at Jean, but making himself heard, "Your friend made a wrong step and it cost him. Be sure not to make the same mistake." Her father tried to take Freya back home, but Jean pulled something out

of his coat pocket.

"Pappa!" Freya shouted as the yellowish powder was thrown into the air and reeked of rotten eggs. Her father used his body to shield her as a blue feathery fire carpeted his back and made him drop to his knees.

"Draoi!" The crowd screamed as they scrambled around for their life. Freya quickly peered over to see a blazing red ring surround Jean as he cried out in agony, "Meurtier! You didn't have to kill him!"

"Jean, stop! What if the Sanctus Venatores show up?" one of his crewmates said, grabbing onto him.

"Get out of my way!" Jean shouted as the ring turned into a pulse of green and a gust of wind blasted everyone around him away.

Freya's father tried to get back to his feet, but they were both coughing violently. Freya noticed a little bit of blood coming out of her father's mouth.

The green ring under Jean's feet was burned by the red as he took out another handful of powder. He was about to throw it at her father again, but was tackled by Mister Conall and crashed through a food stand.

***

Brigid hurriedly helped Freya's father to stand asking, "What is going on?" "... Khoff ...! Do not let him reach into his ... khoff ...!" her father tried to say through his coughing. Mister Conall held Jean down, but a bright, wispy green light appeared under him and Mister Conall was sent

flying

halfway across the road by a powerful gust of wind.

"Da!" Brigid shouted as she tried to rush over to Mister Conall but was stopped by Freya's father.

"Take Freya …khoff …somewhere safe!" he instructed before taking a drink out of a pale orange-coloured vial. When she hesitated, he shouted, "Leave now!"

Brigid lifted Freya over her broad shoulders and tried to run. Jean picked himself up and pointed an outstretched hand toward a couple of open drinking water barrels on the side of the road. A deep, wavy blue ring surrounded him, then the water from the barrels rushed out, forming a small tidal wave about to crash into Freya and Brigid.

Her father grabbed the nearest piece of splintered wood and threw it at Jean. Once it left his hand, it flew faster than any arrow Freya had ever seen. Jean jumped out of the way, just narrowly avoiding the lethal projectile, but it broke his concentration. Freya didn't see where the piece of wood landed, but it made a crack louder than fireworks. The wave, which would have crashed into them, dissipated though still strong enough to sweep Brigid off her feet.

Dock guards arrived from the Port District with their spears. Some townsfolk from the rest of the Districts came from every other direction. The richer ones used small swords, and the rest used tools as makeshift weapons. Jean and the rest of his crew were surrounded. Left with no other option, they had to fight their way out.

Brigid picked Freya back up, both drenched from the water.

"We n-needd t-to g-go to the ch-church! No o-one in their r-right mind would d-do anything to a holy place." Brigid shivered, but then someone screamed as a firestorm surrounded Jean, igniting the nearby buildings. The fighting townsfolk fled for their lives. Freya couldn't help but stare at the awe-inspiring and terrifying display of Magic.

"I-I d-don't think he is in his right mind-d at-t the m-moment," Freya said, shivering from pain and the skin-biting cold.

Despite all the chaos, one of Silas's crew headed toward Mister Conall. Brigid dropped Freya and made a mad dash to save him, and Freya could only watch. Mister Conall slammed his blade down at his attacker with all of his strength, batting his opponent's blade in every direction with blunt force. It was clear Mister Conall only knew how to forge swords, not fight with them, as his opponent twisted Mister Conall's sword out of his hand with a simple flick of his wrist.

Before the attacker could kill Mister Conall, Brigid charged at him, screaming with the ferocity of a battle cry. As Brigid tackled the attacker's leg, Freya's father flicked his wrist. Brigid looked surprised and horrified as instantly the attacker's leg snapped painfully backward at the knee with an audible pop. He let out a blood-curdling scream as he fell to the ground with tears welling in his eyes.

"Holy shite!" Brigid could only say. Mister Conall grabbed her under his arm and ran toward Freya, scooping her up in his other arm. He charged like a bull toward the church and kicked a pattern of knocks on the door. Saint Orlaith unlocked and opened the door, allowing Freya to see other people sheltered and cared for by the priestesses.

"Why is there no one defending the church?" Mister Conall asked, panicking, as he looked at all the entrances.

"Misssess Aibrean will be back ssoon. She ssaid she needed to grab Ferguss," Saint Orlaith answered as she grabbed blankets for Freya and Brigid.

"Her husband or her crossbow?" "Yes."

One of the priestesses answered.

"Where iss Jacinta?" Saint Orlaith asked, looking around.

"I don't know. I lost her right before all this chaos happened, but I'll look for her while I get weapons for the people fighting," Mister Conall answered.

"Let me help, Da! We promised!" Brigid offered.

Mister Conall put both her and Freya down as he told them, "I need you two to help keep everyone inside the church and keep them calm."

"But Da—"

"No buts. Stay here. I'll be back with Jacinta soon," Mister Conall said before he ran back out.

***

The only light in the church was a few candles. The aisles echoed with the muffled sounds of battle from outside and the reciting of the Libri ex Dii.

"But one day, an ancient being came to us and said Fraxineus's star would fly through the cosmos. That Fraxineus's prison is not eternal. The Star of Ash will collide with the Known World, bringing chaos and war beyond any measure. Fraxineus shall return. And when he does, we must be ready, for only we can save ourselves this time." - Partus Vitae 1:42-46

Freya sat in one of the pews, wrapped tightly in blankets to dry off and get warm. Brigid had found a pillow for Freya to lay her wrists on. It had helped a little bit, but Freya felt tear -jerking pain anytime she moved them or was bumped into. Brigid was busy helping the priestesses pass out water to people who needed it. Freya would have liked to help, but she couldn't lift anything with her injuries. Instead, all she could do was sit idly with little to preoccupy her thoughts as they darkened.

"That Draoi looked so powerful and dangerous. Pappa can't use too much Magic to fight or else the town will notice. What if he gets hurt and I'm stuck here? What if he's kil—" Freya had to stop herself as she noticed her heart was pounding.

"Are you all right, Freya?" a familiar irritatingly cocky voice said. Freya was sure it was in fake concern only meant to grind salt in the wound.

114

Freya looked up and it was Ronan, his face bruised up from whatever Silas's men had done to him. Freya had bit back her tongue before she called him something that should never be uttered in a church.

"Brigid told me about your wrists. How can I help?"

"You don't want to help. You want to gloat," Freya thought.

"Leave me alone," she said through gritted teeth.

"Not until I can do something to help. I have to hold down the fort while my Da slays all those evil Draoi out there."

Freya leaped with as much force as she could at Ronan. If she could, Freya would have punched his mouth over and over. Until he choked on all of his teeth. The pain in her wrist forced her to roll off him as soon as they made contact. Ronan crawled back from her in shock.

"IT's ALL YOUR FAULT! YOU SPOILED EVERYTHING! I WISHED THEY KEPT HITTING YOU!"

Ronan opened his mouth to say something, and Brigid rushed over to Freya. Before anyone could do anything, skittering and scratching came from under the floorboard beneath her. Freya scooted out of the way, and a pair of clawed hands tore through the wood. Soon after, Jacinta's dirt-covered head popped out.

"You again?"

"Not now, Ronan!" Brigid snapped.

All the anger Freya had faded away as Jacinta climbed out of the hole, but it appeared to transfer over to Brigid as she said, "You better have a good Godsdamn reason why you ran from us, Jacinta! Da and I went searching all over for you!"

Jacinta quickly wrapped her arms around her in a tight hug.

"I'm sorry. Once I saw the fires … I got so scared; I needed to know you two were all right," Jacinta said, choking up a bit as she tried to cover her accent.

"Well … give me a bloody heart attack, why don'tcha?" Brigid sighed, as she returned the hug, not caring about the dirt ruining her dress.

"I'm sho shorry if I shomehow caushed all this."

"No, it's not you, it's all Ronan's fault!" Freya said, trying to point at him, but her fingers couldn't move, and she regretted even trying as the pain flared up.

"I didn't do anything!"

"Liar!" Freya shouted.

"Jacinta apparently ran off and then broke the church floor. How can someone like this not be the cause of all this?"

"It's no one's fault! It's just a series of crappy circumstances mushing together," Brigid said.

Freya didn't feel that was the case, but she didn't want to argue with Brigid, not after how emotionally drained she was feeling.

115

"Are your wrishtsh all right?"

"I don't know. It hurts so much."

"I offered to help," Ronan reminded her.

"I don't want your help!"

"Fine! Just don't go crying to me if you get more hurt while the Elf messes more things up," Ronan said, marching off.

"Brigid, I need you to help the priestesses barricade the back doors while I keep a watch out front," Missus Aibrean commanded as she was being let inside the church. Missus Aibrean was wearing a chainmail shirt and her large crossbow slung on her back as she helped her husband, Fergus, who was missing his cane, to the nearest pew.

"Yes, ma'am!" Brigid said, snapping to attention, and followed her orders. Missus Aibrean looked up and down at Jacinta and asked, "Why are you covered in dirt?"

Jacinta looked back to her hole and said, "The door was locked."

"And you didn't walk in with your friends? Or are you telling me all three of you went through the hole?"

Jacinta couldn't think of a reasonable explanation.

"You are in for quite the lashing when I see you back in school, young lady. Do you understand?"

"Yesh—I mean yes, ma'am," Jacinta said.

"Good. I'm glad you are safe," Missus Aibrean said before leaving Jacinta and Freya alone.

***

Jean threw a bag that smelled smoky and peppery as a wispy green ring stacked on top of a blazing red ring underneath him. Kal had to focus on altering the Rules of Reality so that the bag would land short, but the explosion was powerful enough to knock him off his feet, light some nearby buildings on fire, and severely injure townsfolk and pirates caught closer to it. Black smoke plumed everywhere and Kal's ears rang. He could tell most of his potion vials had shattered, but he kept his focus on Jean. It was clear Jean knew multiple schools of Magic and even more frightening, he knew how to use them to complement each other.

"Even if I was able to use my full power without fear of discovery, this would be a dangerous fight," Kal thought.

Jean configured the Rules of Reality of the local wind so the smoke was pushed away from his line of sight of Kal. Jean grabbed another bag from his belt, but Mister Conall started swinging his sword at him. Jean danced and dodged around his attacks gracefully like a dancer.

"And some sword training as well. I certainly have stood with my beard in the post box." At least Mister Conall's attacks kept Jean too distracted to cast a spell. Kal kept his distance. Looking for something he could use as a weapon while subtly increasing the pull of gravity on Jean, Kal hoped that

the increased feeling of weight would tire him out from moving or have him make a mistake. Despite being slowed down, Jean was still able to outpace Mister Conall. He made a quick back step to grab another pouch, but Kal rapidly altered the pull of gravity on the pouch, forcing Jean to drop it. Kal found a broken plank of wood and charged after Jean. While swinging the plank, he increased the pull of gravity at the end to make it crash down on Jean like a sledgehammer. Jean managed to pull out his sword and deftly parried the plank away.

Jean tried to counter and Kal made gravity pull back the plank in his hand to intercept the chop. The sword got stuck in the wood and Kal hoped he could take control now, but a red ring surrounded Jean and he placed his hand on the flat of his blade. Smoke sizzled from the wood plank and it quickly caught fire. Before Kal could drop it, a green ring surrounded Jean and the fire was blown in Kal's face. Mister Conall came in with another swing before the burns could do permanent damage.

Kal backed away, trying to recompose himself and focus. "I-I need time to think, but he's relentless."

"Are you all right?" Mister Conall asked.

"I will be," Kal answered, ignoring the pain and headache his Magic was causing.

"I'll make sure you won't!" Jean roared as he hurled another bag between them. Kal altered the Rules of Reality on Mister Conall in a split second to make him fall away from the bag before it exploded.

***

The fighting and explosions outside grew louder and sounded closer to the church. The people inside became silent. They drew as far from the doors and windows as they could, making an already-cramped situation unbearable. Missus Aibrean had set herself up on the pew by the door. She rested her crossbow on the rail already cranked with a bolt notched in and trained at the door. A red light shone through the window, and in a flash, the glass shattered, and the door swung open. The barricade they set up fell apart as Freya's father crashed inside.

Missus Aibrean tried to get an aim at Jean, but a red ring under his feet formed, and smoke rose from Aibrean's crossbow and she was forced to drop it on the carpet as her hands started to burn. The carpet soon followed. When the carpet caught fire, it began to spread to the tapestries. The people inside scrambled in a blind panic to the other exits, trying to pull down the exact barricades meant to protect them. The crowd trapped Brigid, and Jacinta went over to try and save her.

Jean simply walked over to Freya's f ather while he was on the ground and slammed his fists into her father's face over and over. Freya realised no one was willing to save her father as his blood started to cover Jean's knuckles. She prayed to the Gods hoping no one would see her as she altered the Rules

of Reality on Jean to fall into the church ceiling. Her father raised his hand, and Freya could see a bright blue light flicker for just a second as a portion of the ceiling could no longer hold the sudden pull on it. Both it and Jean crashed back down to the ground.

Freya sat silently on the church floor as the dust and debris settled. Her whole body ached, and her spine chilled as the realisation dawned on her. They both used Magic in the middle of town.

CHAPTER 9
DAY OF REGRETS

THEN

Kalby did what he was told from then on and more. When they ordered him to learn new formulas, he memorised and perfected them. When they demanded Kalby kill one of their subjects for tests, he did so without hesitation. He made their deaths slow so the masked ones could better examine the victims. When they wanted to cut him open again for more study, he laid down on the operating table before they even asked. When they gave him a potion, he chugged it down and resisted all urges to vomit. He did not know how long it had been since he had last seen his sister. He had no concept of what a year was, but he was becoming taller than the masked ones.

They seemed to trust him more, but not enough to give him their names nor show their faces. Though it seemed they kept this from each other as well. They would often let him explore the testing facilities and the library. They once brought him to the big room and showed him how they observed all the subjects with what looked like transparent walls and light tricks that allowed them to see the subjects but didn't let the subjects see them.

Kalby seemed to have piqued the most interest of the young man in the flat brown mask. He would show Kalby how to read beyond just numbers so Kalby could learn Magic from carefully chosen books. Flat mask showed him how wands and crystal focuses worked and how they could correct errors made in altering the Rules of Reality, increasing the potency and reliability of spells beyond anything Kalby could do before. Flat mask even called Kalby by his name on occasion. Mostly when he was tired of calling him by his long numbers.

***

They seemed pleased with the results of their experiments and even more so with Kalby's cooperation. One day, before sending Kalby back to his cell, the man in the half-skull mask and the young man in the flat brown mask presented Kalby with a mask of his own. It was as black as the fluid they pumped into him with the bright blue ring of equations and chains on the forehead.

"Your miraculous success as a subject cannot be left unrewarded. This privilege is exceptionally rare for non -subjects. To have even been considered despite being a subject … It may never happen again," Flat mask said enthusiastically.

Kalby rubbed his fingers around the smooth surface of the mask. He didn't know what to say.

"It should never have happened at all," said the man in the half-skull mask.

"How can you say that? He has Magic! This is a brea—"

"It is not one of us. It has little education, sub- par aptitude for Magic, and will have no anonymity in our order. At best, this pet project will be a liability."

"Well, it's not your call. Please think about it Kal—subject J16-30," the man in the flat mask said before closing the cell door.

They believed they had made Kalby docile and obedient. They thought they knew everything about him and would let him join them. They were wrong.

When Kalby woke up, another man in a mask he didn't recognize opened his cell to bring him his food and water. Then instantly, the masked man's neck could no longer support the rapidly increasing pull from the side and snapped. There was no light, no colour, and no ring. If he had seen it, he might have been able to stop it. Kalby altered the pull of gravity on the masked man's body before it fell so it wouldn't make any noise. Kalby quietly closed the cell door, swapping his old burlap jumpsuit for the masked man's white robes. Kalby couldn't help but notice it brushing against his skin. It was so soft and smooth, especially on his gnarled wrists. It was both comforting and unnatural to him.

The next thing he needed was the mask. Kalby had finally killed one of them. Killed one of the people who experimented, tormented, crippled, and tortured himself, his big sister Freja, and every other subject here. He felt nothing for killing him. He would never feel anything for the killing because of them. The only emotion he had was the gnawing need to see what they were under the mask.

There was also a building terror the masked one could somehow still be alive, and this was simply another one of their cruel tests. Kalby's shaking hand reached out. He placed his fingers underneath the mask and ever so slowly pulled it off. Kalby froze. He had no idea what he was expecting. The face of one of these monsters was unremarkable. It was the face of a man just like Kalby. He was older, had more hair, and was cleaner, but he was no more a monster than Kalby.

Kalby had no more time to waste. He tried to ignore whatever he was feeling and placed the mask he was given on the dead man. Kalby used the dead man's mask to disguise himself. His vision was limited to the tiny slits of the mask. He could hear his heavy breathing as the mask echoed it back. Kalby laid the dead man as Kalby would appear if he was sleeping. He wasn't sure how long this trick would last, so he needed to hurry.

He walked down the stone halls he had memorised. When other masked ones were nearby, he walked amongst them like he was one of their own. When he got lost, he tried his best to read the directions on some walls. With the mask on, Kalby was allowed access through doors the masked ones would never have permitted him to use before. When a door was locked, he would alter the Rules of Reality to make gravity force the door open.

His Magical abilities alone were hopeless to fight against the masked ones. Their power, skill, and knowledge dwarfed his. But something unnatural was going on with Kalby's Magic that none of the masked people even realised was happening before them. It was like the Rules of Reality for Magic itself were damaged or not working right for him. With a little extra concentration, he could hide his spells. It wasn't always reliable. If he was under a great deal of stress or mentally drained from previous castings, he would have an exponentially harder time keeping it hidden. But with this, he could stand a chance against them.

When Kalby reached the familiar hallway he was often dragged through to be cut open, he knew where to go. He headed toward the door he could finally partially read. All he could get out of it was, "Subject holding fac—" And dozens of other words Kalby couldn't comprehend.

Kalby pushed them open and walked past each of the cells. He could see children with various malformations. Stitched on limbs, tubes pumping all sorts of fluids poking through their stomachs. Unnatural masses seemed to grow out of their bodies and sometimes attached them to the walls, preventing them from moving. There were other cells with healthier-looking children. They had to take care of children who were too young to walk. There were an increasing more of those lately, Kalby had noticed. When Kalby got near them in his mask, they tried to hide in their cells just as he and his sister did before. There was no way to save all of them, and Kalby didn't care. He was only worried about one, and his pace picked up as he looked through cell after cell, trying to find her.

He almost passed it when he found hers. His sister had become so frail

that her already-thin legs were like twigs. Her gaunt face was scarred and burned and started to resemble a skull with what little hair she had and loved was gone. The faint yellow glow of her skin had all but dimmed. Her body shook as she tried to crawl away from him with her weak hands. Kalby didn't have the key, so he configured the pull of gravity to rip the door off the hinges. Her now-greying eyes looked so terrified as he knelt to face her.

He took off the mask to calm her.

"K-Kalby? Er det du? Are you really here?" his sister asked.

"Det er meg, Freja. I am going to get you out of here and I will get you back to your family from before."

"But ... I cannot walk."

Without hesitating, Kalby scooped up his big sister. She was so light in his arms, like holding a book.

"How did you get so much bigger than me, little Kalby?" his sister asked him with a look of hope in her eyes that he had never seen before. He ran as fast as he could back out of the cells.

He put the mask back on, hoping it would buy him just a little more time, but not long after he left the cell room, one of the masked ones came running and shouted, "Everyone stop, there is an imposter here!"

No one knew what each other looked like under the mask, so no one could tell if they were pretending to be someone else. Kalby knew they wouldn't let him leave. Especially when he was carrying one of their subjects, so he used the opportunity to create chaos. Before the running man could stop and catch his breath, Kalby had gravity pull on him so hard he tripped headfirst into the stone floor and cracked his skull. Kalby tried to slip away while the others ran to check if the man was all right. However, he was stopped by another.

"Wait! Where are you going with the subject? Stop!"

There was no way Kalby could effectively lie to them. He still knew so little about what they were, it would be obvious. Kalby got the jump on him and slammed the masked man into the wall with a hidden spell, and made a break for it. The others chased after him, about to cast their own spells. Kalby tried to distract them by throwing anything and anyone he could see at them. His head was starting to hurt, and he only narrowly avoided blasts of fire, crushing water, sharp and fast lights of various colours, cutting winds, and other objects being thrown at him as he dashed from corner to corner.

Adrenaline was pumping and pulsing through Kalby's body, keeping his legs running and letting him ignore the few hits they got on his back and side. Kalby remembered where he was and took an unexpected turn into the library.

Once inside, Kalby used his Magic to drag entire shelves in front of the door through the main hall. There was another exit for Kalby to use, and the masked ones would have to go through multiple hallways to get to him. Even if the masked ones wanted to break the blocked door open with Magic, they would have to spend some time configuring the Rules of Reality without knowing all the variables since they couldn't see what was blocking it and how. If they rushed it, they also risked accidentally collapsing the roof on top of them. It may have slowed Kalby and his sister's escape, but it bought them some breathing room.

"How did you become like them?" his sister asked.

Kalby was too out of breath to respond. Not that he knew much of the process himself to give her an answer. The masked ones' words rarely ever made sense to him when they spoke.

"Are you all right?"

He didn't even notice until she pointed it out. Blood was dripping out of his nose and onto her. He ignored it and jogged out the door at the opposite end of the room.

***

It took him a second to get his bearings and find the closest signs. One of the words Kalby made sure to learn was "Entrance." He followed each sign pointing toward it. Most of the masked people guarding the restricted doors were gone. No doubt looking for him. The occasional one that stayed behind, Kalby was able to kill quickly and quietly with a hidden spell. Each spell took longer and longer to compile and cast and caused his head to pound in pain. Kalby could see the solid metal gate with the word "Entrance" above it. They were so close, but the man in the half-skull mask was waiting for him.

"You thought poorly," Half-skull said in his same cold tone.

Kalby placed his sister on the ground behind him and wiped the blood from his nose.

"There is no way you can join us now. You have made that a clear impossibility; however, if you go back to your cell like a good subject, then your expiration shall be delayed."

Kalby had no words to say to him. The only thing that mattered to him was escape. Everything else, including revenge, was meaningless to him. Kalby tried to catch Half-skull with a gravity spell to snap his neck, but he couldn't concentrate enough to keep his Magic hidden, allowing Half-skull enough time to respond with a simple counter gravity of his own to nullify Kalby's pull.

Half- skull dashed toward Kalby and while he was preparing to defend against a spell, Half-skull punched his nose, causing it to crack. More blood spurted out and Half-skull had a white crystalline ring underneath him. The line of blood from Kalby's nose instantly hardened and Half-skull broke it off to use as a crimson frozen dagger and tried to stab and slice Kalby.

Kalby dodged as fast as he could. Leaving only a minor cut to his shoulder, the dagger shattered into hundreds of ruby crystals after impact.

123

Half -skull kept pushing the attack, and Kalby tried to block another punch only to realise Half-skull had grabbed his arm. Another white ring formed, and Kalby's arm burned with the intense cold. Kalby tried to throw Half-skull off by making gravity pull him away. A light blue ring formed on top of his white and Half-skull simply threw in another counter gravity.

The rapidly increasing pain helped Kalby to focus. It allowed him to hide his Magic to grab one of the frozen crystals and launch it into Half-skull's back. Hel released his grip on Kalby and fell to the ground. Kalby's arm was beginning to numb, and he couldn't get it to move, but he didn't care at the moment. He was busy trying to dig the sharp fragment of ice as deep into Half-skull as he could, but unexpectedly Half-skull formed a light blue ring. Before Kalby could figure out what spell Half-skull was doing, he fell sideways hard against the far wall before natural gravity took over, causing him to crash back to the ground.

Half- skull managed to stand back up before Kalby and pulled the blood from his back with a glassy sword. Kalby tried to force him back with Magic as Half-skull charged toward him, but Half-skull countered it again. Kalby tried using as much energy as possible, but it slowed him down as if walking up a steep hill.

Kalby could feel his mind fogging and zapping up again, becoming harder and harder to think. He could see his sister dragging herself by her hands to a metal wheel contraption. Her hand was bleeding as it squeezed a larger sharp piece of the icy dagger. She reached up to the rope surrounding the wheel, and a heavy tube of metal fell, causing the wheel to spin and the metal gate to pull itself open. Half-skull locked on Freja and with a flick of his wrist and a light blue ring, he slammed her head-first to the ceiling. Getting distracted, Half-skull caused Kalby's spell to take over and launch him hard into the wall. Half-skull didn't get back up as natural gravity caused Freja to fall hard on the stone floor.

Kalby limped toward her as fast as his better leg could take him. His body was in so much pain. He still couldn't control his left arm. His mind was so addled; simple thoughts were a struggle. It took him a while to register that Freja's head was covered in so much blood.

"Freja?" he groaned, though not sure he would have understood a response. But there was none.

"Freja? … Please … wake up …You wanted … to see … your family again? ... Please … do not … leave me … alone out there."

She didn't move.

"Dead." Was the word appearing in his head that he wanted to ignore. Kalby tried to drag her, but he was too weak and he could hear the echoes of other masked ones coming closer. He knew there was no way he could fight them. Kalby could barely walk himself, let alone carry her. Even with Magic, he could only lift her so far before his brain would give out. There was no

other choice, he would tell himself. The masked ones would never let Kalby live after this. There would never be a second chance. There was nothing he could do. Or at least he tried so hard to believe.

Kalby's head ached like it was splitting open as he tried to remember how to say, "I … Love … You," before he walked through the gate.

***

Kalby could feel the familiar damp chill fade with each step further away, and the footsteps grew even louder. He could hear they had passed the gate and were in the winding tunnels after him. Kalby knew he had only enough in him for one last simple spell. When he reached a support pillar, he sat down and waited, writing down all the configurations as he could with the dust on the stone floor so his addled brain didn't forget what to do when it was time.

Their footsteps thundered as they rushed closer and closer to him through the winding tunnel. Kalby waited, staring at all the numbers, symbols, and instructions as he prepared. As soon as one of the masked ones came into view, Kalby read the written spell one last time and used his Magic to split the wooden support beams. Rocks and debris came crashing down, blocking the tunnel. The masked ones would not have been able to clear it quickly lest they cause more collapses. Kalby wanted so desperately to lie down and rest, but every instinct in his body forced him to crawl to escape.

As he turned the last corner, he could see a pale silvery light stretching in front of him. He would have braced himself, but any sense of self-preservation he had was lost along with his sense of self. As his hand reached outside, his fingers dug into the dewy, soft, green ground. He pulled himself further. A warmth surrounded him he had never experienced before. Kalby's muscles wouldn't let him crawl any further, so he laid down on his back.

Kalby looked up, and it was an endless dark blue filled with billions upon billions of glowing lights. Most didn't appear to move, but one flew past his sight. Each one brighter than torches, and in between, a ginormous smoky pillar filled with light and more colours than he had ever seen. It was big. Too big for Kalby to comprehend. For the first time in his life, Kalby experienced freedom. Terrifying, overwhelming, boundless, beautiful freedom. Kalby closed his eyes to rest.

Now

And when they opened again, he was back in his wooden hilltop home. The memory left him as quickly as it came. Leaving him with just a feeling of guilt, fear, and heartache he could never explain, nor did he want to.

He was laying on the floor with Freya snuggled up beside him. Kal remembered last night; the fight he had with the other Draoi. He grabbed

124

Freya from the church and rushed her back to their house. His adrenaline must have given out as soon as they were safe because he didn't remember laying on the floor. Freya must have placed the pillow under his head and the blanket on top of them both.

He tried to hug her, but the pain from all his bruises, burns, and broken ribs stopped him. Kal stared at the ceiling and caught his breath. He was just relieved to have Freya safe and at his side. She was still in the dress Mister Conall's daughter had loaned her, and it was mangled, stained with soot, and damp. Kal believed he ought to pay Mister Conall for the dress before they had to leave, but they may need every penny. Kal brushed his gloved fingers through Freya's long, tangled teal hair. She looked so much like her mother.

"If only she were here now," Kal thought.

Freya began fidgeting in his arms as she woke up.

"God morgen, Pappa. How are you feeling?" Freya asked before yawning. "I have been worse," he said, still staring at the ceiling, his voice a little nasally due to his broken nose covered in dry blood. "Are you hurt, Freya?"

he asked, rubbing his bruised jaw.

***

Freya looked at her wrists, which were still out of place. She yelped in pain as soon as she tried to move them.

"Do not hurt your—" her father tried to warn her before going into a coughing fit. Freya crawled on her knees to her room to grab a waterskin with her teeth. When Freya crawled back to him, her father managed to pour it into his mouth. His breathing eased a bit but was still pained.

"Tusen Takks, vennen min."

"Are you sure you are all right, Pappa?"

He pointed in the direction of his potion vial tray on the counter.

Freya looked back at her father crestfallen.

"I can't. My wrists hurt too much and I can't move my fingers."

Her father appeared lost in thought for a moment before telling her, "You will have to use Magic then. I cannot see it from here and I am having a hard time focusing."

"But what if—"

"It is all right, vennen min," he interrupted weakly.

"But my hands. I can't use Gravomancy very well without them. I'll end up dropping and spilling them all," Freya said.

"You are not actually holding them with your—" "I know. You said that already." "Find a way. Please ..."

Freya wanted to cry as both pain and despair crept in, but her father needed her and it was up to her to help him. She closed her eyes and tried to imagine herself just going over there and picking up the tray as she formulated the configurations of the spell. She could see the blue light beneath her eyelids, but she shrieked when a glass shattered.

"I'm so sorry," Freya said reflexively, but her father was in too much of a daze to respond. Freya looked over and could see one of the vials was knocked over, which caused it to break and spill its contents.

"Pappa could do this, so you can too," Freya whispered to herself. She kept her eyes open this time and reconfigured her spell. The spell looked right and logical in her mind, but so did the last one. She cast again and managed to get the tray to hover slightly above the table. It was wobbling like it was in an earthquake and started to spin. Freya released her hold before the spinning could get faster.

"I-I c- can d-do this … I-I need t-to do this … I will do this!" Freya said to herself as she tried again. She didn't bother to reconfigure the spell. She knew it was correct. "It is not a physical task, but a mental one," Freya repeated over and over. The light blue ring formed underneath her once again. She altered the Rules of Reality, changing how gravity affected the tray. It began to float in equilibrium with natural gravity until Freya compelled the tray to gravitate toward her in a smooth motion. When the tray softly landed near Freya's feet, she ended the spell.

"I … I did it. I finally did it. Did you see that, Pappa? I did it without using my hands!" Freya said. Too excited and relieved to care about the mind fogging she had from the spell.

Some light came back to his eyes as he gazed over to Freya, "Good job, vennen min. I am so … proud."

Freya searched through the collection of vials for the pale orange-coloured Phigs potion and a sharp pang of disappointment stabbed into her when she realised there was only one left.

"What happened to the other ones?"

"I brought some with me … for the festival. They shattered during the fight."

She tried to give it to her father, but he stopped her.

"You are hurt as well. Drink half of it. I will drink the other half and we can go out and make more."

Freya took a sip of the coppery cinnamon -flavoured fluid, being careful only to drink half, and helped her father drink the rest. She laid down next to her father as they waited for the potion to kick in.

"Are Silas's people gone for good?"

"I think so. Their Captain and Draoi are gone, so they probably ran away or were overwhelmed by townspeople."

Hearing this filled Freya with relief, but dread crept right back into her heart. He needed to know, Freya thought.

"Pappa?"

"Yes, vennen min?"

"B-before t-the fight, R-Ronan—"

127

Her father gently stroked her hair before saying, "Take some breaths, vennen min. You are making yourself too nervous."

She did so and with each breath, the potion coursed through her wrists, reducing the swelling and numbing the pain. When she could feel her heart slowing, she continued.

"Silas saw me use Magic."

"What?"

"I'm so sorry, Pappa! Ronan was getting beaten up and then I found out he was playing some evil trick on me! When that other Draoi was punching you, I used Magic to get him off of you in the middle of the church …"

Her father was silent.

"Pappa? Pappa, are the Sanctus Venatores going to take us away?"

"I … The townspeople might not have noticed during the chaos. We won't know until we go down there and see how they respond. Even if they did, I will not let them take you away from me."

"What are we going to do?" Freya asked.

"We are both pretty hurt. It may be best if we get more Phigs potion ingredients from town. It will look less suspicious than hiding in our house all day, and it will let us figure out how much the town knows."

"Why don't we go out to the woods and get the ingredients?" Freya asked, scared about what the townsfolk would do to them if they knew.

"It would be very difficult for us to move around in the woods as hurt as we are. And with winter so close, we might not be able to find enough of the ingredients we need. Also, if any of those pirates ran away, they might be hiding in the woods. It would be too risky."

After a few more minutes, her father was able to pick himself up though still obviously sore.

"I am sorry, vennen min."

"For what?"

"The Phigs will speed up your natural healing, but if I do not fix your wrists, they will heal incorrectly."

"This is going to hurt, isn't it?"

"I am afraid a lot."

Her father picked the blanket off the floor and wrapped a part of it around a wooden spoon.

"Have you done this before?" Freya asked, starting to get scared.

"Yes, during the Crusade. It was a common-enough injury. They had us all learn how to treat it. You will want to bite down on this."

Freya did as instructed and her father placed his hands on her arm and wrist. He made a sharp pull and Freya's wrist popped again. She screamed into the blanket as the pain came back just as agonizing as before.

"I am sorry, vennen min. Just one more."

Freya tried to shake her head no, but her father grabbed her other arm

and wrist and did it again. When it was over, Freya was crying on the floor. "It will be all right now, vennen min," her father told her as he cradled her.

Her father snapped the wooden spoon in two and used cloth scraps to wrap them around her wrists.

"These will help keep your wrists in place. When we get more Phigs, you will not have to wear these for long."

"Tusen Takks, Pappa." Freya said with a sniffle, happy that she could finally move her fingers again.

"When you are ready, let us go. I do not want you here alone."

Freya nodded, her father helped her up, and he grabbed his big pointy hat before they left the house as they used to nearly every morning before.

Freya kept as close to her father as possible, nearly tripping a few times, but she was afraid and getting more scared the closer they were.

"Oh, what if they know? Will they treat us like the Draoi in the play? Will they try to hurt us? This is a bad idea. I want to go back home," Freya thought, her legs practically shaking with each step.

It wasn't long in their walk to town that she could hear her father's breathing becoming laboured. The chilling dry air was not helping, and he needed to take rests before they even got into town. He had done so much for her, and all she could do now was watch.

"If only I was strong enough to carry him."

When they reached the sign just out of town, the roads were mostly empty, which made it easier for her to see Mister Conall coming out of the Starboard Inn and Tavern.

"Mister Conall, you're all right!" Freya shouted before her father shushed her.

Mister Conall noticed them and headed toward them. As he got closer, Freya could see that Mister Conall had a couple of bruises of his own. He was also favouring his left arm.

"Janey Mack! I was getting worried about you two. Good to see you out and about. How's the craic?" Mister Conall asked.

Freya could see her father tensing up.

"We're pretty sore. Da and I wanted to get some ingredients to make Phigs to feel better."

"Aye, I was just getting myself a jar at the tavern to do the same. You may want to stock up quite a bit. A lot of people got tossed and burnt by the Draoi and could really use a Phigs to help them recover. Heck, I'd be willing to pay your highwayman prices myself at this point."

Freya started to notice her father wasn't looking at Mister Conall. Her father was looking at a figure ripped straight from Freya's storybook. The figure was a tall, strong man covered head to toe in gleaming silver plate

armour. The shoulders and tassets were covered in metal plates that slid and allowed him to move and twist as freely as if he weren't wearing it. His helmet was rounded with a tiny fish-like fin on the top and a single line slit for the eyes on his upturned visor. His short sword was in its scabbard, but Freya could see the pommel was replaced with a set of prongs used to hold any enchanting crystals. His metal heater shield had a depiction of himself riding his horse and slaying a giant by slashing its ankles. Its style was like the tapestries in the church and nearly hid a slot for another enchantment crystal.

Freya was in both awe and horror as she realised what he was.

"Right, this would be your first time seeing one. Pretty exciting huh? I almost forgot to mention that word got to the Sanctus Venatores about what happened, and so they came to investigate and provide aid however they can. Thank Gods we live on the First Third River. Would have taken them days to get here otherwise. You two might want to talk to them since you both got the best look at the Draoi before he escaped."

"He got away?" Freya asked, shocked the rubble collapse didn't kill him. "Aye. Nobody's telling me much. I got tossed around too much to get a look. What about you, Kal? He seemed—"

"There you are, Tom! I was—" Mister Gallagher interrupted as he came out of the tavern and before noticing Freya and her father.

"Hey, uh, Tom. We need to hurry back. I just remembered I, uh, need to get something from the house."

"All right, Fao, I'll be with you in a bit." "It's rather urgent."

"What are you getting on about?" Mister Conall asked.

"Godsdammit! Just come on."

"Fine. By the Gods you would think his dinner was burning. Well, I'll see you two later."

"Mister Conall!" her father called out.

"Aye?"

"Come by our house later. You can have any Phigs left over. I won't charge you."

Mister Conall looked as though he had to make sure pigs weren't flying before he could answer, "Oh? I'll take you up on that. Thank you, Kal. Hopefully, today will be better than yesterday, but not as good as tomorrow, right?"

When Mister Conall went after Mister Gallagher, Freya asked, "I thought the price was not negotiable."

"I want to pay him back as much as I can before it is too late." "What do you mean?"

"He has been helping us for a long time. I should have done more, but …" her father trailed off as he led Freya to a route away from the Venatores Knight.

***

130

The rest of the day was spent searching around town, trying to find ingredients at any store still open. This wouldn't have taken so long any other day, but her father needed to stop by and rest at nearby benches and catch his breath more and more frequently. At their current pace, Freya was worried he wouldn't be able to make it back home. Freya suggested they stay at the nearby inn, but he wouldn't have it. They had managed to avoid most of the Knights as they wandered and only had saltwater left as their final ingredient. Luckily for them, there was more than plenty by the docks.

All of the dock guards were on edge from last night, closely inspecting any and every newcomer they saw. A couple even tried to stop her father until they recognized Freya walking beside him and let them be. He had to lay on his stomach to reach over the docks and scoop up as much water as he could with his waterskin.

"Vennen min?" her father asked, still laying on the docks.

"Ja, Pappa?"

"Your school lessons are done around this time, right?" "They've probably been done an hour or two by now."

Her father took in a few breaths, "Do you think the main roads will be clear?"

"I don't know," Freya answered, worried he was asking because his strength was failing him. What if he was too weak to walk any farther? Freya couldn't lift him or drag him far even before her wrists were injured. If they couldn't get back, then getting those ingredients would be for nothing if they couldn't get to his apothecary table. There was no way he would heal if he didn't die sleeping outside in the icy cold. Freya knew there was no way she would let that happen. She could go to Mister Conall's and beg for his help if she needed to.

"Are you all right, sir? Are you suffering a bad dose?" asked a voice from behind, interrupting Freya's thoughts.

Whoever he was, he helped her father to his feet, and when her father turned, she got a good look at him. He was a young man with a freshly shaved head with barely a green stubble on his chin. He wore a suit of chainmail covered a long purple-and-green patterned gambeson. Freya was fairly sure he used to go to her schoolhouse and must have graduated a year or two ago.

"We are fine, squire," her father told him.

"Are you sure?"

"Ja."

"If you say so, sir. The name's Murphy. What's yours, citizen?" "Kal."

"Pleased to meet you. And who might you be, young lady?" Murphy asked, not remembering Freya from their relatively short time in class together.

131

"Freya," her father answered before she could.

"Oh. All right then. What do you do around here, Mister Kal?" "Apothecary."

He waited for more details and decided to break the silence when it appeared that her father wouldn't continue, "Don't talk much huh? Are you a foreigner? You don't sound like you're from here. I always wanted to travel myself."

"I have a house nearby."

"I see ... Well, Mister Kal, in case you didn't know, my fellow Venatores and I were sent because we heard your town had a Draoi attack last night. Did you see what happened?"

"I was just trying to get my daughter to safety."

"Daughter? Oh, I thought—Never mind. Were either of you hurt?" "Not as bad as others."

The young squire looked at Freya as he said, "Your Da seems tough. It must have been scary to have that happen huh? Especially on Souls of Saints Day. You must be pretty tough too since you made it through alright."

Murphy tried to ruffle Freya's hair, but her father instinctively stepped between them, nearly stumbling over from the pain.

"I'm sorry. You all must still be a little jumpy from last night. Are you sure you're all right, sir? We have medical supplies if you need them."

"We are fine. We need to return home."

He was clearly unconvinced but didn't want to push further, "If you say so, sir. Have a good evening."

***

The journey home took them longer than it did to leave. Freya's fingers were numb from the cold once they reached the centre of town, and the sun was gone by the time they passed the sign. When they finally made it back to their home, her father plopped Freya in front of the stove and collapsed on the floor, gasping just as he did this morning.

"Are you all right, Pappa?"

"I will ... be okay. Just ... catching my breath ... Could you please ... light up the stove?"

Freya nodded and walked over to the stove. After a few minutes, she managed to get a fire going. The two laid by its warmth until her father could stand again and brew up some potions. By the time he finished, he had enough for six vials. They each had one, and not long after, Freya's wrists were as if she had never fallen, and her father was moving around closer to his old self, and his face looked fresh as ever. Her father removed the splints and insisted they eat a light dinner of a small bowl of salted mashed potatoes. He said Phigs could make you sick on a full stomach, but Freya couldn't recall him saying this before when he taught her. No matter how hard she tried.

By the time dinner was finished, it was well past her bedtime. Her father

helped her get to bed.

"Hopefully when the morning comes, your wrists will feel as healthy as ever," her father said as he tucked her in. "If you need anything, I will be awake in the other room in case Mister Conall comes by.

"Pappa?"

"Ja, vennen min?"

"Could we read a story together?" Freya asked, making her pleading eyes as big as possible.

"Are you scared?" her father asked, and Freya nodded.

He looked like he was going to say something, but instead chose to ask, "Which storybook?"

Freya gave him the book she had bought last night and they read until Freya could no longer keep herself awake.

CHAPTER 10
NIGHT OF HUNTING

Freya was able to sleep, but Kal couldn't. He kept a brave face for Freya, but he was terrified. Kal would have already taken her out of Valour were they both not so injured this morning.

"He who waits like a sheep shall be eaten by the wolves," Kal said to himself and got to work on some more potions. He scavenged every scrap of ingredients he had left until all his jars and shelves were barren. Kal hoped the absence of some of the ingredients wouldn't have severe side effects. Even if nothing were to happen this night, this was an adequate distraction for a few hours. It almost made Kal nostalgic for the late nights he stayed awake brewing potions for Freya's mother. She often encouraged him to get some sleep and said his health was just as important as hers, but Kal didn't see it that way and he had a similar feeling with Freya.

"I hope you would forgive what I might have to do," Kal whispered to someone whom he dearly wished was with him now.

His thoughts were interrupted by a soft knock on his door. Kal quickly injected the Aplite potion into his wrist and was able to get some drops of Eye of Eyda into his eyes before the second knock came. The former numbed the remnants of pain he had left and with luck kept him from feeling the potential pain he may experience soon. The latter let his eyes better adjust to the darkness.

Kal walked over to the door expecting to see a Venatores Knight about to read their decree of arrest in the hope Kal would simply surrender. Since Kal had not committed a crime, as far as they knew, if he willingly submitted to them, then according to the Doctrine of Amnesty they would register him as a Draoi and let Kal live in Valour so long as he never performed Magic again. Of course, the Venatores would also alert the entire town how Kal was a Draoi and inform the townsfolk they should report any instance of Magic they witness. Kal would also not be allowed to have any profession a Draoi's innate mathematical knowledge would give him an edge in, so potion selling would be impossible. If someone were to report Kal of breaking any of these rules, he would be imprisoned or potentially killed depending on the degree of the crime claimed.

Were those the only punishments Kal could tolerate it. But because Freya was born with Magic as well, she would be registered and taken from him to be raised in Charity where they would force Freya to fear what she was. As a Draoi himself, Kal would not be allowed to see her lest he diminished the fear of Magic in any way for her.

There was no way Kal was going to lose Freya as well. He formulated a spell in his head when he opened the door. Kal was ready to catch them off guard to make a way for him and Freya to escape, only to see that it was Mister Conall at the door holding a lantern.

"Good evening, Kal. Hope I didn't wake you."

Kal looked around Mister Conall, making sure he wasn't leading any of the Venatores here with his improved night sight. When the coast looked clear, Kal stepped outside and quietly closed the door behind him so as to not wake up Freya with their conversation.

"You are here for the Phigs, right?"

"If the offer is still open."

Kal reached into his jacket pocket and pulled out the vials. Such curious things. So valuable yet mass-produced more than anything in the Known World. It saved lives yet perpetuated wars. So revolutionary yet the ingredients were deceptively simple.

Kal handed them over.

"Thanks again. But I can't stop myself from asking why? No offence, but as long as I've known you, you weren't the generous sort."

"I guess … It is thanks … for everything you and your family have done … for myself and Freya. I have only met such kindness in few."

"Huh," Mister Conall said awkwardly, scratching the back of his balding head.

"Hard to believe you're the same nervous kid in the ragged uniform with a babe on his back my dear Dana let in. You've grown to be a good father to Freya and a good friend. … Welp, I better head on back. Brigid seems to still be pretty spooked from last night. Didn't even want me to come here, but she didn't say why. Good night, Kal."

"Good—" Kal was about to respond, but he managed to spot some Venatores Knights approaching, with a couple on horses. They were hoping to use the darkness for cover, but Kal's night-enhanced eyes allowed him to spot them early. He slammed the door on Mister Conall and ran to get Freya. ***

The banging sound of the door woke Freya up in alarm. Her heart

was beating as if it were going to explode.

"PAPPA!" Freya screamed before a tall shadowy figure rushed into her room and covered her mouth and nose.

Freya couldn't breathe, but she tried to scream.

"Hold your breath, Freya!" her father yelled at her as he scooped her up under his arm. He lifted her out to the main room, and through the light of the stove, Freya could see the whole room covered in a yellow, smoky haze coming from broken shards of clay. Her father began sprinting toward the table sidewall, and Freya thought he would try to ram the door, but instead, a blue light lit the whole room from beneath his feet, and he pushed out his hand. Nearly half the wall shot out like it was blasted by a cannon, and he jumped through the hole carrying Freya.

As soon as they were outside, Freya's face stung with the icy cold wind. Freya couldn't hold her breath any longer and pried off her father's hand to get a quick gasp, but he covered her face again before she could fill her lungs further as he sprinted with her toward the woods. Torchlight began to blaze and reflect from the Knights' dark steel armour. Their breaths rasped like starving wolves through their jagged helmets, which grinned maliciously. Their tooth-edged swords gleamed crimson as wet blood.

"What are you doing? They haven't done anything!" A familiar yet distorted voice shouted. Freya turned back to see a bald, bearded, portly malformed creature pull his arm away from one of the young men in clanging chain mail. He punched a Knight who tried to restrain him. The clang his fist made against the Knight's helmet was louder than a war drum. Before the portly creature could do anything else, it was tackled and beaten by the dark armoured knights. Then all of a sudden, Freya and her father were consumed by the black woods.

The moon was nowhere in sight, her father allowed her to breathe again, and the air was freezing from the winter night. Nearly every day, Freya and her father would wake up in the morning and venture deep into these woods, away from their town. But tonight, it was nothing like the woods she remembered. Crows screeched and screamed, followed by thunderous stomps of pursuing horses frothing at their mouths. The thorned branches of every tree violently convulsed, each one looking nearly about to grab Freya and rip her apart. Freya wanted to use Magic to get them away, but she was petrified with fear. All thoughts turned to horror.

As Freya and her father reached closer to the clearing, she could see the dark knights gaining on them in seconds on their wild horses.

"They're going to catch us! They're going to catch us!" Freya screamed. Her father stopped, to her horror, once they were in the centre of their clearing.

"No, these woods are our weapons!" he said as he turned to face them. The horsemen were going to charge into Freya and her father. Instantly a

blue ring exploded from underneath her father. It was brighter than she had ever seen, lighting up the whole clearing as if in daylight.

"Gravomancy, be careful!" one of the horsemen shouted. His voice was quickly drowned out by the sound of dozens of trees being ripped from the dirt. The roots vainly held on for dear life before the trees flew toward the horsemen like giant arrows. One after the other, the trees soared and crashed into the ground, splitting and splintering as they made contact. The horsemen continued their charge. A few were hit, their armour crunching from the intense weight and force. Some of their horses were taken out, causing them to crash to the ground wailing in pain.

A few skilled riders managed to make their horses dodge, duck, and jump over the trees. Her father held tightly to Freya and dashed farther into the woods, knocking over trees behind them to slow the horsemen down. Crossbow bolts launched right at them. One nearly pierced the back of her father's head, but even without a ring underneath him, the arrow promptly reversed course back at the horseman. After letting out a blood-curdling scream, the rider became lost in the darkness.

Her father managed to plunge them farther away from the horsemen's torchlight as he hopped off a nearby boulder and pressed his back on the other side. He rasped heavily, trying to catch his breath and clutching at his rib injury from the night before. Freya looked up and scars crawled around her father's face and cut deeper into him like razor wire.

"PA—" Freya screamed, trying to warn him of it, but he quickly covered her mouth.

"Did you breathe in before we got to the woods?" her father whispered.

Her whole body shook as she nodded.

"Keep your eyes closed. It will be all right, it's just a—" her father said before having another coughing fit.

"Over here!" one of the Knights hidden in darkness shouted. In a rush of fear, only a single spell would come to mind, and before the Knight could pull the trigger of her crossbow, a faint blue light glowed underneath Freya. Snow, leaves, sticks, and rocks instantly and violently gravitated toward the Knight, puncturing and pulverising her.

"Did I just kill someone?" The thought crept into Freya as she trembled.

Her father turned her away before Freya could know for sure.

The Knight's screaming gave away their position, but Freya and her father had a solid lead through a brush and into another clearing, where they found the stream now frozen over.

"The ice is still thin, but we can cross it," her father said, putting Freya down.

"What if it breaks?" Freya asked, keeping her eyes closed as he suggested and trying to forget what she might have done.

"Just be careful. I will not let you fall in. The Venatores will have a harder time with their armour and weapons, and there would be no way for them to bring their horses."

But before her father could take one step, a flash of light glowed behind her and a thunderous boom came right after. Her ears started to ring, and she tried to see where it came from before a dark figure approached them. There was a glowing crystal in the hilt of his sword and the blade crackled with white lightning. Each flash revealed dozens of other dark Knights and horsemen with their own weapons drawn and crossbows aimed at them. One of the men in chain mail slowly approached them with shackles in his hands.

"I am Sir Liam Walsh, Knight Lieutenant of the Sanctus Venatores. By the authority granted to me by the Grand Masters divinely chosen by the Gods, I order you to submit!" the knight with the lightning blade said.

Freya looked up at her father and watched him relax. Taking slow and deep breaths, he let the knight with shackles approach them.

"Is father too tired? Are we really giving up?" Freya wondered. Tears burned her eyes as she realised she would never see her home again. She would never see her friends, Brigid and Jacinta.

"Will I never see Pappa again? Will we never practice Magic together again? Will he never read me bedtime stories again? Will he never hug me again?" Freya tried using any and all Magic she could think of against the Knights, but her brain was getting more and more muddled; not a single spell came through. It was hopeless.

The Knight was within arm's reach of Freya, and she could see blood dripping from the thorned shackles.

"Are they going to hurt us? Is that what happened to Pappa? Is that why he has nightmares?" Freya thought, trying to hide her hands from the Knight, but unexpectedly he fell sideways toward her father. A lightning bolt shot from Sir Liam's sword but was pulled toward the falling Knight and struck him. Steam simmered off him, but he appeared to still be breathing as he floated between her father and the other Knights.

"You will not take her away from me!" Her father roared when everything from ice, rocks, and trees orbited around herself and him. It was as if they were in the eye of a storm that would rip apart everything in its path. Knights who got hit were merely debris added to the carnage. Freya thought she was awed by the power of Jean. She realised now her father may not know much about any other Magic, but he was the master of gravity.

Sir Liam tried shocking her father more, but each bolt was redirected by the ever-growing metal-armoured Knights adding to the storm. When that didn't work, the Knight pulled out another crystal. He placed it in the slot on his shield and rushed her father. Her father was prepared to pulverise Sir Liam with debris. In a flash, a light brighter than the morning sun flew at Freya and her father. It disoriented her, but her father appeared to have been blinded by it. They were surrounded by the yellow smoke again and she smelled something foul, and soon she could feel her heart racing worse than before. When she was able to see her father better, his face was leaking blood like a fountain, and all Freya could do was scream when Sir Liam appeared to grow larger and bashed her father with his shield. All at once, everything in orbit simultaneously dropped to the ground.

Freya wanted to go over to her father and save him. Yet her body refused to do anything except scream even as her throat burned. She only stopped when another Knight kicked her in the head, and everything went black.

***

It wasn't long before Freya had awakened. Or so she thought. If it wasn't for the terrible pain in her head, Freya would have thought this was a horrible nightmare. She couldn't see anything but something was tightly wrapped around her eyes and ears. Freya tried to pull them off but quickly realised her hands were bound to her ankles. She wanted to scream again, but her mouth was gagged. Freya couldn't have heard herself anyway with her ears covered. She tried rolling around to get some sort of sense of where she was but was getting nauseous.

"Am I rocking?" Freya wondered. The only thing she could feel was a thin blanket wrapped on top of her. She still shivered from the cold; it didn't help that she was still in her sleeping clothes.

Something pressed against her, and at first, she was startled, but it seemed to be breathing uneasily. She had nothing to prove it, but she was sure it was her father and tried to lay up against him to let him know she was nearby. Freya was getting sick to her stomach. The whole world was spinning. The nothingness made it impossible to tell how long she was waiting. It could have been hours or even days, for all she knew.

Then all of a sudden, the world stopped moving. Its absence of motion made Freya feel worse than when it spun. Something or someone picked her up. She tried to fight, but it was too strong, and it pulled her away from what she believed was her father. There was no way for her to use Magic without any semblance of bearing to base any configurations on. She might have been on a boat, a cart, or even on the ground. She had no way to know what to grab. She was carried away for some time. The cold wind seemed to disappear. Was she indoors now? Before she could even guess where she was, she was placed on a chair. Her arms were pulled forward on a table or slab. There were two clicks, and then she could not move her arms and legs. How long will they keep her here? Will she ever see her father again? Will they ever let her see and hear again?

CHAPTER 11
NIGHT OF GATHERING

There was a time when the pure white-stoned Tower of Babel inspired Ava. Made her feel like she was a part of something greater, as she did the Gods' work. She hasn't felt that way for a long time. It was imposing to her. Made her feel small. Like she disappointed the nursery nuns back in Charity again. Ava tried to keep her eyes away from it whenever she returned to Hope castle. Even this late at night, it was near impossible to ignore as it split the moonlight like a shadowy gate.

Ava could hear her horse, Niamh, breathing hard through her bridle. Ava couldn't blame her. They had been sent back and forth from here to way down south of the Fay Forests. Acting as a courier for months now. A task mostly given to squires and not a Knight Sergeant such as herself. Ava would never complain. How could she after what she had done? Ava did promise herself that she would at least request a different horse if she was to be sent back down again. Niamh needed a rest.

"Identify yourself," someone called from one of the towers on the outer wall.

"Knight Sergeant Dame Ava Mulrennan!"

"Understood. Please hold, ma'am," the guard said and a moment later, the drawbridge had lowered over the moat and the portcullis had risen.

Niamh trotted toward the castle, her milky-white coat contrasting with the dark wood bridge. Once they were inside the castle walls, a few young squires were about to help Ava take Niamh to the stables. They halted when the Knight Master of Hope called.

"Don't waste your time. Your chores are more valuable than her."

The squires froze in confusion. It's one of their duties to aid their superiors, and the near-explicit insult only muddied the waters. Ava understood they were too young to know what had happened.

"His orders take precedence. I can take care of my steed myself. I don't want to keep you up later than you have to."

"Uh yes, ma'am. Welcome home and Gods be with you." One o f the young squires said before she and her fellows returned to their work. Ava wondered if either of her former squires were here. Her youngest, Benedict, had been eager to quest alongside his older brother, Terrence, the moment he was Knighted. She hadn't seen either of them in almost a year, and she missed them dearly.

"Do you have the missive, Mulrennan?" Knight Master Cillian asked. "Yes, sir."

"Hand them over."

Ava reached over to one of the saddle pouches and handed him the documents.

"In about two hours, you need to go back and give them my response." Ava's sore muscles ached after hearing that. "Two hours? Is there an emergency?"

"No. Report back here in two hours. You are dismissed, Mulrennan." Ava wished she could protest, but she knew she had no right. She gave

Niamh a gentle squeeze with her legs and led her to the stables. As Niamh ate from the alfalfa, Ava took the armour off her. Niamh neighed appreciatively as she shook and stretched. Ava couldn't wait any longer to do the same herself. Her muscles ached, and her skin chaffed from the week she had to wear it. Even a one-hour break from the armour was a gift. She managed to get the upper part off, letting her gambeson warm her up before someone else came in.

"I was told you were back."

"Terry?" Ava asked, turning and seeing the face of her first squire more grown than before. He had a gentle yet strong face. He had finally grown some stubble since she last saw him. His fiery red hair was almost longer than her own. "It's been donkey's years! How have you and Benny been?" Ava asked.

"I'm fine, but things with Benedict have been tense. Especially after a few hours ago."

"Oh, Gods!" Ava gasped. "What happened?"

"Long story short, I believe he's been getting radicalised by some of the more severe members of the order."

Ava's heart sank as she thought back, "Did I miss the signs? Was Benny like this all along or did I push him away when I told him what I did? It wouldn't be the first. That I haven't lost Terry too is a miracle."

"He and a company of Knights attempted to aggressively apprehend a suspected Draoi without evidence beyond hearsay and without warning. Things got violent," Terrence continued.

"Was anybody killed?"

141

"Yes … a few of the Knights. A couple were injured, some might never recover."

"And Benny?"

"He's fine. Just an injured pride. Was punched by a sympathetic civilian." "Were any civilians killed?" Ava asked, guilt hurting her chest before she even heard the answer.

"Thank the Gods, none. The one who punched Benedict was apprehended. He's being held for questioning."

"Did the Draoi get away? Or were they ..." Ava droned off. It was not the most popular opinion among the order, but Ava and plenty of other Venatores still consider Draoi as people as well. Dangerous people, no doubt, but people nonetheless.

"No, Sir Liam managed to capture them."

"Well, the 'Draoi' should be released! Like you said, they didn't have any evidence."

"We can't just ignore the fact that the Draoi used Magic to defend himself."

"Exactly what the radicals wanted," Ava thought. "'Why bother trying to make sure they actually are Draoi and give them a chance to turn themselves in peacefully when we can just terrorise any suspect and force them to use Magic to defend themselves? Who cares if anybody dies as long as we get the Draoi.'"

Terrence looked around the stables, making sure no one was around. When he looked back at her, his eyes were so full of compassion. Something was unsettling with how her former pupil could be so orderly and selfless. It was as if he was incapable of being anything less than an exemplar of the order. No matter how hard she tried to remember, there wasn't a single moment she could think of where he broke a single rule. Even Knight Masters would have some vice. Ava certainly had a few unforgivable flaws. Despite knowing what she did, Terrence never judged her. Perhaps the only one who hasn't.

"What aren't you telling me?" Ava asked, her fears rising up again.

Terrence coughed. "Ava. I was told that the Draoi wasn't alone. He had a little girl with him."

Ava's throat tightened. "Was the child a Draoi too?" she managed to squeeze out.

"They suspect she is, but no one witnessed her use Magic. They have her in one of the interrogation rooms. I've managed to keep those animals away from her for now, but I really think you should be the one to interview her before they get a chance. Just in case ..."

Ava nodded, unable to say anything else. Terrence led her the way. Each step down the hall terrified her, but she couldn't tell what outcome she was fearing.

142

"She's inside this one," Terrence said as he stopped outside the door.

"How long has she been in there?" Ava asked.

"Less than an hour, I think."

Ava reached for the door handle, but Terrence held it.

"Just be prepared in case it is … what we think," Terrence said, moving out of the way.

Ava took a shuddered breath before opening the door.

***

Something slithered on Freya's right arm then soon after the left and she screamed as loud as she could through the coverings. "These are the giant worm vampires Ronan was talking about!" Freya thought. Without notice, she could move her hands and feet again. Before Freya could rip the covers off her eyes and ears, somebody made her drink something foul. She tried to fight it, but they held her tightly. After a few minutes, Freya gave up and sobbed into whatever was holding her.

Stranger still, something removed the coverings on her ears, then someone sang,

"Bless you, oh sleepy child.

I'll sing you a lullaby

So that you may soundly sleep through the night.

Gods bless you, oh sweet child.

May Umba protect you

Embraced with Gillian's nurturing.

Gods bless you, oh dear child.

Underneath the stone tower so white

sleeping all long through the night."

***

It was a woman's voice Freya did not recognize. It was a voice both lilting and beautifully haunting, making Freya's heart and breathing steady. The hold turned into a gentle hug and the singer gently stroked her hair.

"Who is she?" Freya wondered, trying to fight the urge to fall asleep. The singer stopped hugging her and helped Freya out of the eye coverings. After Freya's eyes adjusted to the torchlight around her, she could see a woman sitting in front of her. She had a narrow jaw, but wide cheekbones. Fair skin, with thin eyebrows and long eyelashes. A perky nose and neck-length teal-coloured hair. Her eyes were grassy green and were watering like Freya's were moments ago.

"Is she crying? Why is she crying?" Freya thought to herself.

The singer gave Freya a warm smile until she looked at Freya's forehead. She quickly placed Freya back on the chair, and it was only then Freya realised they both had been sitting on the floor.

"Blessed Gods! How did this happen?" the singer asked.

"'Make sure not to use Magic around them and refuse to say or do anything until they let you see me.'" Her father's lessons echoed in Freya's head, so she stayed quiet.

"Was it one of those Knights? What they did was horrible. To leave you here stewing under the effects of the gas was beyond cruel."

Freya agreed but still didn't say anything. The singer simply smiled again and kissed the bruised spot on her head. If Freya was confused before, this certainly didn't clarify anything.

The singer wiped her eyes and laughed a bit as she said, "I'm sorry. That was pretty odd for you, huh? My name is Ava Mulrennan. And you must be Freya."

"How did they already know my name? Did someone from Valour tell them?"

The panicked look of confusion must have been plain on Freya's face as Ava asked, "You don't recognize me, do you?"

Freya shook her head no. Technically not speaking to them.

"I guess that makes sense. You were too young. Your Da and I were … close friends during the Second Grand Crusad e." Ava started tearing up again and it was so awkward for Freya. She didn't know what to do, so she held Ava's hand. She would have said, "There, there," but that would be speaking.

After a brief moment, Ava looked at what Freya was doing and laughed again as she said, "I'm so sorry. I … I've wanted to see you for so long ... I'm sorry this must all seem so, so strange." She took a deep breath before continuing, "Let's take you to your Da, he will clear things up for you."

"You'll take me to Da?" Freya bl urted and covered her mouth after realising she just spoke to a Venatores, but Ava just smiled at her.

"This must be a dream. They wouldn't just let us go free, would they?" Freya thought, right before another Knight with long red hair burst into the room.

"Ava!"

"What's wrong, Terry?" Ava asked, putting her hand on her scabbard.

Freya noticed the young handsome knight was staring at her and Freya couldn't help but bashfully look away.

"The Draoi escaped," he said.

"That's not possible. He would have breathed at least the same amount of gas as she did."

"I'm not sure. The other Knights said the gas didn't seem to work on him when they captured him."

"Oh, Kal," Ava said under her breath.

"We need to hurry, Ava!"

"Hold on." She looked back at Freya. "I need you to stay here." "I want to see Da!" Freya protested.

"You will soon, I promise," Ava said right before following the other Knight out the door.

Freya wasn't sure what to do in this empty room, and she was getting impatient. She didn't know if she could trust Ava and had nothing to distract herself with in the meantime.

Out of boredom and because she couldn't stop fidgeting, Freya messed with the door only to find it wasn't locked.

"What's going on?" Freya thought. "First this Ava was being super nice unchaining me and removing the blindfolds. Then she says she knows Pappa. Is this some trick? Did they meet during the Crusades? IF it is a trick, I don't see how or why." Freya paced back and forth trying to figure out this conundrum until the solution smacked her in the face.

"Of course! Pappa must have planned all this in case we got caught. Pappa is always planning, and Ava must have been a friend on the inside! But why didn't Pappa tell me about her? Well, Pappa doesn't like to talk about his past. Old friends would be part of the past too, I suppose. Ah, forget it. I can't waste any more time!"

She peeked outside the door to see if the door was clear, and for some strange reason, it was. It was completely empty, with not a single guard in sight.

"What's happening out there?" Freya wondered as she ran down the hall. It took her a while to find her way out. Her feet ached from walking barefoot on the cold stone. She opened the door and just as quickly closed it again after being blasted by the cold.

"Nope. Not going anywhere without something warm," Freya thought, so she cracked the door open ever so slightly to get a peek.

"This is a castle, right? They have to keep their clothes some … where?" Freya's thoughts were interrupted when she noticed the tower in the centre that went skyward without end. She had to close the door again before it made her vomit.

"Was that the Tower of Babel? Am I in the castle of Hope?" If this was the case, then Freya was right. They were taken on a boat down the First Third River. She peeked out the door again. She tried her best to ignore the gargantuan tower, which blocked most of her view, except for a building with black smoke that came out of its chimney, contrasting with the heavy snowfall.

She couldn't put her finger on why this detail was important to her until something clicked, "It's just like Mister Conall's forge! He has black smoke coming from his chimney all of the time!"

If there was a place where clothes and armour would be made, that ought to be it, Freya decided. But a new issue emerged. How to sneak across the courtyard? Especially when Venatores ran around as if a massive sale was happening in the Valour markets. She needed a plan. She thought about hiding in one of the barrels in a nearby cart and using Magic to make it roll to the other side, but they might stop it if they thought it was valuable. However, it might work in her favour.

"Think of it like the power exercise Pappa had us do. Keep the spell simple and only use as many alterations as needed. Overdo it and the ring will glow too bright." She configured her spell, made the pull of gravity double, and then tripled on a few barrels inside until the cart's back wheels could no longer hold the crushing weight. It collapsed and spilled all of the barrels. The potential energy released made the barrels roll like a rock slide and knocked down a couple of fully armoured Knights nearby. Others rushed to their aid, which gave Freya just enough time to sprint over to the smithy before anyone could look back.

Freya nearly lost herself in the warmth of the forge. It was almost like relaxing in a bathtub especially when her bare feet had to go through the snow to get here. But she couldn't enjoy it for long. The smith was still in the building, and Freya had to crawl underneath her table as she checked who opened her door and let the cold in. Freya was able to sneak in to the storeroom and inside was a bunch of chain mail, plate armour, gambesons, and all sorts of weapons.

"Brigid would have killed to see all of this," Freya thought, until guilt crept in for stealing this woman's hard work.

"Why should I care! They kidnapped Pappa and me in the first place!" Freya thought. She put on a warm thick pair of trousers and a gambeson with as little noise as she could. They were most likely made for short Demi-Humans like Leprechauns to be used by the Emerald Knights branch. Freya took a dagger as well in case she needed to cut a rope or something. She would have loved to take a full suit of armour with her, but there was no way she was going to sneak out clunking around in that. Freya tucked her long hair inside the gambeson to keep it from getting caught on anything. She tried crawling back under the same table, but before she reached the door, a pair of armoured boots walked in.

"What's with all the maggotry outside?" A raspy woman's voice shouted.

"A Draoi managed to escape. We're opening the gate to go after them.
We need you to help out with dispensing the gas shells."

"Oh, for Gods sake! I'll be out in a moment."

"Pappa escaped? He must be waiting for me outside!" Freya realised and waited for the two to leave before sneaking out the door. Outside, she had to walk for fifteen minutes before circumnavigating the Tower of Babel enough to see the rising portcullis and stables with Knights running in and out of each.

"I won't get far if I just run for it. But perhaps with a horse I can pick up Pappa and we can ride away."

There was no way of sneaking her way through all of them, but she was

dressed like them. She walked her way across, keeping her head down, and tried her best to stay a reasonable distance, hoping they wouldn't notice how short she was to them. But as she was closer to the stables, it became harder to avoid the crowds. Her heart nearly stopped when she bumped into one of the Knights.

"Eyes front, squire!"

Freya nodded and kept walking, holding her breath until she was finally inside the stables. There were dozens of strong horses stomping around and neighing. Some were still in silvery armour, and some looked like they were trying to sleep as stable squires were swiftly saddling them. Freya looked around for one that could be ready to go and be calm enough to handle. She took a glance at every stall she passed. Some were too sleepy to ride, some looked too scary. However, as she hid behind one stall to avoid being spotted by a squire, the horse inside reached over its fence and nuzzled Freya with its snout.

Freya was startled at first, but when she turned around, a beautiful milky-white horse with big, soft brown eyes tried to nuzzle her. Freya had to stifle a chuckle from the tickling while reading the name, "Niamh," on the fence and below it, "Ava Mulrennan."

"You must belong to the nice Knight. You're so sweet, but I shouldn't steal you from her."

"Then again, what if this was part of the plan? The horse was already saddled and tacked up as if ready to go," Freya thought as she opened the fence and grabbed a small stool to help her onto the horse. Once Freya had her hand on the reins, Niamh started trotting out of the stables, following a routine she had done hundreds of times before without even being given a single command. Freya gripped the reins as tightly as she could as her feet were too short for the stirrups, and she had never ridden a horse before.

"The storybooks make it sound so different," Freya thought as she tried desperately to look like she knew what she was doing while also trying not to fall off. As soon as they were out of the stables, the only thing Freya thought was, "Oh crap! I'm right out in the open!"

Freya tried pulling the reins to steer Niamh toward the gate, but she already seemed to know where to go and wasn't appreciating the tugging and started stomping in protest.

"I'm sorry, please act normal!" Freya whispered into Niamh's ear and luckily everybody else was too caught up in their rushing to notice.

***

Niamh took Freya just under the portcullis and was right about to cross the drawbridge when a sharp yell caused her to stop.

"Mulrennan, get your arse back here, Gods dammit!"

Freya couldn't help herself and turned her head for a quick peek but turned away as she realised the Knight in fully decorated armour was looking

right at her.

"I did not give you leave to go after that bastard! Get back here and I will only have you flogged for this."

Freya wasn't sure what to fear more, being caught as a Draoi or caught as Ava. Either way, Freya leaned forward and desperately kicked against Niamh until she abruptly bolted into a gallop. Freya fell from the saddle, but her ankle got caught in the stirrup, her head dangling just barely above the ground. Niamh's hooves thundered next to her ear, nearly drowning out the desperate shouting of the Knight chasing after her, "Roll your body toward the horse!"

Freya tried to get up herself, but she was too disoriented and not strong enough. The Knight sprinted at her like a bear after prey. Freya's head was pushed upward by the Knight. Freya was able to get back on the saddle just before the Knight stumbled to the snowy ground.

"Stop, girl!" the Knight shouted, but Freya didn't know how to stop a horse nor did she want to at the moment. She held onto Niamh's neck as tight as she could as the darkness of night enveloped her.

CHAPTER 12
DAY OF JOURNEYS

"Why isn't Da back?" Brigid wondered all throughout the night. Too wracked with worry to sleep and it only compounded when the sun began to rise as she hid in a corner holding one of the swords she made with her father. Brigid could always put on a brave face for her friends when bad things happened in the past because they needed her too and because they made her feel braver. But now she was all alone. No doubt the Venatores got Freya and her father. If Jacinta had another opportunity to run away again, she most certainly did.

"But where was Da? He was supposed to get the potions and be back in forty minutes, but it's been over twelve hours, and he hasn't returned. Did Mister Pantar kill—" Brigid was about to ask herself, but suddenly skittering and scratching came from under the floorboard.

Brigid held the sword up high, ready to swing down like a hammer blow. If he came to get her too, then she wasn't going to go down without a fight. Her hands started to shake, though, as the floorboards began to crack, and Brigid was nearly unable to stop herself when a clawed hand broke through, and Brigid realised who it was.

"Holy crap, Jacinta! Did you make that hole for my grave? What are you doing?"

Jacinta's head popped out of the hole. She shook some of the thicker patches of dirt out of her hair.

"Get your shmithing shuppliesh and follow me! We need to reshcue Freya!" Jacinta gabbled so fast her thick southern accent took over, making it hard to understand her.

"Jacinta, what are you talking about? Speak normally."

Jacinta rolled her eyes and spoke slowly for Brigid, "Those Knights took Freya and her father."

Brigid was a little relieved knowing they got him. "Right, because her Da is a Draoi. I saw him use Dark Magic. He was going to collapse the whole church on us."

"Why didn't he then?"

"I don't know. You don't pay attention in Missus Aibrean's class. She explained that they don't think like us. They see people and the world as toys. Remember what happened to Mister Gallagher? What if her Da used Dark Magic to break his hand? No way a scrawny guy like him could do that on his own."

"Gallagher deserved it. Freya doesn't. She's been taken from her home just as I have. I won't go back to mine until she's brought back to hers."

Brigid's head had been heated for a while, but now it was burning so hot not even a quenching bucket could cool it. She screamed, "Freya lied to us! She's been lying to us for as long as we've known her! She knew her father was Draoi and she lied! She is a liar and I never want to see her again!"

"And you wouldn't for your family?" Jacinta snapped back.

Brigid was too angry to admit Jacinta was right and said, "We're not grown-ups, Jacinta. We can't go all the way to Hope ourselves."

"Where's Mister Conall? He's friends with Mister Pantar, right? Maybe he would help?"

"I don't know where Da is. He went to Mister Pantar's place and never came back and it's freaking me out."

"Did he know?" Jacinta asked.

"I don't think so. I wanted to tell him, but if Mister Pantar knew that we knew, he would have attacked us."

They both wondered what might have happened and after a few seconds Jacinta clicked her tongue and said, "If he hasn't come back, then the Venatores might have taken him too!"

"What? Don't be ridiculous, my Da isn't a Draoi!"

"But everyone knows he and Mister Pantar are friends. Maybe they thought he was hiding him?"

"Gods dammit." Brigid thought. "I guess we have to now, huh? But how would we even get them out? Hope is a fortress. Their walls are taller than our houses."

Jacinta had a sly grin to her that Brigid had never seen before.

"What is it?" Brigid asked.

"They don't build walls underground."

***

Freya's whole body ached as she woke. She didn't even remember falling asleep, yet here she was, lying on the snow, cuddled up next to a horse. Her fingers and toes were numb. She needed to walk around and get the blood flowing in her body, but she had no idea where to go or where she was. She looked for footprints of where she came from, but the snowfall from last

night buried them.

Niamh woke up after sneezing, and after she rolled for a bit, the horse was back on her feet and walked through the woods.

"Where are you going?" Freya asked, but Niamh just kept walking. With no other ideas about where to go, Freya decided to follow her. It didn't take long for them to reach the edge of the forest and see the castle gates of Hope in the far clearing. Niamh tried to continue to walk back to her home, but Freya managed to grab her reins before she could be seen by someone on the watchtowers.

"I can't let you go back just yet. I need to find Pappa first. He's probably waiting for us around here." Though she had no idea where he would be. Freya wasn't sure what the next step of the plan was supposed to be. She tried looking around the clearing for a smoke signal or something but quickly realised that would have been a fast way to get caught again. If he had left a trail, it would have been lost in the snow like her footprints.

"I wish you would have told me what the plan was," Freya said to herself before seeing the portcullis open again. Freya pulled Niamh further back and hid behind a tree. She peeked around the corner and there was a procession of Venatores on horseback. They gathered on the bridge. In the centre of them was her father shackled and sitting on a black horse behind Ava.

Freya's voice quivered, "But he … he was s-supposed t-to escape. He was s-supposed t-to save me … What d-do I … What d-do I do?" Freya clamped her hands against her mouth to keep her crying from giving herself away. Her legs became jelly and gave out beneath her.

"This couldn't happen. Pappa always has a plan." Freya thought and a question bore into her, "Why does Ava have him chained? She was supposed to help us … That must be why the plan failed. She betrayed Pappa!" But the despair passed as Freya uttered a thought she needed to hear out loud, "Pappa can't help. And crying won't change that. I can't save him alone and no one would help a Draoi escape except … except … other Draoi!" Freya grabbed Niamh by the reins and ventured forth south to Sagacity. The biggest city in Bastiel.

Then

Kalby wasn't sure how long he had been walking Kalby wasn't sure how long he had been walking nor where he was walking too. Perhaps he was avoiding that huge round light in the sky. It seemed to always follow him in the long stretches of the soft, green ground. He wasn't sure about anything. He woke up after being uncomfortably warm, like standing too close to a torch, and he needed to get away from where he was for reasons he couldn't explain. It wasn't until the sound of running water was near that he realised his throat was dry.

He scooped up as much water as his hands could fill. He kept drinking repeatedly until the dryness in his throat was gone. When Kalby looked back at the river, someone looked back at him in the water. The figure barely had short blonde hair, flat eyebrows, a pointed, crooked bloody nose, and a squarish jaw. Kalby had no idea who this was. He looked around, but the only other people he could see were a massive crowd marching in the distance. Figuring where they were going was most likely where he ought to head, Kalby decided to walk with them.

It took him a bit to catch up, but when he got a careful look at them, he didn't know what to make of it. Some were dressed in metal, some in pa dded clothes, some in ornate robes, and some in simple dirty clothes. There were all sorts of strange animals carrying boxes on wheels with more boxes or food inside. It was hectic, to say the least. And uncomfortably noisy, but one sound seemed to pierce through the others.

"Kid! Get your lazy arse moving and put those crates in the wagon! The Crusaders aren't going to tolerate anyone who doesn't pull their own weight." A man with a covering on one of his eyes yelled at Kalby while aggressively pointing, correctly assuming Kalby had no idea what he was talking about.

It was a stack of five crates and after a bit of configuration, Kalby used Magic to lift each one into the wagon. As Kalby was levitating the final crate into the wagon, someone screamed, "Magic!" causing Kalby to drop the crate and spill all the food in a panic. A group of men wearing random bits of metal and carrying sharp sticks of metal came toward him. Kalby froze, not sure what to do. They surrounded him, each one shouting and shoving.

"You're a spy, aren't you?"

"We need to make him confess!"

"String him up! Make an example to all the other Magic users!"

One of the men knocked Kalby on the ground and before Kalby could kill them, one of the men fell to his knees after a young woman in a chain robe kicked him from the back of his legs.

"Who do you think you are, sow?" one of the men shouted incredulously.

"She is my Venatores squire," said another man, who was covered head to toe in golden-and-black metal and had a purple cloak.

"I'm very sorry, Sir and Dame! We have a Magic user right here though.
Want to take care of him for us?" one of the men asked.

"He is our comrade in arms!" The woman snapped.

"What? We caught him using Magic red-handed!"

"Doesn't matter. All who fight for the Gods are welcomed in the Crusade. Those who attack their fellow soldiers are traitors. And I believe you know the penalty of treason?" the young woman said. Her grassy green eyes beamed at him.

"Ye-Yes, Dame," the other man said before the rest stomped off.

When the men were out of eyesight, the young woman let out a breath she had been holding and approached Kalby. She had a narrow jaw, but wide cheekbones. Fair skin, with thin eyebrows and long eyelashes. A perky nose

and long teal hair she kept tied in a bun.

"By the Gods, your nose, wrists, and your feet! Did those men hurt you? Are you alright?"

Kalby looked down at his bare feet. They were bruised, sore, and bleeding, and his wrists were torn and gnarled, but they had been like this for as long as he could remember. Which was when he woke up earlier today.

"Permission to take him to the infirmary, Sir Quiñones?" the young woman asked.

"Very well. Meet with me in the front, with the cavalry division, once you're done, my young squire," Sir Quiñones said.

The young woman helped Kalby to his feet and placed his arm around her neck while putting her hand around his waist to help support him. The position was a tad awkward, considering he was significantly taller than her, but she was dedicated all the same.

"What's your name by the way?" She asked.

After thinking, only a set of numbers and a couple of words came to mind. He chose one of the words, "Kalby."

"It's nice to meet you, Kalby. I am Squire Ava Mulrennan."

END

THE STAR OF ASH: A CHILD FROM FAITH

THEN

The sudden stop of the ship swung Ava on her hammock, waking her with a startle.

"We're finally here!" Ava thought eagerly as she climbed down and ran to her foot locker. She got herself dressed in her green-and-purple gambeson of Bastiel, and in her haste, got her long teal hair caught while throwing on her chain robe and accidentally tossed herself to the hardwood floor with a thunk.

"Gods bless you this morning, my sweet Ava. It seems like you need their blessings more than usual today," Ava's best friend said, speaking softly in the same accent as Ava's.

"Oh, good morning, Aoife!" Ava returned, looking up at Aoife's beautiful, pale, freckled face and emerald-green eyes through the neck hole of her tangled chain robe.

"How's the craic, the soldiers making you nuns wake up early?"

"No, my dear, we got up ourselves. We wanted to pray for all of you just before we docked."

"Ah, thank you. I'll be sure to do the same for you," Ava said as she struggled to get her hair unstuck.

"Do you need help with that?"

"Don't worry, I almost got it … and there! Never had my hair stuck in chain mail before."

"It's the humidity down here. Not even the Fay Forests get this humid, so your lovely hair is all frizzy."

"What?" Ava asked before she felt her hair had turned straw-like. "Oh wow, that's pure quare. Thanks for the heads-up."

"Any time. Oh, I saw Sir Quiñones up on deck. I think he is waiting for you," Aoife said as Ava found some string to tie back her hair and pulled up her mail coif.

"Yep, I was just on my way there. See you ashore!"

"Be safe!" Aoife called back to Ava as she climbed up the upper deck and saw her mentor, Sir Luis Quiñones.

He was an older man of sixty-nine with dark tan skin, a long, grey pointed beard, and twirled moustache, but he stood just as strong and proud as a Knight in their prime.

"Ah, buenos días, my young Squire."

"Good morning, Sir!" Ava greeted only just realising how sweaty she was. "Drink plenty of water and take off the coif until we are in combat. You're

not used to the heat, are you?"

"No, Sir. This is the farthest I've ever been from home."

"You're fifteen, right? Perfect time in your life to see the world. I left my home in Reino del Sol when I was your age."

"Thank you so much for letting me join you in the Divine Militia." "You may feel differently when this is all over."

"I don't believe so. This crusade is going to save everyone! It would be selfish to refuse that honour."

"I hope the Gods prove you right. … Come, let us join the other officers ashore and meet with our guides while the rest of the troops get everything deployed."

***

As Ava and Sir Quiñones walked down the boarding ramp, she could see the Knight officers speaking to a woman and man with deep sepia skin. The woman had extremely short black hair and wore a blue beaded dress with diamond patterns. The man had long braided purple hair and wore vibrant orange clothing and carried a spear and wooden shield.

"Sawubona, Divine Militia. Welcome to Edene, the motherland of humanity. And welcome to the Ukufika Ezulwini Empire. Our Umbusi wishes you swift victory and safe travels," the woman said, with a more closed-mouth accent with a mix of dark, pulled-back sounds and bright forward sounds.

"Umbusi?" Ava whispered to Sir Quiñones.

"She is their elected leader. Think of it like the Grand Masters of the Venatores," Sir Quiñones answered before approaching the man in orange.

"And I believe you will be our guide through the Sand Sea, correct?" Sir Quiñones asked.

The man spat in his hand before extending it toward Sir Quiñones and he responded in kind and shook his hand.

"Keyaa! You are correct. I am of the Sailing Ilmorran and you can call me Legishon. Just tell your people to listen to me and I can guarantee most of you won't die." His accent was different. It had stronger Rs and was sing-songy.

"Well, I'm glad to hear that. How soon can we travel?" Sir Quiñones asked.

"The sooner the better. The Binzia have been getting bold. They might try cutting through the Sand Sea."

"Can't we do the same?" one of the Knight officers asked.

"Too dangerous. Your supply lines would be too far out in the open. Easy to ambush. Assuming you survived that far anyway."

"Understood. We shall get everything unloaded and set up camp at the border. Then we shall begin our venture at dawn," Sir Quiñones said.

"Kuhle. Umbusi will be glad to hear it."

***

Ava watched in amazement as their massive company of forty thousand marched toward the border. Over a thousand cavalry, hundreds of wagons, giants and small folk, Knights, priests, peasants, and everything in between, with creatures of all sorts.

"Makes you wonder just how close are we to the size of the First Crusade nine thousand years ago?" Sir Quiñones pondered, barely audible over the thundering footsteps.

Ava was too stunned to answer. "All these people. Under one banner, under one goal. The world will never be the same," Ava thought as she watched.

"We need to make him confess!" She heard someone shout through the crowd. Ava looked around and saw a scared young man getting surrounded by an angry mob.

"Shouldn't we do something?" Ava asked.

"Indeed. What will you, do I wonder?"

"Well, I'm not going to sit here and let these bullies hurt him," Ava said as she dismounted her horse and stomped toward them.

"String him up! Make an example to all the other Magic users!" another man in the mob shouted.

Ava hesitated upon hearing that. But once she saw the young man get shoved down, Ava continued forward. "It doesn't matter if he is Magic or not. He wasn't hurting anyone."

As soon as she was behind the shover, she took a deep breath and gathered her courage before she kicked the back of his leg.

"Who do you think you are, sow?" one of the men shouted as he buckled over. They all turned toward her now. Ava kept her hand tight on the sword on her side.

"She is my Venatores squire," Sir Quiñones said. His black-and-gold armour blocked the sun like an eclipse from atop his horse.

"I'm very sorry, Sir and Dame! We have a Magic user right here though.

Want to take care of him for us?" one of the men asked.

Ava looked down at the young man. He looked to be around her age, very tall but half-starved. His skin was sickly pale and he had buzzed blonde hair. His face was rectangular and he had a broken pointed nose. His dusty brown eyes stared at her frightened and confused. "This boy volunteered to risk his life for us and you just expect me to kill him for no crime at all?" Ava thought as her blood boiled.

"He is our comrade in arms!" Ava snapped, biting back the harsher words she had in mind.

"What? We caught him using Magic red-handed!"

"Doesn't matter. All who fight for the Gods are welcomed in the Crusade. Those who attack their fellow soldiers are traitors. And I believe you know the penalty of treason?" Ava replied, sliding her sword just slightly out of its sheath so that the blade could glimmer in the sun.

"Ye-Yes, Dame," the other man said before the rest stomped off.

When they were out of eyesight, Ava let out a breath. It was only then that she realized her heart had been racing. Ava approached the young man to help him up, but noticed his wrists were gnarled and his feet were bleeding.

"By the Gods, your nose, wrists, and your feet! Did those men hurt you? Are you alright?" Ava asked, frantically checking him over making sure he wasn't hurt anywhere else.

He didn't say anything and after almost getting lynched by his own comrades, Ava could understand why.

"Permission to take him to the infirmary, Sir Quiñones?"

"Very well. Meet with me in the front, with the cavalry division, once you're done, my young squire," Sir Quiñones said.

Ava nodded and helped the young man to his feet and placed his arm around her neck while putting her hand around his waist to help support him just as she was trained.

"What's your name, by the way?"

He still remained silent as they trudged onward.

"How many of our Draoi allies have been attacked by our own men?" she wondered.

"Kalby." Ava heard him whisper. His voice sounded hoarse.

She smiled. It was a unique name to her. Though Ava had heard plenty already and will no doubt hear plenty more during the Crusade. She'll have to remember his. Let him know that he has a friend in this Militia that has his back.

"It's nice to meet you, Kalby. I am Squire Ava Mulrennan."

FOLLOW THE AUTHOR

Follow me on Facebook, Twitter, or Tik Tok to learn more and ask me anything. Please don't spoil the book though.

https://www.facebook.com/profile.php?id=100090512516536

https://twitter.com/PDJs_Creations

https://www.tiktok.com/@parkers_creations?is_from_webapp=1&sender_device=pc